BIG CORPSE
ON CAMPUS

What Reviewers Say About Karis Walsh's Work

Sit. Stay. Love.

"A cute and fun romance set in a small town. Great main characters that are easily relatable."—Kat Adams, Bookseller (QBD Books, Australia)

"This is a sweet romance about two lovely people growing together and falling in love as they help the people and animals around them."—*Rainbow Reflections*

"This is an easy romance to read. It's not overly fraught with angst, but there is some light drama to keep the plot moving forward. The obligatory separation of the leads near the end of the book didn't feel eye roll worthy, because, though dramatic, it was set up almost from the beginning of the book. I loved the characters, pacing and plot of this book. Very recommended."—Colleen Corgel, Librarian, Queens Public Library

Love on Lavender Lane

"Gentle romance, excellent chemistry and low angst. …The two MCs are well defined and well written. Their interactions and dialogue are great fun. The whole atmosphere of the lavender farm is excellently evoked."—*reviewer@large*

"[*Love on Lavender Lane*] was very nearly my perfect romance novel. Lovely human beings for main characters who had fantastic chemistry, great humor that kept me smiling—and even laughing—throughout, and just enough angst to make me feel it in the heart. And a cute doggie, too!"—*C-Spot Reviews*

Seascape

"When I think of Karis Walsh novels, the two aspects that distinguish them from those of many authors are the interactions of the characters with their environment, both the scenery and the plants and animals that live in it. This book has all of that in abundance..."—*The Good, the Bad and the Unread*

Set the Stage

"I really adored this book. From the characters to the setting and the slow burn romance, I was in it for the long haul with this one. Karis Walsh to me is an expert in creating interesting characters that often have to face some type of adversity. While this book was no different, it felt like the author changed up her game a bit. There's something new, something fresh about this book from Walsh." —*Romantic Reader Blog*

"Both leads were well developed and you could see them grow as characters throughout the novel. They also had great chemistry. This slow burn romance made a great summer read."—Melina Bickard, Librarian, Waterloo Library (UK)

You Make Me Tremble

"Another quality read from Karis Walsh. She is definitely a go-to for a heartwarming read."—*Romantic Reader Blog*

Amounting to Nothing

"As always with Karis Walsh's books the characters are well drawn and the inter-relationships well developed."—*Lesbian Reading Room*

Tales From the Sea Glass Inn

"*Tales from Sea Glass Inn* is a lovely collection of stories about the women who visit the Inn and the relationships that they form with each other."—*Inked Rainbow Reads*

"A wonderful romance about starting all over again in middle age. Karis Walsh creates an affirming love story in which relatable women face uncertainty and new beginnings, with all of their promise and shortcomings, and come out whole on the other side."—*Omnivore Bibliosaur*

Love on Tap

"Karis Walsh writes excellent romances. They draw you in, engage your mind and capture your heart. …What really good romance writers do is make you dream of being that loved, that chosen. Love on Tap is exactly that novel—interesting characters, slightly different circumstances to anything you have read before, slightly different challenges. And although you KNOW the happy ending is coming, you still have that little bit of 'oooh—make it happen.' Loved it. Wish it was me. What more is there to say?"—*Lesbian Reading Room*

"This is the second book I have read by this author and it certainly won't be my last. Ms Walsh is one of the few authors who can write a truly great and interesting love story without the need of a secondary story line or plot."—*Inked Rainbow Reads*

Sweet Hearts: Romantic Novellas

"I was super excited when I saw this book was coming out, and it did not disappoint."—Danielle Kimerer, Librarian, Reading Public Library (MA)

Risk Factor—Novella in Sweet Hearts

"Karis Walsh sensitively portrays the frustration of learning to live with a new disability through Ainslee, and the pain of living as a survivor of suicide loss through Myra."—*Lesbian Review*

Mounting Evidence

"[A]nother awesome Karis Walsh novel, and I have eternal hope that at some point there will be another book in this series. I liked the characters, the plot, the mystery and the romance so much." —Danielle Kimerer, Librarian, Reading Public Library (MA)

Mounting Danger

"A mystery, a woman in a uniform and horses. ...YES!!!! ...This book is brilliant in my opinion. Very well written with great flow and a fantastic plot. I enjoyed the horses in this dramatic saga. There is so much information on training and riding, and polo. Very interesting things to know."—*Prism Book Alliance*

Blindsided

"Their slow-burn romance is a nuanced exploration of trust, desire, and negotiating boundaries, without a hint of schmaltz or pity. The sex scenes are sizzling hot, but it's the slow burn that really allows Walsh to shine. ...The deft dialogue and well-written characters make this a winner."—*Publishers Weekly*

"This is definitely a good read, and it's a good introduction to Karis Walsh and her books. The romance is good, the sex is hot, the dogs are endearing, and you finish the book feeling good. Why wouldn't you want all that?"—*Lesbian Review*

Wingspan

"I really enjoy Karis Walsh's work. She writes wonderful novels that have interesting characters who aren't perfect, but they are likable. This book pulls you into the story right from the beginning. The setting is the beautiful Olympic Peninsula and you can't help but want to go there as you read *Wingspan*."—*Romantic Reader Blog*

The Sea Glass Inn

"Karis Walsh's third book, excellently written and paced as always, takes us on a gentle but determined journey through two women's awakening. ...Loved it, another great read that will stay on my re-visit shelf."—*Lesbian Reading Room*

Worth the Risk

"The setting of this novel is exquisite, based on Karis Walsh's own background in horsemanship and knowledge of showjumping. It provides a wonderful plot to the story, a great backdrop to the characters and an interesting insight for those of us who don't know that world. ...Another great book by Karis Walsh. Well written, well paced, amusing and warming. Definitely a hit for me."—*Lesbian Reading Room*

Improvisation

"Walsh tells this story in achingly beautiful words, phrases and paragraphs, building a tension that is bittersweet. As the two main characters sway through life to the music of their souls, the reader may think she hears the strains of Tina's violin. As the two women interact, there is always an undercurrent of sensuality buzzing around the edges of the pages, even while they exchange sometimes snappy, sometimes comic dialogue. *Improvisation* is a true romantic tale, Walsh's fourth book, and she's evolving into a master romantic storyteller."—*Lambda Literary*

Harmony

"This was Karis Walsh's first novel and what a great addition to the LesFic fold. It is very well written and flows effortlessly as it weaves together the story of Brooke and Andi's worlds and their intriguing journey together. Ms Walsh has given space to more than just the heroines and we come to know the quartet and their partners, all of whom are likeable and interesting."—*Lesbian Reading Room*

By the Author

Harmony
Worth the Risk
Sea Glass Inn
Improvisation
Wingspan
Blindsided
Love on Tap
Tales from Sea Glass Inn
You Make Me Tremble
Set the Stage
Seascape
Love on Lavender Lane
Sit. Stay. Love
Liberty Bay
Love and Lattes

Mounted Police Romantic Intrigues:
Mounting Danger
Mounting Evidence
Amounting to Nothing

University Police Romantic Intrigues:
With a Minor in Murder
A Degree to Die For
Big Corpse on Campus

BIG CORPSE
ON CAMPUS

by

Karis Walsh

2025

BIG CORPSE ON CAMPUS

ISBN 13: 978-1-63679-852-3

THIS TRADE PAPERBACK ORIGINAL IS PUBLISHED BY
BOLD STROKES BOOKS, INC.
P.O. BOX 249
VALLEY FALLS, NY 12185

FIRST EDITION: JUNE 2025

CREDITS
EDITOR: RUTH STERNGLANTZ
PRODUCTION DESIGN: SUSAN RAMUNDO
COVER DESIGN BY TAMMY SEIDICK

CHAPTER ONE

Cappy Flannery spread peanut butter and strawberry jam on a piece of wheat bread and folded it over to make a half sandwich. She took a bite of her usual speedy breakfast and turned when she heard her grandmother enter the small, galley-style kitchen.

"Morning, Gran," she said as soon as she was able to swallow her sticky mouthful. She gestured with the sandwich. "Want some breakfast?"

Edith Flannery was wearing a pink robe and slippers, but she already had on a hint of makeup, and her hair—a gray-streaked version of Cappy's dark, almost black hair—was carefully brushed and contained in a tidy bun. She looked ready to face the day, while Cappy was still wearing a ragged Seahawks jersey, and even though she hadn't checked in a mirror yet this morning, she was willing to bet her hair was sticking up in the back. Gran looked at the concoction Cappy was waving as if she had just been offered a wedge of moldy cheese.

"You're too old for lectures, I suppose," her grandmother said with a sigh.

Cappy grinned. "Yep," she said. "I'm a hopeless cause."

Gran laughed and playfully swatted her on the arm. "We bought plenty of groceries this weekend. Why don't I make you a real breakfast. Eggs and toast? Some fruit?"

"Maybe for dinner," Cappy said, putting the lid on the jar of peanut butter and returning it to the cupboard. "I'll be late if I don't get going soon." She paused, feeling the mood shift for both of them. She was getting used to the swings they had been experiencing in the few weeks since her grandfather died. Laughter and smiles one moment, then the inevitable return to sadness. Cappy had gone to California to help her gran with funeral arrangements but hadn't been able to leave her there alone when she returned to Seattle, so they were currently crammed together in Cappy's tiny apartment until they decided what to do next. "Are you sure you'll be all right here alone today?"

"Don't you worry about me, I'll be fine," Gran said, opening the fridge and taking out a carton of eggs. "I've got books and television. Plus, I might wander down to the market later."

Cappy had been about to leave the kitchen, but those words conjured up images of her gran wandering the streets of Seattle lost and confused, getting attacked by street gangs with knives. Taking a wrong turn and falling into Puget Sound...

All right, the last one was unlikely. And Cappy hadn't seen any knife-wielding gangs roaming near Pike Place Market, but still.

"Maybe I should take some more time off work," she said. Her sergeant might be gruff and terrifying, but Cappy had no doubt she would give her as much leave as she needed. "Or I could find someone to come by the apartment and keep you company while I'm gone."

"A babysitter?"

"Sure," Cappy said. "Something like that." She had actually been thinking of calling the Seattle Police and having an officer stop by. Her partner Clare surely knew someone from her former precinct who would be willing to help her, although they would probably be frightened off by the glare her grandmother was currently giving her.

"Go to work," Gran said. "I'll manage just fine. I agreed to move to Seattle so I'd be able to see you more than once a year, not so you would have to monitor my every move. Got it?"

"Yes, ma'am," Cappy said, giving her grandmother a mock salute, and then rinsing her plate and knife and putting them in the dishwasher.

"Thank you." Gran reached over and gave Cappy a pat on the cheek. "Now go comb your hair, then get to work."

Cappy grinned and went into her bedroom to change into her university police uniform. Funny how her grandmother could make her feel like a child again when she bossed her around, and Cappy didn't mind a bit. Even before she had moved away from California, she hadn't seen her grandparents often—a week or two a year, at the most—but when she thought of childhood and home, their house was often the one that came to mind rather than her dad's, where she had spent the majority of her young life. He had done his best to be a good parent, to fill in the empty space when her mom left, but still... Cappy shook herself mentally and checked her watch. She really was going to be late if she didn't stop thinking and start moving. She quickly brushed her teeth and hair before yelling good-bye to Gran and rushing out the door.

Cappy quickly navigated along familiar back roads from her downtown Seattle apartment to UW's campus. Even though she had only been away from her job as a campus police officer for a few weeks, she had missed being at work every day. These people were her true family. Her colleagues, and even Sergeant Kent. Cappy would give her life to protect any one of them, especially her partner, Clare Sawyer. They hadn't known each other long, and they'd gotten off to a rocky start the first time they had been forced to work together, but once Cappy had realized that Clare wasn't selfish and willing to climb over anyone in her way to get to the top—and once she'd convinced Clare to work *with* her instead of struggling on her own—they had formed what had the potential to be a great partnership. Solving a string of murders together and watching Clare get hit with what could have been a lethal bullet had cemented her as part of Cappy's team. Still, murders didn't happen every week on campus, and the officers rotated through shifts in varying combinations, without permanent partners, so Cappy was eager to get back to the comforting routine of patrolling on campus, no matter who was assigned to be with her.

She parked in a garage near the station and walked along the Ave. Most of the stores and restaurants had Halloween decorations in their windows, and even though many of the trees still held on to their bright fall colors, the pavement was coated with trampled yellow and brown leaves. Autumn was Cappy's favorite time of year on campus. Nestled between the chaos of the beginning of the school year and the chill of winter, there was always a settled feeling to the season. She felt her world righting itself as she turned off the Ave and entered the glass-fronted police station.

"You're back!" Clare appeared in front of her as if she had been catapulted out of one of the conference rooms. She gave Cappy a quick hug, then glanced over her shoulder. "Uh-oh. Don't look behind you."

Cappy, surprised by the warmth of Clare's welcome, naturally turned around to see what Clare was talking about. She saw her sergeant, Adriana Kent, standing outside the door and talking to a woman Cappy recognized as one of UW's classics professors and a friend of Clare's girlfriend, Libby Hart. She couldn't remember her name, but she was strikingly pretty even though she was dressed in what Cappy liked to call Campus Camouflage. Neutral-colored tweed jacket and beige slacks, designed to make any professor blend in with the dirt paths on campus. The two of them laughed at something Kent said, then leaned closer and bumped their shoulders together before walking separate ways. They probably meant the move to be casual, subtler than the kiss they obviously wanted to share, but instead the touch somehow seemed more intimate than a passionate kiss would have been.

"Is she…no, she can't be…is she *smiling*?" Cappy hissed in a stage whisper as Kent pushed through the door into the foyer.

"She does that a lot these days," Clare said with a nod. "Creepy, isn't it?"

Kent just shook her head, not even trying to hide what looked suspiciously like a lovesick grin. "Good to see you back, Flannery. I hope everything went smoothly on your trip home?"

"Yes, thank you," Cappy said, appreciating Kent's circumspect way of asking about her situation. Kent knew why she had been on leave and about her grandmother moving to Seattle, but she was making sure that the information was Cappy's to share or not.

"Good. If you need more time off or anything, just let me know. Sawyer can fill you in on what's been going on around here, and I'll see you in turnout in five."

"So, since you've been gone, Sarge started dating Professor Tig Weston," Clare said loudly as Kent walked away. She merely shook her head and kept walking, though, so Clare laughed and tugged on Cappy's sleeve, pulling her into a small room off the lobby. Clare sat down on one of the hard plastic chairs and ran a hand through her short, reddish-gold hair.

"Five minutes, huh? Where to start...Have you been keeping track of local news?"

"No," Cappy said, settling herself in the chair next to Clare's. She usually was obsessive about following local newsfeeds whenever she was away from campus, but this time had been different with the funeral, seeing her dad, getting her grandmother's belongings packed and her house ready to sell. Cappy had fallen into bed each night physically exhausted and mentally drained.

"Okay, here's the SparkNotes version," Clare said before swiftly recounting her most recent murder case, and Cappy struggled to keep up with the rushed, convoluted story.

"I think Kent's been missing real police work," Clare said. "So she decided she was going to be my partner while we solved the case. You know, she's even bossier than you are."

The last statement was said with a playful smile, and Cappy tried to find an appropriate response to the teasing, but the only words that came to mind were *That should have been me.* She should have been the one investigating the murder with Clare while Kent stayed in the background and yelled at them to hurry up and solve the mystery. In the past, she could easily have taken a year or more of leave without needing to worry about missing a murder case, but apparently now even a few weeks was too much.

"Anyway," Clare continued, seemingly oblivious to Cappy's confusing train of thought, "Tig and Kent ended up falling in love, although—and don't tell Kent this—Libby and I think Tig might be tempted to swap her for one of those ancient vases we found, if she had the chance."

She paused to catch her breath after the rushed account, and Cappy regarded her skeptically. Ancient artifacts and fistfights in the Classics Department? "Are you sure this really happened here, or are you just telling me the plot of a movie you saw? Or a dream you had?"

"It really happened," Clare said, putting her hand over her heart as if swearing a vow. "You can read the report. The romance part is true, too, even though Libby had been trying to set Kent up with her other friend Jazz."

Cappy frowned, trying to place the name. She was fairly sure Clare was referring to Libby's librarian friend, whom she hadn't yet met. "The one with the axe in her office?"

"Yes. Well, there's obviously more to her than that, but that particular possession seems to stick in one's mind." She glanced at her watch. "You'd better get going. You have about fifteen seconds to get to turnout."

"You're not coming?" Cappy asked, trying to keep the wistfulness out of her voice. How could so much have changed in less than a month?

"I'm just coming off shift," Clare said, standing up and arching her back in a stretch. "But we should be working together next week, I hope." She gave Cappy's shoulder a squeeze and went out of the room, leaving Cappy sitting in a daze.

She stood up and headed toward the turnout room. It was all a bit much to handle, with changes in both her personal life and now her work life. She pushed aside the feeling of being left out of all the action and focused on the morning ahead. All she needed was a nice, routine day to get her back on track. She was reaching for the door handle when Kent's sharp voice made her stop, her hand outstretched.

"Flannery," Kent said. All traces of love and smiles had vanished from her face. "Wait here."

Kent stepped in front of Cappy, opening the door and calling for Derek Landry. He joined them in the hall, giving Cappy a quick nod in greeting before they both turned their attention to Kent.

"I need you two to go to Stadium Court," Kent said. She gave an audible sigh before continuing, and Cappy could see a hint of what looked like grief behind her stern expression. "A student was found dead this morning. Suicide. Brian Keyes. He's...his body has already been taken downtown for an autopsy, but I have permission for you two to go over the scene. Make sure everything is...well, just check it out."

So much for her hoped-for routine day at work. Derek went to the front desk to grab keys for a patrol car, but Kent put her hand on Cappy's arm, gently keeping her in place.

"Will you be all right with this?" she asked. "I hate for this to happen when you just got back, and I can send someone else, but I'd rather have you there if you can handle it."

"I appreciate that," Cappy said, forcing the words out of her suddenly tight throat, and referring both to the compliment and the compassion. "I'll be fine." Whatever the hell *fine* meant.

Kent nodded and let her go. She joined Derek in the hall, and he slung his arm over her shoulder and gave her a quick sideways hug as they walked toward the back door that led to the garage. The two of them had joined the campus police about the same time, nearly a decade ago when she had just moved to Washington. They had bonded at first out of desperation as the only two rookies in the department, and gradually had become friends.

"Good to have you back, Cap," he said, entering the stairwell and jogging down the steps. Even though there was no point in rushing to get to the scene, he seemed to feel the same sense of urgency that she did.

"Good to be here," she said, before giving a small shrug and quietly adding, "I guess."

He pushed open the door and led them into the garage. "Yeah, not the easiest assignment to welcome you back. Do you want to drive?"

She shook her head and got into the passenger seat of the patrol car, forcing her focus off her own feelings and onto the tragedy that lay before them. Brian Keyes. Star running back of the UW Huskies, and practically guaranteed a shining future as a pro football player until the car crash that had taken his leg and ended his career.

"Did you ever see him play?" she asked as they drove.

Derek shook his head. "No. I'm more into baseball than football, but I've heard of him, of course. Who hasn't, though, at least on campus? Was he as good as the rumors made him sound?"

"Better," Cappy said. She had either volunteered to work as security or had sat in the stands as a fan at almost every home game since she had come to UW. She hadn't admitted it during her interviews, but she had chosen this campus department as much for its football team as for its excellent reputation as a positive and inclusive place to work. "He made it look effortless. It was such a shame about the accident."

Derek nodded, his face reflecting the sorrow she felt. "I guess the loss was too much for him to handle. A future filled with millions of dollars and adoring fans, all gone in an instant. I can't imagine how he must have felt."

The trip to the new student housing apartment complex near Husky Stadium only took a few minutes. There were two Seattle PD cars parked in front of the building, and Derek pulled in behind them. They took the elevator to the seventh floor, the top of the building, and easily found the room marked off with crime scene tape.

One of the Seattle officers welcomed them with a grim expression and introduced herself as Detective Ellingsen. "I'm sure you know the drill," she said. "Wear gloves, don't move anything, and if you notice anything suspicious, report it to us before you go. We'll be right outside, so take your time."

She ducked under the tape and left them standing in the small entrance hall. Yes, Cappy knew the drill—the scene would be guarded and kept in its current state until the autopsy and forensic reports confirmed that this was a suicide—but only academically, not from personal experience. She had never been called to examine a suicide scene before, and she didn't think Derek had either. They looked at each other, then walked into the room.

Cappy exhaled quietly as she entered the airy, spacious living room. Without a body, she could almost fool herself into thinking this was just another college apartment, and that nothing horrible had happened here. As long as she ignored the lingering smell of death and the tape outline on the hardwood floor, of course. She walked over to the window and stared at the gorgeous view of Mercer Lake, with the hazy top of Mount Rainier in the distance. This was ridiculously prime real estate for college kids, but football players were in a whole other category of students. She gazed at the water for a few seconds, composing herself, before she turned away from the window and looked around the living room.

The alcohol and pill bottles had been taken away, along with the body. There were several photos on the walls of Brian in his uniform: studio headshots and action photos from games and team photos, along with two pictures of him hoisting the Rose Bowl trophy over his head in victory, from the past two years. A glass case full of trophies ranging from middle school to college stood against the wall, with miniature copies of the Bowl prominent on the top shelf.

She wandered into the kitchen next, pulling on nitrile gloves before she opened the fridge and cupboards. Instead of stereotypical takeout containers and beer bottles, she found a crisper full of fresh vegetables and several packets of chicken breasts. She shouldn't have been surprised since until last month he had been a premier athlete in the middle of an important season, but still, she expected more beer and pizza from a college kid. He must have kept up the habit of healthy eating even after his accident, which had happened right before Cappy left for the funeral.

She went into the bedroom next, where Derek was standing next to a desk holding a model of a stegosaurus. "Kid liked dinosaurs," he said unnecessarily. There were several other models on his shelves, and a world map of paleontological digs. Somehow, this glimpse into a hobby of his made him seem more real to Cappy, and she found it difficult to breathe properly until she turned away from the paleontology books piled on the desk. She ran her finger over the titles in a small bookshelf near the door, which held standard college texts for a student who was either taking the liberal arts idea seriously, or who already had a career mapped out and didn't need to specialize academically. She assumed he fell in the latter category. Used paperbacks for an English lit course, basic math books, and a second-year German text were crammed next to some unused plastic binders. Nothing unusual, but all so very sad.

She didn't see a laptop anywhere—his was likely now in the possession of SPD—but she found a daily planner on the desk, open to the current month's calendar. She flipped through it, but he must have purchased it after the accident—maybe because it was too difficult to look back in the old one on the pages full of practices and games. She took a couple of photos, but all she saw were some due dates for papers and weekly tutoring sessions.

They spent another half hour poking through drawers and closets, but nothing seemed out of place or incriminating. The story was pretty clear to read, in the trophy case and the framed newspaper articles about the football prodigy and the apparent vagueness of his college career. The only evidence of the accident was the pair of crutches leaning next to the bedroom door. Cappy gave them one last look before she and Derek left the apartment.

CHAPTER TWO

Jasmine Harald carefully measured out a quarter cup of muesli and sprinkled it on the blueberries and skyr in her bowl. She drizzled some wildflower honey over the top in a wavy pattern, then put the tub of Icelandic yogurt and the rest of the berries back into the library breakroom's fridge. Most of the other librarians were downstairs, opening the Suzzallo Graduate Library for the day, and the hallway and offices around her were blissfully quiet. She carried her breakfast back to the office and placed it on her desk next to her phone, settling into her chair with a contented sigh as she prepared to eat and scroll through some newsfeeds before tackling the busy day ahead.

Which was, of course, the cue for the hallway outside her office to erupt with voices and laughter. If the noise had been coming from her staff or from students who had lost their way and mistakenly entered the Employees Only area, then she could have shushed them and sent them on their way. But she recognized the voices of Professors Antigone Weston, Libby Hart, and Ariella Romero, so she slid her phone to one side and prepared herself to face the consequences of having chosen these women as her best friends. She smiled as they piled through the door and took up their customary places around her office—Libby in the chair across from her, Ari perched next to Libby on the edge of the desk, and Tig leaning against the window frame. They were disruptive and made it difficult to enjoy a meal in peace, but she wouldn't trade them for anything.

"Ooh, breakfast," Libby said, leaning forward and resting two coffee cups on the desk. They were marked with the logo from Libby's favorite café, in the basement of Odegaard Undergraduate Library. "Anything good? Can I trade a tiny little bite for this entire double espresso con panna?"

Jazz shook her head and laughed, pushing her bowl across to Libby, accepting the coffee in exchange. "Go ahead and eat it. I'll make more later."

Libby grinned her thanks and stirred vigorously, turning Jazz's carefully layered meal into a soupy concoction. Libby took the role of reluctant cook very seriously, rarely eating anything that wasn't borrowed, bought, or prepackaged. Jazz had thought she might change her ways now that she was living with Clare, but that wasn't happening. Jazz had seen the inside of their fridge. Neither one of them was making any move toward domestication, at least in the kitchen.

"Which one of them is winning this morning?" Jazz asked Ari.

"It's a close one so far, with Tig leading twelve to eight," Ari said, removing a tea bag from her own to-go cup and tossing it neatly into the garbage can beside Jazz. She was the bright spot in the room, with Libby and Tig in their customary neutrals and Jazz all in black. Ari had on a simple navy top and ballet flats, but her pants were a silky swirl of jewel tones, edged with gold lace on the cuffs. Her entire wardrobe seemed to consist of pieces from the brand This Would Look Ridiculous on Anyone but Ari.

"What am I winning?" Tig asked.

"I'm losing? What am I losing?" Libby asked at the same time.

"We're keeping track of how many times the two of you mention your girlfriends," Jazz said, holding out her hand with her palm facing up. Ari sighed and fished a dollar out of her bag, slapping it onto Jazz's palm.

"Hey, we're not that bad," Libby protested. "Well, Tig is obviously worse than I am, at least."

"I am not," Tig said, looking as if she was torn between being indignant and trying to recall how many times she had talked about Sergeant Adriana Kent. "I mean, twelve times doesn't seem unreasonable, does it? Is that over the past week?"

Ari shook her head. "This round started when I ran into the two of you near Odegaard, about ten minutes ago. Who knows what the score was before I got there."

Tig and Libby exchanged a guilty look. "Zero to zero," Libby said in an unconvincing tone. She jabbed her spoon toward Jazz and then Ari. "And just wait until one of you falls in love. I'll bet you'll be worse than both of us combined."

"Oh, I'll be awful," Ari agreed with a happy grin. "After the education I've had, I'm programmed to fall in love with someone broody and emotionally unavailable who probably has a past lover locked in the attic or a couple of creepy kids who hang out in deserted corridors. I'll drive the three of you crazy with all my pining and wailing."

"You don't have to sound so excited about that," Tig said, but Ari just shrugged her off.

"I always suspected that your fixation on gothic literature could prove dangerous," Jazz said. "Still, you're usually a very calm person. It might be a nice change of pace for you."

"What about you, Jazz?" Libby asked. "I suppose when you fall in love, you'll give yourself an allotment of times you can mention her name in public. Once per day?"

"And twice on her birthday," Tig added.

Jazz gave a derisive snort, ignoring their laughter. "I'm constitutionally incapable of caring for anyone beyond the level of acquaintance." She paused, then waved her hand at the others. "Well, except for you."

"Oh, please," Ari said, reaching across the desk to slap at Jazz's hand. "That's not true."

Jazz paused, as if contemplating Ari's words. "Yes, you're right. I really don't like the three of you all that much, either."

Jazz leaned back in her chair as her friends' laughter died down and they—thankfully—moved to a new topic of conversation. Her comment about being incapable of love was an exaggeration, and one that Jazz wasn't interested in exploring too deeply. She could feel the emotion but had failed miserably in the follow-through. The kind of love Tig and Libby had found with Kent and Clare seemed to require more mutual support than Jazz could handle. She was fine with being the rock, the one person her partner could rely on, but turning the tables and coming to another person for help or comfort was the part that tripped her up. She had learned that girlfriends tended to want a partner who was emotionally vulnerable on occasion. Go figure.

Tig and Ari left soon after, heading to their morning classes and leaving Jazz and Libby in the office. Jazz leaned back in her chair and sipped her espresso while Libby finished off her breakfast.

"You're good at that," Libby said, her attention on the bowl as she scraped the sides with her spoon, getting the last bits of yogurt and muesli.

"Thank you," Jazz said. "Good at what?"

"Good at deflecting the conversation away from topics that might make you emotional. You make a joke, then get very quiet and still so the conversation moves on without you."

Jazz laughed, hiding how accurate Libby's comment was in this particular case. This once. "I'm not deflecting. I'm just ready to move on to a new topic."

Libby moved a file folder in front of her from the pile on Jazz's desk and set the empty bowl on it. "No. In those cases you just bring up a new subject. I'm talking about emotional triggers for you."

"Like what? Love? You and Tig talk about that all the time, and I don't make jokes or give you the silent treatment."

Libby shrugged. "I don't mean love in general. But if someone mentions you falling in love, you do your…thing."

"Do not," Jazz muttered under her breath, even though she realized how much she sounded like a child on a playground. She paused, fighting her curiosity before finally giving in. "With what other subjects do you erroneously believe I do this *thing*?"

"Labeling children with reading levels," Libby said, not even pausing to think. "Defunding libraries. Wagner's *Ring of the Nibelung* operas."

"I love the *Ring* cycle," Jazz said. She might admit to being slightly opinionated about the first two topics, but the Wagner one was ridiculous. "I go every time it's performed nearby."

"I know," Libby said. "I've been to the four-night extravaganzas you throw in the conference room on the years it's not performed. The Jazz version of an extended Super Bowl party. But what do you do if anyone happens to call the cycle boring or insufferably long?"

Jazz paused for a moment, searching for a response that wouldn't prove Libby's original point. She was already recognizing the urge to run through the same routine in order to end this particular conversation. "Fine," she eventually conceded. "I would make a joke, then stop talking about it."

Libby spread her hands in a *told you so* way. "It's okay," she said. "It's your cute little quirk. I just wish falling in love wasn't on the list of topics to avoid. I don't want you to be lonely."

"I am not cute," Jazz said indignantly. "And not lonely, either. How could I be, with this library full of people and my amazing—though somewhat annoying—friends?"

"Amazingly perceptive, but somewhat nosy friends," Libby corrected. "I've been on the receiving end as well, remember?"

Jazz nodded, thinking back to their intervention with Libby, when they had been worried about her being in a rut, which had resulted in her taking an interest in a murder case and falling in love with Clare. Did Jazz need to trust Libby, now, too? Maybe not the falling in love part, but in learning to be more comfortable with her stronger emotions? No, definitely not. The very thought made her uncomfortable. She was self-aware enough to recognize that her avoidance was more proof for Libby's point, but she didn't care. She was quite comfortable ignoring it altogether.

"I know you love this library," Libby continued, "but it's become home to you. I sometimes wish you had a person in your life who would be your home. You're here late every night, and you eat breakfast here even though you know I might come in and steal it."

Jazz almost made a quip about having an air mattress under her desk to save on rent, but she stopped herself. She couldn't remember the last time she had done more than grab a few hours of sleep in her apartment. It was merely a storage space for her clothes and bed.

"Maybe I like having you steal my breakfast," she said, instead of the joke.

"I know you do," Libby said with a smile. She stood and picked up the bowl. "I have to get ready for my first class, but I'll wash this before I go. Just promise me you'll think about maybe opening yourself up to your emotions, even if they don't happen to be love."

"Sure," Jazz said, mentally adding a sullen *whatever*. It was too petulant to say out loud.

"Good. See you at lunch. Love you."

"Love you, too," Jazz said. She sighed and leaned back in her cushy chair after Libby left. Friends. They could be exhausting. Luckily she had her monthly programming meeting in a few minutes. She'd keep her promise to Libby and give her opinions some thought, but it would have to be later. Preferably much later.

She gathered her tablet and handwritten notes before heading downstairs. The library was busy now, as opposed to the echoing emptiness that had greeted her when she first arrived this morning. Library staff were shelving carts of books and guiding patrons as they helped them locate research materials. Students wandered through the stacks or sat at the tables and carrels, studying calmly for classes or frantically trying to complete assignments left until the last moment. Jazz loved the quiet blend of peace and urgency that always permeated the graduate library.

She waved at a few of the students who were most familiar to her. She had her regulars—both graduate and undergraduate—who routinely spent mornings or evenings surrounded in one layer by their books and in another wider sense by the stacks and wisdom-saturated walls of the library. She didn't get to know as many of them as her friends did, in their roles as professors, but she believed she knew them more deeply, perhaps. She could identify each one by name and major, as well as by how much confidence or lack thereof they felt in their studies and what fears and dreams they might hide from their professors. They were her kindred spirits.

She circled around the circulation desk on the first floor and entered the small meeting room where four of her senior staff members were already assembled. She sat on one side of the long table and opened her calendar app.

"Let's start with community events," she said, readying her stylus. "Denise?"

Unlike the larger planning meetings, when her entire staff would come together and create a programming schedule for the year ahead, Jazz didn't need to do more than facilitate at this one. Her two associate directors and two project coordinators handled most of the meeting, merely running through the month ahead to make sure that the plans they had made before the academic year started were organized and ready to run as smoothly as possible. Jazz insisted on a high level of organizing up front to minimize how many changes would need to be made at the last minute. These meetings were usually more about confirming her detailed planning than they were about sharing information.

"I have two community groups scheduled to use the downstairs alcove this month, but I can switch them to study rooms instead," Denise said. "Liane, I thought you might want to use that space for a memorial display."

Jazz had been admiring the neatly color-coded calendar on her tablet, but she shifted her attention back to the meeting.

She held up her hand to stop Liane, who was about to respond. "Wait, why are we changing rooms when the alcove was already reserved? And whose memorial?"

"Brian Keyes, that young football player who was injured last month," Denise said, sounding surprised that Jazz didn't know the news. "He died by suicide. The police found him yesterday."

Liane nodded solemnly and handed out a printed page to everyone. "Here are some ideas I had, but I'm open to suggestions…"

Jazz took the piece of paper but didn't register what was written on it. Brian. Dead? Suicide? She couldn't accept the news, wouldn't believe any part of it was true. There must have been a mistake, or Denise had misunderstood. That was it. Brian would be in his usual carrel tonight, with his crutches propped against the wall, wearing the slight frown he always did when he was reading his textbooks…

And if it wasn't a mistake?

Jazz couldn't accept that. She would do the research and find out the truth herself, but for now she remained quiet and let her staff plan their tribute display. What did it matter, when they wouldn't need to make use of those ideas once Brian showed up, and they had to admit they were wrong? She felt an unfamiliar urge to fidget but somehow managed to make it through the rest of the meeting without letting her emotions show. The effort required to simply remain still in her seat pushed her to her limit, and her participation from then on was limited to nodding and saying *yes* a lot. She had no idea what other programs and ideas she had authorized, but she supposed she would find out in the coming weeks. For now, she just had to get through the moments standing between her and her research into this rumor.

She finally was able to end the meeting and dismiss her staff, walking back to her office on autopilot. She sat at her desk, suddenly wishing her friends would come barging back into her office, filling the space with their laughter and comfort. But what good would that do if the news was true? None at all. Jazz opened a browser and started her search.

CHAPTER THREE

Cappy walked into the changing room at the station in the morning and saw Clare sitting on the bench by her locker, pulling off her black work boots. She held back a sigh. Obviously their shifts weren't overlapping again today so they wouldn't be patrolling campus together. It wasn't that Cappy disliked working with Derek or the other officers in the department, but she had still been hoping for a return to normalcy. After such a short time knowing each other, Cappy's baseline had apparently become her partnership with Clare.

She hesitated in the doorway for a moment, making sure that her disappointment was buried deep. She loved having her grandmother in Seattle, honestly she did. But they had made the decision for Gran to move more rashly than was normal for Cappy. It seemed her gran felt the same way. They got along well, but they were trying very hard to be respectful of each other, and the result was an overly conscious politeness bordering on stiffness. Cappy had lived on her own since she was eighteen, and her grandmother had been in charge of her own house and family for even longer. Now, they bumped their way through the too-small apartment, apologizing more than they should and awkwardly searching for compromises in television shows and meal plans.

Cappy really needed work to be her predictable, unchanged safe place. After yesterday's suicide call and now with another day of a partner who wasn't Clare...well, she was having trouble getting her bearings. She had work, and she had her home. Neither one felt familiar anymore.

"Hey," she said, sitting next to Clare on the bench. Happy smile, she reminded herself. "Going home?"

"Yes, I…are you okay?" Clare turned at Cappy's greeting, but her expression changed to one of concern when she looked at Cappy's face.

Less happy smile, Cappy decided. Her first attempt might have been more of a grimace. "I'm good, I'm good. Any exciting plans for your free afternoon?"

Clare laughed and leaned forward to shove her boots into her locker. "Well, I've always wanted to see the Great Wall of China, but I think time might be a little tight. Libby's got classes all day, so I'm going to do some studying."

"Studying?"

Clare shook her head. "I forget sometimes how much you missed while you were gone. Did I tell you how glad I am that you're back? Anyway, I'm planning to take the sergeant's test in January. I'm not sure if I'll pass the first time through, but I figured I'd give it a shot, especially since Kent's going for lieutenant, and a spot will be opening if she makes it."

Cappy was silent as she absorbed the information. She felt as if she'd missed a year, not just a little less than a month. She wasn't surprised about Clare since she'd always known about her ambitions to rise through the department ranks, but Kent, too?

"I thought Kent would stay in that sergeant's office until she retired," she said, working to keep her tone light. She figured that was working about as well as her happy smile had.

"Me, too," Clare said with a laugh. "I think Tig has been good for her, plus she was more relaxed and cheerful while she was away from all that paperwork and on the streets chasing a murderer. She has some good ideas about training her officers in different areas of detective work, so we have a sort of task force on hand when those crimes occur. She can't make those kinds of changes until she gets more authority."

"Huh, that's a smart plan," Cappy said, pulling off her gray sweatshirt and buttoning her wool uniform shirt over the thin white T-shirt she had underneath. She liked the idea. She'd found it intellectually stimulating to work on Professor Turnbow's murder with Clare, and she'd appreciate having more thorough training in solving homicides and other types of crimes. This potential promotion for Kent might be beneficial to Cappy, plus she was glad to see her sergeant following her dreams and being happy rather than stagnating in her office with her usual expression of irritated resignation on her face. And Cappy was always going to support Clare and be proud of her accomplishments. She really did wish both women the best as they worked toward their goals.

But still...couldn't they have waited just one more month before making all these big changes and plans, so Cappy could have come home to some stability, no matter how short-term it was going to be? Was that too much to ask? Apparently so.

She stood up and buckled her duty belt on her hips, settling its heavy weight into a more comfortable position. "If you need someone to quiz you before the test, I'm here for you," she said, shutting her locker and spinning the combination lock.

Clare stood as well, slinging the strap of a stuffed-looking backpack over her shoulder. "I will definitely take you up on that," she said. "Test-taking isn't my strong point, so I'm a little intimidated by the prospect."

Cappy had no doubt that Clare would study harder than anyone else who was sitting for the test. Her dyslexia was a challenge, but it had made her resourceful and determined, and Cappy was sure she'd surprise even herself with her results. "You'll do great," she said. "I'll bet five dollars you end up in the top ten percent."

"Deal," Clare said, shaking her hand. "It's risky to make a bet with the person who's taking the test, though. What if I do poorly on purpose just to get that five-dollar bill?"

"Please," Cappy said, as they walked toward the door. "You wouldn't throw the test even for a million-dollar bet."

Clare laughed. "True," she said. She hesitated once they reached the lobby. "You're off this weekend, aren't you? You should come over Saturday night. Libby's friends are coming over. Nothing fancy, but we're going to watch a movie, and probably order some pizza."

"I'm not sure," Cappy said, feeling the awkwardness of having her grandmother at home. Would she be upset if Cappy didn't spend time with her on her first weekend off, or would she be secretly glad to have some peace and quiet with Cappy gone?

"We'd expect you to bring your grandmother, of course," Clare said, as if she understood what was making Cappy hesitate.

Cappy searched her expression, but Clare looked as if she honestly meant what she was saying, and not just making an offer out of obligation.

"Good, then, it's settled," Clare said with a grin, without waiting for Cappy's reply. Did she even need Cappy in the same room for them to have a conversation? "We're looking forward to meeting her. We're expecting plenty of embarrassing Baby Cappy stories."

She waved and headed out onto the street, leaving Cappy standing in the lobby, still in silence. She wrinkled her nose, going over any potential stories her grandmother might tell. Yeah, she was going to have to set some ground rules before they went to Libby's. The key was setting those rules without accidentally reminding her grandmother of something better left unshared with Clare and her friends.

Nearly eight hours later, Cappy was back in the station's lobby, leaning against the counter on the civilian side while Lea Keaton finished up her last report from their shift. Miles Larson was just starting his shift as on-duty desk officer, and he was sorting through a stack of handwritten reports from earlier in the day while Lea sat at one of the desks behind him, typing on her laptop. Cappy and her partners usually alternated who did the paperwork for each call, and Cappy had lucked out with a minor altercation, leaving Lea with a shoplifting incident from the student union building's gift shop. Cappy's had been little more than a squabble between roommates, which likely wouldn't have required police interference if they hadn't had the misfortune of walking around a corner and nearly colliding with the two angry students. She had finished the incident sheet in less than five minutes, while Lea likely had another half hour before she would be done. Cappy would technically be off work in half that time, but she didn't like leaving her partners like that, even if there was nothing she could do to help. Solidarity.

She was mentally checked out, though, and thinking about her dinner plans. Her gran had cooked the night before—an excellent pot roast—so tonight was Cappy's turn. She was trying to decide which burger place to stop at on her way home when the front door of the station burst open, startling her out of her thoughts and making her snap her elbows off the desk and stand upright, as if Kent was springing a surprise inspection on the ranks. She felt a little foolish about her reaction to a citizen coming through the door, but Miles and Lea had been startled as well, which helped her feel less overreactive.

Even once her initial surprise wore off, though, her heartbeat seemed reluctant to slow down. The woman was gorgeous. Tall, dressed head-to-toe in expensive-looking black pants and turtleneck, with only her rectangular maroon glasses providing a hint of color, aside from her jewel-bright blue eyes. Her long blond hair was pulled back in a sleek ponytail. Cappy didn't recall ever applying the term *statuesque* to someone who wasn't a model or actress, but no other word would quite do her justice. She seemed upset, but most civilians who came into the station—unless they were Libby, or maybe her friend Tig coming to kiss Cappy's sergeant—had similar shell-shocked expressions on their faces.

Miles was on duty to handle walk-ins like this, but the woman focused on Cappy instead, probably because she was closer. And maybe staring, just a little. Cappy thought the woman in front of her looked vaguely familiar, as most people who belonged on campus did, but not enough that Cappy thought she had dealt with her before while on the job. She would not have easily forgotten her if she had.

"I need to see Clare," she said, her words clipped, as if she was forcing them to stay under her control. "Clare Sawyer."

"Officer Sawyer isn't here," Cappy said. She was about to gesture toward Miles, sending this woman and whatever trouble she was bringing with her in his direction, but the woman sighed, audibly expressing her disappointment with Cappy, the station, and likely the world in general.

"Fine, then. Kent. Sergeant Kent. She'll do."

"She'll be ecstatic to hear that *she'll do*," Cappy said, torn between wanting to pass that statement on to Kent just to see her reaction, and being terrified of being near when said reaction occurred. "Unfortunately, she isn't here, either. I'm not at liberty to give out their schedules, but I'd be glad to give one of them a message."

"No, I need to…You'll be fine. Who are you?"

"Cappy," she said, disarmed by the way the slight catch in the woman's voice had imbued her previously haughty tone as she demanded to see Clare or Kent with a new thread of despair. "I mean, Officer Flannery."

"Oh yes. Clare's partner. I'm Jazz Harald, Libby's friend. She likes you." She didn't add *So I guess you'll do*, but it was implied.

Something clicked in Cappy's slightly befuddled mind. "Jazz. The librarian with the axe. Of course."

"It's a priceless family heirloom that provides a significant connection to my cultural heritage," Jazz said with the air of someone who had needed to say those words many times in the past. "Do you want to see the paperwork giving me permission to display it in my office?"

She started to reach into her black leather bag, and Cappy had absolutely no doubt that she would be able to produce the appropriate documentation.

"No, I don't need to see it. As long as you don't bring it into the station and wave it around, we're good. Now, I'm going to hand you off to Officer Larson here. He'll be able to assist you with whatever complaint or issue you need to report."

She turned to the desk, prepared to pass Jazz along to Miles, but neither he nor Lea were anywhere to be seen.

"They left," Jazz said unnecessarily.

"About the time I mentioned the axe?"

"Yes."

Damn. Cappy ran her hand through her hair, then tried to flatten out the curls she had made stick out. "Okay, then I guess we're stuck with each other. How can I help you? Did someone dog-ear the pages of one of your library books? Or were they whispering too loudly in the stacks?"

Jazz didn't bother to respond to Cappy's facetious comments, although her glare was comment enough. "I'm here to report a murder," she said evenly.

Cappy just stared at her for a few heartbeats. What was it with Libby and her friends? Was Jazz the latest wannabe detective, imagining mangled corpses lining the sidewalk outside her library? "Really? A murder? I must have missed the call on the radio about a dead body."

"Brian Keyes," Jazz said. "He didn't die by suicide, he was murdered."

Cappy took a deep breath, instinctively changing modes from snide bystander to comforting cop. She had thought she would be able to leave yesterday's visit to Brian's apartment behind once they closed the door behind them, but apparently not. She pointed toward the hallway. "Let's go into one of the meeting rooms, and we can talk about this," she said, leading the way into a small interview room. She sat on one side of the steel table and gestured for Jazz to take the plastic chair across from her. She trusted Miles—who had either been under his desk or hiding behind the filing cabinet—to turn on the cameras in case there was anything they needed to record. Unlikely, since she was convinced this would be a case of calming a distraught person rather than an informational session about a real crime.

She took a small notebook out of her breast pocket and flipped it open, detaching its little pen and setting them in front of her.

"Did you know the deceased well?" she asked.

"Yes," said Jazz confidently. "I mean, fairly well. He came in the library almost every night to study. We talked."

Cappy nodded and wrote that down. "You talked. About…?"

"His studies. His plans for the future."

A future that had disappeared the instant the passenger door had been hit, crushing his dreams along with his legs.

"You're aware of his circumstances, aren't you? His promising football career, his accident?"

"Yes, I know," Jazz said, her voice sharp again. Cappy was starting to recognize when emotions made Jazz's tone have a brittle edge. "I know everyone thinks he took his own life because he couldn't handle the loss, but they're wrong. He was strong, and he was determined to fight back. To make a new life for himself."

She paused and closed her eyes. Cappy watched in silence as Jazz breathed deeply, fighting for control.

"Look, Ms. Harald," Cappy started, speaking softly. "I know what it's like to lose someone you care about to suicide. You might feel anger or guilt. You wish you had seen the signs, or that you could have changed things, but it's not your fault. You saw him for what, an hour or so a day when he was in the library? Talked to him for maybe five minutes at a time? You couldn't have been expected to fully understand the pain he was keeping inside. I don't know if anyone did."

Cappy flipped her notebook closed and leaned forward. "Let's go back to the lobby. I have some information with community resources that might help. There are professionals who will be there for you if you need someone to talk to about what you're feeling."

"I'm the *librarian*," Jazz snapped. "You have that information because I compiled it and distributed it to all campus locations that might need it. I don't need a brochure on dealing with grief, and I don't need to talk to anyone about..." She paused and rubbed her temples. "Well, I probably do, but I have a therapist I can call. I can cope with my grief, I can research the issue of survivor guilt, but I can't launch an investigation when everyone assumes this was a suicide and they refuse to see it as anything else. I...I need your help."

Cappy watched the muscle in Jazz's jaw twitch as she ground out that last sentence. "Wow. That was physically painful for you to say, wasn't it."

Jazz gave a humorless laugh, and Cappy's breath caught as she saw the first glimmer of a smile—weak though it was—on Jazz's face.

"You have no idea," Jazz said.

Cappy opened her notebook again. "Okay. I'm here and I'm listening. Convince me that this should be investigated as a murder."

CHAPTER FOUR

Now that she had Cappy's full attention, Jazz struggled with what to say. She was unfamiliar with the feeling—words had never let her down before. After a few false starts, she made herself sit still and search for the right combination of sentences to convince Cappy to believe her.

She was annoyed with herself for not leaving when Cappy said Clare wasn't there. She could have gone to look for her—starting and ending at Libby's apartment, no doubt—but instead Jazz had stayed. And instead of approaching the young officer with his carefully combed hair and wire-rimmed glasses, who was obviously the person on duty specifically for handling people coming in off the streets, she had aimed directly at Cappy as if pulled by a magnet, the person leaning against the counter and—just as obviously—not there to greet invading civilians.

Libby liked this one, though. As soon as Jazz had put a name with her face, she wasn't about to let Cappy shuffle her off to another officer, even if the other two hadn't conveniently disappeared before she was able to do so. This had everything to do with Cappy's connection to Jazz's best friend and Clare, and absolutely nothing to do with the way her hair looked so sexy and tousled when she ran her hands through it in exasperation or the way her very soft-looking lips seemed as if they were always on the verge of a smile—whether it was a teasing one or a gentle one, like when she was trying to comfort Jazz.

Yes, she was good-looking, and nearly as tall as Jazz, which was pleasant and not very common, but Cappy was appealing for more reasons than that. It was something about her eyes, Jazz decided. Her own were blue without question, no mistaking them for anything else. Cappy's were blue, too, but in a more complicated way. Sometimes gray, sometimes green, depending on the way she tilted her head or—and Jazz hated the whimsy of this thought because it was so unlike her—the emotions and moods behind what she was saying. Here in the harsh lighting of this plastic box of a room, they looked almost teal. Complicated. Jazz had a feeling Cappy herself was the same way. Jazz had always found complexity to be very attractive in a woman.

Cappy sighed and tapped her notebook with her pen. Jazz tried to focus. She was using her attraction to Cappy as a way to avoid this discussion that she had just demanded that they have.

"This is difficult for me," she confessed, rubbing her forehead. Her headache had started during the staff meeting and had been getting progressively worse. She felt as if she had been squinting into the bright sun for an hour, and her jaw was tense as well. "I'm accustomed to dealing in facts, not feelings. I don't have proof about Brian, but I just *know* he didn't take his own life. I need you to find the proof."

"So, describe your gut feelings," Cappy said with a barely hidden sigh. "Most people would hear this news and feel very sorry for Brian and his family, but you came down to the station. Why?"

"He seemed happy," Jazz said after a short struggle with herself. She thought back to those short conversations with him. Cappy was correct that they hadn't spent hours in in-depth discussions but had merely shared a few words when she passed by his carrel. But he was one of her regulars, and she didn't need hours in order to really understand them. "Not like he was hiding his pain behind a smile, but there was a sense of…I think he felt free. Free to explore his passions. Free from the expectations everyone had of him."

"He told you this?"

"Not in so many words, but it was a feeling I got from him," Jazz admitted. She was very uncomfortable with her own words as she floundered through the mess of emotions while knowing there was no foundation of facts and research supporting her declarations.

Cappy paused, looking through the few notes on the page in her little book. "You said you understood what he lost after the accident, but do you really? You're a librarian and an academic, so books and study mean the world to you, but do you think they could replace what he had lost? We're talking millions of dollars. Fame. Huge mansions and fancy cars and people clamoring to get his autograph. Do you really expect me to believe that he was relieved to have lost that and to finally have the chance to study dinosaurs?"

"Dinosaurs?" Jazz echoed. She hadn't mentioned Brian's new focus on paleontology, so how had Cappy known? Maybe she wasn't the only one who thought his death was suspicious, and she grabbed on to that hope.

"Oh," Cappy said with a frown as she ran her hand through her hair again. All her curls were going to be standing on end by the time she finished interviewing Jazz. "I was in his apartment yesterday as part of the investigation. He, um, had a lot of dinosaur stuff."

Jazz nodded. "He was changing majors. He had been taking basic classes, working toward a business degree because that's what some of his teammates were doing. School was just a background to football until the accident, but then he had the chance to make his own decisions. He always was fascinated by dinosaurs and natural history, and he was excited about the chance to study them in his own right, not just as the star football player going through the motions of taking classes."

"And are there paleontology professors who can confirm this newfound passion?"

"No," Jazz said. "He was planning to start taking those classes next semester."

Cappy nodded, fidgeting with her notebook. She hadn't written anything in it since they had been talking. Jazz knew her words weren't enough proof for her, but she didn't have anything else to offer.

"Look, Ms. Harald, I believe what you're saying," Cappy said, pushing the notebook aside and leaning toward her again. "I can accept that there were times when Brian was excited about learning something new, about following a childhood dream. Maybe you encouraged those thoughts in him, and he was responding to your enthusiasm. And that's great—it's a wonderful gift to be able to inspire students. But those feelings of his were momentary, and they weren't enough to get him through nights when he felt despair and loss. You should be proud of the way you touched his life, but you need to accept that there was more going on with him than you saw in the library. None of his other professors or friends or even his family have expressed any doubts about what happened, and as long as the forensic reports agree, we don't have any reason not to rule this a clear suicide."

Jazz stared at her, trying to let Cappy's words sink in and convince her, but they didn't. She felt cold, and it only made her headache worse. "So just accept it and move on? I don't think I can do that."

"There's not much I can do to help," Cappy said. "But I promise that I'll let my sergeant know about your concerns. And when the autopsy report comes in, I'll go over it very carefully. If I see anything suspicious, I'll bring it to her attention." She spread her arms, palms up, in a gesture of surrender. "That's the best I can offer."

Jazz nodded, not trusting herself to speak. It would have to be enough. She felt tight with anger, not directed at Cappy, but at herself. If she had more proof, if she had expressed her feelings more precisely, maybe she would have been taken more seriously. Maybe not. She stood and left the room without another word.

❖

Jazz sat at her desk fiddling with a three-hole punch. She wasn't sure why she had gotten it out in the first place, but now she was turning it end over end, watching tiny circlets of paper fall out every time it went upside down, like she was winning prizes on the most depressing slot machine ever. She felt hopeless. She had gotten nowhere with the police. Sure Cappy had said she'd look into the report, and Jazz had believed her earnestness, but what did it actually mean? Probably nothing. People saw what they expected to see. If everyone was expecting a suicide, they'd be inclined to notice all the facts that corroborated that assumption and ignore anything contrary to it. It was human nature.

She heard a tap on her door and looked up to see Tig standing there, hesitating on the threshold. "Are you okay?" she asked.

Jazz shrugged. "Not really. The grapevine worked fast. Did Cappy call Clare and have her call you to come check on me?"

Tig came in and perched on the windowsill, ignoring the chair even though their other friends weren't there. "Kent, not Clare."

Libby appeared in the doorway before Tig could say more.

"Kent called you, too?" Jazz asked in disbelief. She thought Kent had been actively trying to dissuade Libby from getting involved in police business.

Libby shook her head and took the empty seat. "Cappy called Clare. She told her you swooped into the station like a Valkyrie demanding justice."

Jazz hid a smile. She liked that image. "I just wanted someone to listen to me. I had been hoping to find one of your girlfriends there, but I got stuck with Clare's sidekick instead. She didn't believe anything I said."

Tig and Libby exchanged a glance. Jazz looked at one, then the other. "They don't believe me, either, do they," she said.

"They believe that you're upset about his death," Tig said. "Grief is difficult to handle, and sometimes we try so hard to come up with a logical reason why...Oh, stop looking at me like that, Jazz. Kent just wanted to help, so she gave me some talking points."

"Taken directly from the information packet the librarian gave the police department," said Jazz. "And when I say *the librarian*, I mean me."

"Well, if you're the one who researched the information, then it's probably damned good advice. Maybe you should pay attention to it."

Jazz stared at Tig, letting her words seep in. What she said made more sense than Jazz wanted to acknowledge—not that her research was flawless, but that Jazz really was reacting to Brian's death in predictable ways. She felt a glimmer of doubt forming in her mind. Was she convinced he had been murdered because she couldn't believe that one of her students had been harboring those dark feelings without her being able to discern them?

She suddenly realized that she hadn't yet allowed herself to feel the sadness of Brian's death. She had been so focused on getting someone to believe her that she had managed to ignore the reality that a young man, a student, someone who had confided in her was dead. However it had truly happened, it was a tragedy. She wished she had been alone when this realization hit, and she blinked hard to stem any tears that might dare to roll down her cheeks. Her friends were watching her with obvious concern on their faces. They rarely saw her this vulnerable, and it made her uncomfortable. Had she ever cried in front of them? No, never. She didn't need to spend much time searching her memories to know that.

"I suppose you're regretting telling me to feel my emotions more," she said to Libby with a weak smile. "You both look terrified, like I might collapse into a weeping mess."

"No regret," Libby said, but then she paused. "To be honest, I had hoped you'd start with an emotion like joy or fascination before moving to grief, but I suppose you had to start somewhere."

"Well, I'm finding this fascinating, at least," Tig said. "I had my suspicion that if you ever cried, the tears would melt you, but you seem to be remaining solid. That's good."

"I didn't think she'd melt," Libby said. "I thought she would need to sacrifice one of us to some Norse god in order to banish her weak human feelings and regain her inhuman strength."

The three of them laughed, and Jazz appreciated them sharing the kind of laughter that didn't wipe away pain but made it a little more bearable.

"We understand how you feel," Tig said when the brief laughter had faded away. "We know what it's like to lose a student."

Jazz remembered all too clearly when Tig and Libby had lost their former student and friend, Laura. Jazz hadn't known her when she was at UW, only having spent a little time with her the night she was murdered, but she had been there for her friends while they mourned her.

Libby nodded. "Even though Laura was a grown-up and had graduated, it still felt different. They're our responsibility while they're here, and well, it's just different."

Tig walked over to Libby and put her hand on her shoulder. Jazz knew Libby still struggled with her feelings of guilt about Laura's death since the student who killed her had been in love with Libby and saw Laura as a threat.

"You know it wasn't your fault," Jazz said fiercely, needing Libby to believe her.

Libby shrugged, her eyes sad. "And it's not your fault that Brian made the choice he did. We can understand these things logically, but that doesn't change the way we feel."

"Come on," Tig said to Jazz. "Let's get out of here. We can go for a drink. Or at least let us walk you to your car."

Jazz shook her head. "No. You two go on. I have a few things to finish here before I leave for the night."

Libby stood up, and the two of them hesitated before leaving. "You're sure?"

Jazz nodded. "I'll be fine. But thank you for coming. It helped to talk. Really."

They left with promises to see her in the morning. Once they were gone, Jazz sent a silent thank-you to Cappy, too, for alerting Kent and Clare about Jazz's visit to the station. She probably knew that her calls would trigger a response from Jazz's friends. She'd rather that Cappy had believed her and was furiously investigating Brian's death, but she would accept her compassion as a poor substitute for that.

Maybe Jazz would try again tomorrow, with Clare or Kent. She still didn't fully believe that she was wrong about Brian, but she felt helpless to convince anyone else about her suspicions. This wasn't a debate she could win with logic and research, but if no one else would believe her, then she'd somehow have to try investigating on her own. She was surprised Libby hadn't offered to play detective and take the case, but that was only further proof that even her friends thought she was wrong.

Jazz sighed and stared at her full inbox. She could stay here and do some work, like she'd told Tig, or maybe just play with the hole punch some more. She sighed and pushed away from her desk, standing up and hooking her bag over her shoulder. She had been avoiding walking through the library, but she needed to force herself to do it anyway.

She closed and locked her office, turning out a few lights along the way since the library would be closing soon. She left the hall with all the staff offices and turned right, circling around the perimeter of the library's upper floor. A few students were still seated in the wooden carrels or searching the stacks, and she greeted the few she knew personally by name. She hesitated by the next corner before turning resolutely and walking past the desk where Brian had always studied. She had known him before the accident, but they had talked more often after.

Jazz sat in the chair next to Brian's space. She wasn't a professor, so she didn't have the same type of relationship with students as her friends did. She got to know the ones who worked at the library during the school year, and the occasional ones like Brian who studied on the edges—in the early morning or late at night. She was an adult, but not a teacher or parent, and she had prided herself on how she was able to be there for these students, almost like a priest listening to confessions because they knew they could trust her to listen and not scold or judge or grade.

She shook her head and stood up. How foolish she'd been to think so highly of herself. She'd failed Brian no matter why he had died. Either she hadn't been able to recognize the signs that he was facing suicidal thoughts, or—if he truly had been murdered—she had failed to convince the police to investigate.

So far. She went downstairs and said good night to the librarians and staff members who were closing up for the night before leaving and walking to her car along the darkened paths. She had to trust herself, to trust that her instincts were right about Brian. Otherwise, what good was she to these students, if she never got to know them as well as she thought she did? If she never saw them for who they really were? She got in her car and drove home, forcing those questions out of her mind, not yet ready to face them.

Chapter Five

Cappy was at the small table in her tiny dining nook the next morning when her grandmother came out of the bedroom. She was eating a bowl of cereal with the box propped in front of her on her coffee mug, searching for the various cereal shapes in a picture of a meadow. The puzzle wasn't nearly challenging enough to keep her mind off the past couple of days at work, but the sudoku next to her elbow had been too much for her preoccupied brain to comprehend. She needed the Goldilocks, just-right puzzle but was stuck instead with too-easy and too-hard.

"Breakfast?" she asked her grandmother, waving at the cereal and carton of milk on the table. "I'll cook."

She was expecting a lecture on her childish eating habits, but her gran surprised her by getting another bowl and spoon from the kitchen and setting them on the table.

"Yes, please," she said, sitting across from Cappy as she poured cereal and milk into the bowl. "I haven't had these for ages. I wish they'd get rid of the oat bits and just keep the marshmallows."

"Me too," Cappy said. "Even if they have to keep the oaty part to appease parents, their ratio is way off."

"When I was a child, I asked my mom to call the company and suggest that they make a cereal with just the marshmallows, and to add chocolate chips. She said she'd call, but I don't think she really did."

Cappy pointed her spoon at her grandmother. "You're brilliant. I would so buy that cereal."

"Who wouldn't? I should have gone into product development." She rested her chin in her hand and looked at Cappy. "It's good to see you smiling, dear. You've seemed…well, I know you love your job, but you haven't seemed happy to be back there."

Cappy sighed. She had eaten all the oat pieces first and now chased the last of the marshmallows with her spoon. "It's been a tough couple of days," she admitted. "I feel like I missed a lot, and now everyone is changing course, and I'm just drifting along. Plus, there was a call on my first day back. A student died by suicide."

Maybe, said a voice in her head, sounding suspiciously like Jazz. Their conversation had affected Cappy in more ways than one. Yes, she was beautiful, and Cappy had been surface-level attracted to her. That had happened to her before, although admittedly not always this powerfully, and Cappy had always been able to deal with it by pushing those feelings aside and concentrating on her job. She could do the same in this case. Most likely. But the real reason Jazz seemed stuck in her head was the message she had been trying to communicate to Cappy. This woman who seemed to be driven by order and logic and facts had sat across from Cappy and struggled to express thoughts based on unverifiable intuition. Jazz had asked for help—which had been in itself a challenge for her—without any other reason than *I just have a feeling about this*. Would someone like Jazz push out of her comfort zone that way if there wasn't, just possibly, something to what she was saying?

Maybe, and maybe not. Cappy had said she would carefully look over the autopsy and forensics reports when they were released, and she would keep her promise. That would be the extent of her involvement in this case.

Gran reached over and patted Cappy's hand where it rested on the table. "I'm sorry you had to go on that call," she said. "I know it's still a painful memory for both you and your father, even after so many years."

Cappy nodded, relieved to have someone who understood. "I think I would have been less affected by it if I hadn't just been to Gramps's funeral. And hadn't just seen Dad."

Her relationship with her dad had been strained since childhood. She knew he loved her, and she knew—and had witnessed firsthand—what lengths he would go to in order to protect her, but conversations with him were always stressful to her. There was too much lurking below every interaction, and they had never dealt with their past in an open or healthy way. Too many things unsaid, unhealed, unresolved. He had been weepy and maudlin at his father's funeral a few weeks ago. If Cappy hadn't known better, she might have thought he was roaringly drunk, but he hadn't touched a drop since she was a toddler and never would again. He was sad about Gramps, naturally, but they had never been especially close. He was even sadder about the past. Funerals were difficult for everyone, of course, but they were very triggering for her and her dad.

"But I got through it," Cappy said, resolutely. It was over. She had survived and could put this case behind her soon, unless Jazz invaded the shores of the station again. She got up and rinsed her cereal bowl, wishing she didn't feel a little thrill of hope that Jazz might do just that. She gave her grandmother a kiss on the cheek, then grabbed her work bag and headed to the door, stopping when she remembered her conversation with Clare the day before.

"Oh," she said, turning back to the dining nook. "My partner Clare and her girlfriend are having some friends over for a movie this weekend. They want me to bring you, if you'd like to come?"

"How kind! I'd love to meet your friends," Gran said. She paused, tapping her finger against her mouth. "Where was that? Oh yes, I remember the box. I'll need to go by the storage locker before then, dear."

Cappy frowned. "Okay, but you don't need to wear anything special. It's just a casual get-together in their apartment."

Edith laughed. "I'm not looking for clothes. I just need the box with your baby pictures. We can go by the locker when you get home from work."

"Oh darn. I forgot to tell you," Cappy said, slapping her hand to her forehead. "The storage place burned down. To the ground." She held out her hand, palm up. "But if you give me your key, I can go by and see if anything is salvageable."

Her grandmother laughed and made a shooing motion at her. "I'm not giving you that key. Now get going, and I'll see you after work."

❖

By the time Cappy rushed through the station door, nearly late for turnout, Clare was already in civilian clothes and heading out. They paused together for a moment, an island of stillness in the chaos of the lobby during shift change.

"Hey, thanks for talking to Jazz yesterday," Clare said. "Libby said she was pretty upset about the Keyes boy."

"Oh sure, of course," Cappy said. "Not that I had much choice since everyone else went into hiding and I was the only one left."

Clare laughed. "Yeah, Jazz can be kind of intimidating at times. She's just a big softie at heart, though."

"Really?" Cappy asked.

"Maybe?" Clare echoed Cappy's questioning tone. "Softie might not be the right word. She's very kind, and she loves her friends."

Cappy shrugged. She hadn't been intimidated by Jazz at all, even without imagining some hidden teddy bear side of her. She liked women who were strong and confident. Not that she needed to *like* Jazz. At the moment, she would be content with forgetting all about her and her allegations of murder. "Jazz is a capable and intelligent woman," she said, raising her voice slightly as Officer Keaton walked past them. "Miles and Lea were terrified."

"I was not!" Lea said in an indignant voice. "We merely thought you were handling the situation in a satisfactory way, so we decided to leave you to it."

"I can imagine," Clare said, as if Lea hadn't spoken. "I'm surprised they had the presence of mind to hide and didn't faint dead away."

"They might have," Cappy said with a laugh, dodging Lea's mock punch. "I couldn't see over the counter."

Clare returned to her normal tone of voice as Lea walked away from them, heading toward the turnout room. "One thing Jazz *isn't*," she said, "is impulsive. This seems like it was an impulsive thing to do."

"Grief can mess with any of us," Cappy said. "She seemed to really care about the boy, and hearing about his death made her act out of character. Happens to the best of us."

She had been trying to convince herself since yesterday that grief was the only motivation behind Jazz's accusation of murder and that there was no truth to her convictions. She was succeeding most of the time. The only thing she knew for sure was that she had done her part. She had talked to Jazz, she would read the report, and she had handed the problem off to Kent and Clare, who in turn had handed Jazz over to their girlfriends. Jazz had a support system around her now, and Cappy could walk away from this case without guilt.

"Flannery!"

Cappy jumped at the sound of Kent calling her name from the entrance to the hallway. She hoped her startled squeak had been inaudible, but judging by Clare's laughter it hadn't.

"I know, Sergeant," she said. "I'm late. I'm going."

She was about to jog toward the turnout room, but Kent raised a hand and stopped her in her tracks.

"You're excused from turnout. I need to talk to you." She looked between Cappy and Clare and heaved a long-suffering sigh that was visible even halfway across the lobby. "Sawyer, you might as well come, too. Save Flannery the trouble of calling you afterward."

"I'm in trouble," Cappy said under her breath as they walked toward Kent's retreating back. "Why am I in trouble?"

"I don't know," Clare whispered back. "But you managed to drag me into it, too. Thanks a lot, partner."

"Anytime," Cappy said as they walked into Kent's small office. As usual, there was little in the room besides her plain desk and the piles of paperwork on top of it. Cappy wondered fleetingly why she had so much paper to handle when the department was nearly completely digital, but she didn't ask. She was more interested in keeping her job and all her limbs attached than she was in finding out the answer. If Kent wanted to print out every report and sign it by hand, she was welcome to it.

"Sit," Kent said when they were all inside and Clare had shut the door behind her. Cappy and Clare looked at the single chair, then at each other.

"Arm wrestle you for it?" Clare asked.

Kent rolled her eyes. "One of you sit, one of you hover near the door. Standard protocol for you two."

Clare got the door, and Cappy settled herself on the very edge of the chair so the back legs came off the ground slightly. She seemed to be the one who was going to be reprimanded, so it was only fair that Clare had easier access to an escape route.

"Sit like a normal person," Kent suggested. "I'm not going to yell at you."

Cappy settled deeper in the chair. At least enough so all four legs were on the floor.

"I'm pulling you from active patrol for half days," Kent said to Cappy without any sort of warm up to the conversation. "The rest of your on-duty time will be spent investigating Brian Keyes's death to determine whether it was suicide or foul play."

Cappy's eyes widened in surprise, and she wondered if she could ask Kent to reconsider and yell at her about some minor infraction instead. She blinked a couple of times, trying to come up with something to say in response.

"Is there new information from the autopsy? The forensics report?" Clare asked, when Cappy seemed incapable of speaking.

"No. Cause of death was an overdose of anabolic steroids and amphetamines, along with enough alcohol to knock out a horse. Based on the bottles found in his apartment, that's what we expected. I want you to find out if he took that cocktail on purpose or not."

Cappy shook her head, finally finding her voice. "Wouldn't there have been signs of a struggle if someone had been pouring pills and alcohol down his throat? Most people don't just say *Oh well, whatever* and let it happen."

Kent leaned her elbows on her desk. "Do you really need me to answer that question?"

Cappy sighed and shook her head. Of course she didn't. Grind up some pills and mix them with alcohol. Get Brian drinking enough to loosen his inhibitions and keep encouraging him to have more. Start with some drinking games to get the concoction into his system as quickly as possible, before he could realize what was happening. It was all possible, but highly unlikely.

"He would have needed to trust the person in order for that to work," she said, surprising herself by playing along with Kent's game.

"Exactly," she agreed. "So, find out whom he trusted. Then find out if they had any reason to want him dead."

"Why me?" Cappy asked, pleased that she managed to keep even a hint of petulance out of her tone.

"Because this is your case. You went to the apartment, and you're the one who got a tip from a civilian. I can't spare both of you for this since we're short-handed, but we can handle one person on half shifts for a week or two. Plus, this will give you more time to spend with Jazz and dig a little deeper into her reasons for suspecting a homicide."

Cappy had plenty of excuses for why she should get out of this assignment running through her head, but she managed to reject each one before saying it out loud and having Kent do the rejecting for her. Because of her past, she shouldn't have to work on a suicide case. Well, she had chosen to become a cop, and handling difficult assignments was part of the job. She didn't want to deal with Jazz and her unfounded declarations of murder. Well, she had been the first point of contact for her in the department, and she should be the one who followed through with her. She found Jazz to be too distracting, with her statuesque beauty and the way she had allowed herself to be vulnerable for the sake of a student, when Cappy was certain she wouldn't have done so for herself. Well…yeah, she wasn't going to bother refuting that one because she'd never admit it in this room. And she was permanently striking the word *statuesque* from her vocabulary as of this moment.

Unfortunately, her brain got fatigued from keeping those excuses inside her head and not letting them out of her mouth, and she spoke the last one that came to mind. "Are you sure you're not taking me off shift and assigning me to this case just because Jazz is your girlfriend's friend?"

Clare made a slight hissing sound, as if she was trying to make Cappy stop before she finished her question. Kent laced her fingers together and rested her chin on them, watching Cappy without speaking while Cappy wished desperately for time to unwind so she could claw the words back into her mouth.

"I'm sorry, Sergeant," Cappy said, after the three of them had sat in tense silence for a few heartbeats. "I shouldn't have—"

Kent held up one finger to stop her. "Don't apologize, Flannery," she said. "You have every right to ask that question, especially considering the circumstances." She sighed and leaned back in her chair.

"I asked myself the same thing, and I have two answers for you. First, I hope that I would give any one of our community members the same respect if they came to the office and said a crime had been committed. It's our responsibility to investigate no matter who comes to us for help." She tapped her fingers on her leg as she paused for a moment. "My second response might almost be seen as an affirmative answer to your question. Clare and I have gotten to know this group of women quite well, and I've learned to trust their instincts. They're intelligent and thoughtful, and they have an understanding of this campus and the people on it that we, as outsiders, don't always share. If Jazz truly believes we need to investigate this death, then I don't want to take a chance of ignoring her intuition and possibly letting a murderer go free."

Kent laughed and sat up again. "Now, if it had been Libby making these accusations, I might have been worried that she was just trying to drum up another murder case to solve. No offence, Sawyer."

"None taken," Clare said, waving off her concern. "It's totally something Libby would do. She even said so last night, and I think it bothers her that it's Jazz who's acting this way. The idea that this is a murder seems farfetched, but…well, it's Jazz."

Cappy crossed her arms over her chest. She was convinced enough to spend a few hours a day looking into the circumstances of Brian's life, but she still wasn't prepared to give up all her peace of mind.

"If you both love her so much, why don't we have one of you work with her? I'll do the legwork on the case, and you or Clare can give me a transcript of Jazz's interviews with you."

"You'll be fine," Kent said in a not-very-reassuring tone. "Just don't make Jazz mad."

"And don't say anything negative about books," Clare added. "Ever."

"Maybe we should change your name, too," Kent suggested. "Flannery sounds Celtic. Historically, that hasn't gone so well. How do you feel about Smith?"

Clare frowned. "I think the Celts and Vikings got along in some places. We should ask Tig. She'll know."

Cappy ran her hand through her hair and stood up. "You two, carry on," she said. "I'll go start my futile investigation, keeping my name as it is, thank you."

"Good luck, Freya," Clare said as Cappy passed her. She snapped the door shut behind her, muting their laughter, and didn't allow herself to smile at their jokes until she was far down the hall.

Freya Flannery? She scoffed at the name, then frowned thoughtfully.

Actually...

She'd remember that one. In case she ever had a daughter.

CHAPTER SIX

Cappy started her investigation by walking over to the registrar's office to get Brian's transcript, then settling into one of the tinier meeting rooms in the back of the station with her laptop where she read the forensics report and made a list of potential contacts and their relationships to Brian. In short, doing everything she could think of to delay going to the library and talking to Jazz.

Not that she had anything against Jazz. She wasn't afraid of her, like Clare and even Kent seemed to be, at least a little. Jazz was strong and confident, and Cappy found those traits sexy, not scary. This case was geared to push Cappy's buttons, and she needed to be careful not to let her personal feelings about the issues involved show. She could do that without problem while hiding in the depths of the station, but might not be able to once she was working more closely with another person, especially since Jazz was emotionally invested in the case in her own way. Cappy wasn't comfortable with the personal nature of the investigation, and she had a feeling Jazz felt the same. The campus police department—namely Clare and Kent—didn't have a great track record when it came to maintaining personal boundaries when it came to working on cases with civilians. Cappy was determined to heed the warnings from their experiences and keep her distance from Jazz.

She'd eventually have to talk to her again, of course, but first she wanted to get to know Brian on her own, without Jazz's bias influencing her gut reactions. Cappy was familiar with him as a football player—one of the most naturally gifted she had ever seen—and she had walked through his apartment one time. His space had been typical of a college student, aside from the healthy food, and even the dinosaur models weren't unusual, judging by the other dorm rooms she had visited as a cop. The only things that stood out to make him distinguished from an average student were his football career and his accident. And those things weighed heavily on the case for suicide.

Cappy skimmed through his grades for the past three years. Average, again. Mostly Bs, with some Cs and As sprinkled in. The higher As and Bs were clustered in the math and science classes, while the lower grades were mostly for anything to do with languages and literature.

"Are his grades that bad?" Miles Larson asked from near her shoulder. Cappy hadn't heard him come in. "You're scowling at his transcript."

She handed him the paper, and he sat across the table from her, his eyes skimming rapidly across the page. He shrugged.

"Looks normal, just a smidge over a three-point average. Nothing spectacular, nothing really bad."

"Exactly," Cappy said, sighing when he didn't seem to understand why she was surprised by Brian's grades. "It's a normal spread of grades that indicates either an interest or talent in STEM classes. I was expecting to see something higher. Less differentiated, I guess."

Miles nodded. "Ah, I see what you mean. These don't seem indicative of someone who had all As handed to him, with maybe a B or two for show. It looks like he earned these grades, decent and mediocre as they were."

"Exactly," Cappy said. "So either he made the ethical decision and did his own work, or the football world isn't as corrupt as I thought, and he was never offered the option of automatic grades."

Miles laughed. "Score one for ethics."

She smiled in return. "So, what do you have for me?" she asked.

"Well, to get into a graduate program in paleobiology, he'd need to switch his major to biology, with paleo as his specialty." Miles looked at the transcript again. "He has all the basic requirements done, so he'd be able to focus on the coursework for the major. I'd say possibly extending college for two years? More like three, probably. Difficult for someone who was set to graduate next spring, but doable."

"I only saw one biology class on his transcript," Cappy said. "And the deadline for registering for winter quarter isn't here yet, so we don't know what he was planning to take next term." She paused. If he had been planning anything at all for his future, beyond this week. "So it's a possibility, but nothing more. He was working with a tutor, so I'll check with her and see what he was studying. Is there a graduate program here? I wouldn't think an undergrad biology major would be enough for this career."

Miles nodded in agreement. "You're right. UW has a paleobiology graduate program, but it's very select and small. There are other programs, though, so he'd likely apply to a variety of other schools for either paleontology or paleobiology, depending on the career path he had chosen, if he even had gotten that far."

He paused. "Would have applied. Sorry."

Cappy shrugged. "I do the same thing," she said. "Wishful thinking that he's still here and could follow this dream, if it really was one."

"Yeah." Miles wafted the transcript in the air. "This was the college career of someone who was just going through the motions. The minimum number of classes in his major, and mediocre grades in them. The rest are basic survey courses, ones that would have a lot of sections and wouldn't be full if you happened to register right at the deadline and took whatever was still available. It would have been interesting to see what he could have accomplished if he had passion behind his choices. There's no passion here."

Passion. She really need to go talk to Jazz.

Cappy cringed, as if she'd said those words out loud and Miles heard her make the connection between the two. She only had done so because Jazz had said dinosaurs were Brian's passion. Not because there was any passion between…

Cappy slammed her palms on the table, making Miles jump. Why the hell was she trying to explain herself to herself?

"Sorry," she said. She sighed and stood up, gathering the papers and stuffing them into a file folder. "This case. It's getting to me."

Miles nodded, standing as well and handing her the transcript to add to the folder. "I know," he said softly. "People call the accident and the loss of his career a tragedy, but the real tragedy is that this normal young kid is gone. It sucks."

"Big-time," Cappy agreed. "Thanks for your help with this, Larson. I'm going to talk to the librarian, but I'll be back in about an hour."

"I'll be at the desk until then, staying nice and dry before we have to go get soaked on patrol."

It was already drizzling as Cappy left the station to go to Suzzallo Library, and Miles was likely correct that it was only going to get rainier as the afternoon wore on. She had thought she might have a reprieve for an hour or two, but her wool uniform was already feeling soggy before she crossed Fifteenth and arrived on campus. She jogged along the wet pavement of the university paths until she reached Suzzallo, ducking under the archway and into the shelter of the portico. She ran her hands through her hair, flicking away droplets of rain.

She couldn't even pass by the graduate library anymore without thinking of the murder investigation she and Clare had successfully solved at the beginning of the school year. It felt like ages ago, not merely a couple of months, when she had stood close to this very spot, outside the crime-scene tape and on the brink of working her first homicide. And her first case with Clare. Now she stood here alone.

Cappy knew Clare would be involved in this new investigation, just as Miles had helped her and other officers would lend their expertise, but for the most part she was on her own since there was no tangible indication that this was in fact a homicide. She felt the responsibility of that very keenly. She wasn't about to fully accept Jazz's theory about Brian's death, but at the same time she owed him her full attention to the case. She was the only person standing between the two verdicts. If she did a half-assed job and missed something, it was unlikely that anyone else would launch an investigation to uncover the truth. She wanted to be certain before she gave a final report to Kent.

Plus, if she didn't do a thorough job, Jazz would probably form a vigilante detective agency with her friends and terrorize the campus with their interrogations. It was best that they had a professional cop leading the charge, for all the good it would do them in the end when proof of foul play was nowhere to be found.

Cappy stopped by the circulation desk and was directed upstairs to the staff offices. She climbed the grand stairway, marveling at the architecture in this beautiful building—mostly aware of it thanks to Libby's lectures. She realized that in all her time as a campus officer, she hadn't been upstairs in Suzzallo. Maybe during an orientation tour when she first started doing patrol? She had been on several calls downstairs, removing patrons who were fighting or causing scenes, and twice to called-in bomb threats, which had turned out to be backpacks full of books left by forgetful students.

Once she entered the hallway where the staff offices were located, the building changed tone. The grand reading room, with its soaring, arched ceiling and the intricately carved marble of the staircase gave way to a plain, narrow hallway with several doors opening off it. She poked her head in the ones that didn't have a person's name on the door, finding a utilitarian break room, a closet full of cleaning supplies, and a meeting room with a long table and walls covered with posters of celebrities holding books, exhorting the viewer to READ. Preaching to the choir in this room, but good advice, nonetheless.

Cappy closed the meeting room door and continued to the end of the hallway, where she found Jazz's office. Her door was ajar, and Cappy could see her sitting at her desk and staring out the window with a distracted air. That was exactly what Cappy did when faced with a desk full of paperwork, but she had a feeling it wasn't usual for Jazz. She seemed more like the frenzied activity type, furiously attacking every form or report and beating them into submission with her keyboard.

She rapped gently on the door, and Jazz turned slowly to face her, giving Cappy the impression that Jazz had known she was here even before she knocked.

"Come in, Officer Flannery," she said.

Cappy pushed the door all the way open, not sure if Jazz's formal way of acknowledging her was natural for her, or because she knew Cappy hadn't believed her accusations last night. She guessed it was the former.

"Hello, Ms. Harald," she said, equally formally. "I'm here to... oh wow."

She lost track of what she had been about to say when she got the full view of Jazz's office. The desk was massive—a huge wooden structure that could double as an ark in case of a flood. But the objects vying for space on the office wall behind it were what caught Cappy's attention. There was the axe, of course, lethal looking yet delicately carved, and Cappy really wanted to swing it around. Maybe take a swipe at one of the desk's legs, just for fun. The objects around it were equally amazing, though. Ancient knives, thick and dulled with time or use, jewelry, and even a dented helmet hung on the walls. Chunky wooden shelves held carvings of animals and gods, in varying sizes and materials. There were books everywhere, too, but Cappy had been expecting those. The rest looked like a display in a museum.

"Are these real?" she asked, reaching toward a thick torc with raven skull terminals, but not touching it. She rarely wore any jewelry, but she'd make an exception for this. "Authentic, I mean?"

"Some are ancient pieces, like these figurines," Jazz said. She got up and stood next to Cappy, pointing at several of the small, worn statuettes. "Most of the jewelry, too, but many are replicas, and the originals are in museums, like the raven torc," she said as she took the object off its hook, twisting it slightly and slipping it around Cappy's neck. "When my maternal grandparents passed away, my sisters and I found a house and attic full of family heirlooms. We loaned the rare and more academically significant pieces to a museum in Oslo and had replicas made for us to keep."

Cappy gently fiddled with the torc as Jazz continued to talk about a few of the other artifacts. She felt the heavy weight of it against her collarbones, cool where her neck was still damp from the rain, but the most distracting sensation was the ghost of Jazz's touch where her fingers had brushed Cappy's skin.

"It suits you, with your raven hair," Jazz said, as Cappy removed the torc and handed it back to her.

Cappy smiled, hoping she appeared as composed as Jazz seemed to be. "I'll have to borrow it next time I'm meeting with the Morrigan." Jazz smiled at that comment, and Cappy suddenly realized how close they were standing. She wasn't going to be able to keep up the pretense of composure much longer, so she gestured vaguely at the desk and two chairs and then walked over to sit down. She felt more in control once the massive desk was between them.

"So, Ms.—do you mind if I call you Jazz?"

"That's preferable. And I can call you Caprice?"

"What? No, you can't," Cappy said, throwing composure out the window. She really didn't like that name. "No one knows my name, except…Hey, did Clare tell you?"

Jazz looked amused at her outburst. "Clare didn't tell me anything. I'm a librarian."

"Yes, you've mentioned that. Well, all the librarians I know call me Cappy. How about we stick with that."

Jazz held up her hands in mock surrender, and Cappy struggled to get her thoughts back on track. This case was messing with her already, and not even for the reasons she had anticipated. She needed to dive in and get it wrapped up as soon as possible.

"I'm here because I'm going to be digging a little deeper into Brian's death, and I wanted to get a more detailed statement from you."

Jazz sighed audibly. "You believe me."

Her expression showed such obvious relief that Cappy hated to deny the statement, but she also didn't want to lie to Jazz.

"I'm…skeptical," she said. "But my sergeant asked me to look into this more carefully. This isn't an investigation. I'm just going to ask some questions, talk to other people who knew him. If I turn up something suspicious, then we'll open an official investigation."

"You're on a fact-finding mission, then?" Jazz asked. Cappy nodded. "Good. I'll help. Where do we start?"

Cappy had walked right into that one. "All I need from you is some more details about your interactions with Brian. The rest I can do on my own."

Jazz dismissed her protest with a wave. "You're gathering information, researching his life, and verifying facts. That's what I do. I'm a—"

"A librarian," Cappy finished for her. "Yes, I've heard. And I'm a police officer, so this is my job, not yours."

Jazz looked at her in a calculating way, as if she was figuring things out about Cappy. Cappy did her best to keep her face expressionless, but she would have preferred to run out of the office if she could have found a dignified way to do so.

"One day," Jazz said.

"What?"

"Give me one day to help. One interview, or one research project. If I don't add value to the investigation, or pre-investigation, then I'll leave you on your own."

Cappy wanted to say no, but Kent and Clare had already set a precedent for this kind of collaboration. She'd probably have those two and Jazz's friends hunting her down if she said no. Besides, Jazz knew Brian at least a little better than she did. Cappy would let her tag along for one quick interview, then thank her and send her on her way. She could do this.

"One day," she agreed. "And don't make me regret that."

"Oh, you probably will," Jazz said with a laugh.

It was the first time she had seen Jazz laugh, and it completely transformed her face. Where before Jazz had been beautiful in a sort of distant, serene way, now she had a warmth and vitality to her that made Cappy's breath hitch. She decided she would do just about anything to make her laugh again and to see her nose crinkle in that adorable way.

Oh yeah. She was regretting it already.

Chapter Seven

"So, how do we start?" Jazz asked as she drew a black leather folio across the desk. She needed to get to work on this case and do her best to convince Cappy and the rest of her police department that she had valid points. Then she could find justice for Brian and restore her faith in the relationships she was building here with the students who used her library. And also, she would be able to get away from Cappy, with the smell of her damp uniform that made Jazz imagine curling up under a wool blanket with a book on a rainy day. And her skin that had felt smooth but slightly textured like a fine piece of parchment under Jazz's fingers.

And the smell of her hair—yes, she had smelled Cappy's hair when she put the torc around her neck, and she wasn't proud of herself for doing so—reminded Jazz of one of those shampoos with some ridiculous name like Tropical Breeze or Mango Delight and a scent that someone never thought they liked until suddenly they realized they *did* like it. Very much. Why had she put the torc on Cappy, getting close enough to touch her? Better question, why was she so fixated on that brief moment? It was an old torc, not a fucking wedding ring. She needed to focus and—

"You're going to break your pen," Cappy said. Jazz raised her eyes and looked across the desk at her, and Cappy pointed at her hand. "I mean, do what you want, but it looks like an expensive pen. Be a shame to ruin it."

Jazz pried the nib of the fountain pen out of the notebook, where she had apparently imbedded it through several layers of paper, and set it down on the desk with a sigh.

"I am feeling some stress," she said carefully, not bothering to mention that Cappy herself was currently making up a significant portion of it.

"Understandable," Cappy said. "Why don't you leave the notebook impaling for later and let me take notes now while you talk about Brian. This doesn't count as your one probation day, so don't worry about adding value or whatever the hell you're planning to do. Just answer some questions for me, okay?"

Jazz nodded, relieved. She wasn't at her best, with her thoughts scattered and her attention drawn to inappropriate areas of Cappy's... She sighed again. "Go ahead. Ask your questions. I can guess what the first one will be, by the way."

"Oh, good. Clairvoyance," Cappy said, rolling her eyes as she jotted something down in the notebook she took out of her breast pocket. "That will come in handy. What is my first question?"

"Since I recently watched two of my friends assist the police in solving murders, am I talking myself into seeing a crime where one doesn't exist, just to have my chance at detective work?"

Cappy's lips quirked into a small smile for a moment before she bit her lip and met Jazz's gaze. "Are you? Jealousy is a common human emotion."

"So I've heard," Jazz said, and she was rewarded with a real smile from Cappy. "But no, I'm not fabricating a case for myself, nor was I jealous of theirs. I'm proud of both Tig and Libby for what they did, but solving crimes looks...messy, I suppose. I prefer to do my detecting in the pages of a novel, not on the mean streets."

"Well, we'll keep you off those," Cappy said. "And for the record, while I'll admit that was the first question that came to my mind, it wasn't the first I was going to ask. I thought you might be insulted, so I was going to lead with some less offensive ones."

"I'm never insulted by logic," Jazz said.

"Good. Now, why don't you stop trying to divine the rest of my interview and let me ask the questions." Jazz nodded, and

Cappy continued, "Did you have any contact with Brian outside the library?"

"No. I only spoke to him when he was here studying." Maybe she had said hello in passing on campus sometime? Jazz couldn't remember doing so, and as she thought back to their conversations in the library, they suddenly seemed short and infrequent. She had been so convinced yesterday, certain she would have known if Brian was planning to hurt himself, but what did she really know about him? About any of them?

"Can you show me where he studied?" Cappy asked.

Jazz nodded and got up, relieved to have a chance to move. She led Cappy out of the staff area and over to the carrel Brian usually used. The row of desks was currently empty, so Jazz sat down at the one next to Brian's. Cappy sat on the opposite side, as if he was sitting between them.

"What are you thinking?" Cappy asked. "My question about where you talked to Brian seemed to bother you. You gave a short answer but seemed to be continuing the conversation in your head. Please don't keep details from me that might help us."

Jazz wanted to keep her thoughts to herself and fend off Cappy's intrusive questioning with a vague, impersonal answer, but she was the one who had brought the police into this based on nothing but intuition, so she had to follow through.

"I'm doubting myself," she admitted. "But that doesn't mean I'm not certain he was murdered, just that I'm not certain I'm right about my conclusion. That doesn't make sense, does it? I hate not making sense."

She hesitated, trying to form a more coherent explanation, then gave up and just started talking. "If I'm wrong about him, then what good am I doing here? I try to make the library a haven. We're part of the university, but outside it at the same time. There's no pressure, no judgment in the library, and it's a place where students can come and research, learn, be themselves. I thought I was seeing them in a more…well, pure state. I can't explain it very well, which frustrates me, but I think I'm able to see them for who they really are. I thought I saw Brian for who he was, outside the template of star football player. Just a kid who was trying to make his way through life, and who saw a new path to take. If I'm wrong, then my interactions with these kids are meaningless."

"Wow," said Cappy, leaning forward in her chair with her elbows on her knees, her hands clasped together around her notebook. "Jazz, you can't put all that on Brian. If he was in pain, he was hiding it from everyone, not just you. You weren't the sole person responsible for seeing the signs and recognizing what he was going to do. And sometimes there just aren't any signs, even if we look back and try to find them. This can't invalidate what you're doing here, or the connections you're making with other students."

Jazz blinked away the sting of tears in her eyes. She hated crying even more than she hated not making sense, but no one was expecting her not to cry, or not to feel grief. "Thank you," she said. "I guess I've been more shaken by his death than I was expecting. I'll try to keep my personal issues out of the way and focus on what really matters here."

Cappy gave a humorless laugh and sat up again, crossing her legs. "This is a difficult case, and it's bound to bring up more emotions than either of us is comfortable experiencing. Just don't expect yourself to be unaffected by what happened. You trusted your instincts enough to come to the station last night, so don't shut yourself away from them completely. They might prove useful as we go along."

Jazz understood two things from Cappy's short speech. One was that this investigation—maybe because it was ruled as a suicide?—was affecting her, too, on a personal level. The other was that, even if Cappy was willing to share hints of this connection with Jazz, this wasn't the time or place for more discussion about it. Cappy seemed like someone who was as skilled at keeping her feelings in check as Jazz usually was. Somehow, sensing that she might not be alone in this difficult situation helped her feel more in control.

She glanced out the window at the view Brian would never see again. The trees outside were beginning to shed their leaves, but the limbs were still far from bare. She could see the wet campus paths below and the students scurrying along them with umbrellas or lightweight jackets held over their heads, but the filter of the green-gold oak leaves gave the scene an impressionistic air. From up here, one felt connected to university life, but sheltered from it at the same time.

She looked back at Cappy. "All right. I'm ready for more questions."

Cappy nodded as she looked around. "Do you know why he kept coming upstairs to study? He'd have to take the elevator or walk those steps, and I would think it'd be an awkward trip with crutches when there are plenty of seats downstairs."

"I don't know," Jazz said. "I didn't ask, but I thought he might have been doing it to prove a point, that the accident hadn't crushed his spirit. I'll admit, I thought it might be a macho football-player kind of move."

Cappy nodded thoughtfully. "You mentioned Brian wanting to change majors and follow his passion, but were those dreams or concrete plans? Did he understand that it would mean not graduating with his class and having to work hard to catch up to students who already had years of study in this field?"

"He had done his research," Jazz said. Of course he had. You don't mention goals like his to a librarian and not get advice on how to make them a reality. "I helped him come up with some questions to ask and resources to locate, but he did the work. He was planning his schedule for the next couple of years, including attending summer terms, and he was researching other paleontology and paleobiology programs for graduate work."

She paused, searching for a way to explain the difference between Brian's situation and that of most seniors. "I don't think he had many friends outside his team, although I recall him mentioning an ex-girlfriend. After the accident, I think it was difficult for him to be around his former teammates. I don't believe that he had enough ties to his senior class for it to make any difference if he graduated with them or not, so staying a few more years wouldn't have been an issue."

"That's one way to look at it," Cappy said gently. "Another is that he was isolating himself from the only support system he had.

Yes, he was able to talk to you here in the library, but that leaves twenty-three hours for him to face on his own. Sounds lonely to me."

Jazz wanted to argue, but how could she? She bit her lip, hating that Cappy was able to take these aspects of Brian's life that Jazz felt so sure about and make her see them in new ways. Usually, she appreciated that in interactions with others, but not in this case.

She looked out the window again, this time up at the gray sky speckled with leaves.

"Yes, I guess it does," she agreed.

"And you mentioned that you thought he was perhaps trying to be macho and prove he was still capable by walking up to this floor to study. Maybe there were other students in here who would put value on that type of strength, so he wanted to demonstrate it. Is there a chance he was trying to do something similar in his conversations with you? Trying to prove his potential as a student and his interest in entering a more complex field of study because he knew you would place value on those type of pursuits?"

Jazz stared at Cappy without speaking for a moment. She was somehow managing to erode everything Jazz had believed about Brian with her cold-sounding questions. "Is Brian's death under investigation here, or my convictions about him?"

Cappy spread her hands as if in surrender. "Right now, I'm trying to get a feel for Brian and your relationship with him. You were the one who came to the station with allegations of murder, so don't be angry with me if I probe into your gut feelings. I want you to see some alternatives to your impressions of him, just in case..."

Her voice trailed off, and now it was Cappy's turn to lapse into silence.

"You're trying to protect me from what you believe is the truth," Jazz said, and her throat felt tight with anger, barely letting the words out. "Are you even going to give this investigation a fair chance?"

"I promise you I will not half-ass this investigation," she said firmly, before pausing and visibly exhaling. "But yes, I want to protect you," she admitted, sounding somewhat surprised at her words, which managed to deflate most of Jazz's anger. They were both struggling here.

"Tomorrow we're going to Husky Stadium to talk to a couple of Brian's coaches," Cappy continued. "You're going to get a glimpse into the life he lost, which was a pale imitation of what he had to gain by going pro. I wanted you to be ready to really see the loss he had experienced."

"I don't deny that his loss was tremendous," Jazz said, blinking back more of those annoying tears. "And I would never make light of the grief he must have felt. But I thought...no, I *know* I saw hope there as well."

Cappy nodded and closed her notebook, tucking it back in her pocket and standing up. "Okay, then. Don't lose sight of what drove you to come to the station, but also recognize that there might be more sides to the story than the one you know."

"Of course I'll look at all sides of this case. I'm a—"

"Yes, yes," Cappy said, waving her hand around to encompass all the shelves and books. "I recognize you in your native habitat. I'll see you in the morning."

Jazz sat alone for several minutes after Cappy left. Cappy had made her feel some doubt, and she carefully thought through her remembered conversations with Brian. She couldn't adequately express the way he looked when he talked about his new plans, or the simmering excitement she sensed from him as he spoke about them to her, and Jazz was beginning to wonder if she had imagined those emotions in the first place. She had been passionate about her own studies when she was his age, and maybe she just hoped to see that same joy and determination in the students she encountered. She wanted all of them to find the same fulfillment she had, no matter what their chosen subject, and perhaps—she clung to doubt, but admitted *perhaps*—she was projecting her own experiences onto them.

Finally she stood up and pushed in her chair. At least Cappy was still going through the motions of this unofficial investigation, even though Jazz was certain that she didn't believe in it. They would go to the stadium tomorrow and talk to Brian's coaches, and maybe some of his teammates. Jazz needed to make herself useful in some way, so Cappy would continue to let her tag along. She needed to be involved because she was the only one who believed—most of the time, anyway—in her allegations of murder. She was afraid that if she wasn't there to keep pressing Cappy to learn more and ask more questions, the case would falter to a stop.

Unfortunately, she had no idea how she was going to be helpful in a roomful of people talking about football. She had a lot of research to do between now and tomorrow to make sure she could hold her own in whatever conversations they had.

She walked into her office, prepared to begin right away, and found her three friends in their usual spots.

She sighed in exasperation. She loved them, but didn't they have homework to grade or something?

"What did she do, send out an alert to everyone as she was walking down the stairs?"

"I haven't heard anything," Libby said. "I'm the one who called this meeting. We saw you out by the windows with Cappy, so we came in here to wait."

Jazz looked at Ari, then Tig, who both shrugged. "Fine," she said, sitting behind her desk. Might as well get this over with so she could get to her studying. "What's the agenda?"

"Well, since you're going to be working with Cappy to learn more about Brian…" Libby had the grace to wince at that and added an aside to Jazz. "Okay, I heard about that part from Clare, and Kent told Tig. Anyway—"

"I want to lodge a protest," Ari interrupted, holding up her hand. "I want in on this phone tree you have with the campus police. I only heard about this meeting because I was going to Denny to see Tig."

"Fine," said Libby. "I'll text you from now on, as soon as I hear anything."

"Are these texts about me?" Jazz asked irritably. She didn't need her every move disseminated to her friends and the entire police department.

"Mostly," Libby said without any shame. "We care about you, and this case is going to be difficult. We need to be prepared."

Jazz knew why Libby was worried about her, and it wasn't just because the investigation with Cappy might take up her time, or because the matter at hand was so sad. She knew her friends didn't believe that this was murder any more than Cappy did. They were worried about her being distraught when her allegations proved unjustified. She wasn't used to having everyone trying to protect her. Usually, they'd opt to hide behind her and let her do the protecting.

"We need to pick a temporary leader of our group while you're focused on the case," Libby continued.

"I don't need you to…wait, what?" Jazz asked.

"We have a leader?" Tig asked at the same time.

Jazz shrugged. Of course they did.

"Of course we do," Libby echoed her thoughts. "It's Jazz. But you're taking over on a temporary basis."

"Why me? You're the one who called this meeting. It seems like you want to be in charge."

"No thanks. I'm the dreamer, you're the practical one."

Tig frowned. "I really don't think that's true, but why not Ari, then?"

"Not Ari," Jazz said.

"Not me," Ari agreed. She shrugged. "I'm easily corrupted by power. I wouldn't want to give up control once Jazz returns to her senses and stops playing detective."

Tig still looked confused by the conversation. "Do I need to do anything?"

"No," Libby said. "Just be bossy."

"And roll your eyes when one of us does something unreasonable," Ari added.

"Like this?" Tig asked, but Ari shook her head at the weak attempt.

"Make it more Jazz-like. You'll need to practice in a mirror."

"You've been on the receiving end enough," Jazz said. "You should be a pro by now. Oh, and you'll need to make sure Libby gets fed," she added.

Libby pointed at her for emphasis. "Yeah, do that."

Tig lifted her hands and dropped them again in surrender. "Fine, I'll be temporary leader and roll my eyes and feed Libby. Do I need to rearrange your bookshelves when I stop by your offices, too?"

"No. I'll still do that," Jazz said. She wasn't about to give up all her responsibilities. "I've seen your shelves. You're definitely not qualified."

Tig picked up a binder clip from Jazz's desk and threw it at her. Jazz ducked, laughing, and they continued their silly conversation. Jazz eased back from it eventually, as she usually did, and watched her friends chat and laugh. She had never been someone who easily formed friendships with her sometimes-brittle edges and her naturally composed demeanor, which a lot of people mistakenly interpreted as coldness or haughtiness. She still had no idea how this group had formed around her, but she was grateful every day for them. They might not truly believe her about Brian, but with words and laughter, they were letting her know they supported her and that they were giving her the space to be less rational and in control than she usually was.

"Here's your first test, Tig," Jazz said when there was a lull in the conversation. "Today is Thursday, and Libby has had two afternoon classes with no break in between. What do you do?"

"That's an easy one," Tig said, flicking imaginary dust off the shoulder of her blazer. "I suggest that we all leave here and go to La Mia Famiglia for Italian food." Tig gave a theatrical bow as they applauded her.

Jazz put on her leather jacket and picked up her bag. She needed to eat, too. Even more than that, she needed to be around her friends. She would research everything she needed to know about football later.

Chapter Eight

Cappy took the elevator to the third floor of Suzzallo, then turned toward the stacks instead of going directly to Jazz's office. She was following the route she assumed Brian took every evening when he came here to study. Jazz seemed to believe he was proving a point by climbing to the upper floor with his crutches, though Cappy doubted he could have managed that sweeping staircase so soon after his accident. He likely took the elevator, thereby negating any he-man statement he might have made. Was it force of habit that made him choose this path rather than picking a seat on the ground floor? Maybe. Jazz wasn't exaggerating when she said people knew this was Brian's usual place. When Cappy walked by the desk, she saw several single roses and bundles of flowers laid on top of the desk, apparently placed there this morning after the official statement of his death had been released.

She paused for a moment by the impromptu memorial. The view from here was pretty, and the side wall behind the stacks made for a peaceful place to read, but Cappy wondered if part of the appeal of this seat was its proximity to Jazz's office. She had been in the habit of walking by and chatting with Brian, and that might have been a significant factor for a young man who was feeling isolated and whose life was in upheaval. Even though Cappy was sure Jazz would have found him no matter where he was sitting, he might have continued to come here to maintain their connection. That didn't necessarily mean Jazz was correct and he hadn't been contemplating suicide. Maybe the opposite, in fact, if he was lacking other supportive figures in his life.

They should be able to find out more about that today. His coaches would have been his surrogate parents here, and they would have been near constant presences in his life since his freshman year. Cappy hoped they would be able to share some insight into his state of mind, whether it corroborated Jazz's opinion or not. For her peace of mind and Jazz's, Cappy wanted this case wrapped up as soon as possible.

She found Jazz prowling through the staff hallway, obviously waiting impatiently for Cappy to arrive.

"Am I late?" she asked when Jazz beelined for her, and they started walking back the way Cappy had just come.

"No," Jazz said, adjusting the shoulder strap of her bag. It looked suspiciously full, as if she had numerous note-taking implements stored in there and ready to deploy at a moment's notice. "I'm just anxious."

"No need to be," Cappy said as they walked down the stairs, forgoing the elevator. "Let's go over some ground rules, and I'm sure they'll put you at ease."

"Fine," Jazz said shortly.

"Rule one. No more rolling your eyes like that."

"I'll try," Jazz said. "But since I don't have any control over what you might say, I can't make any promises."

Cappy laughed. Jazz being snide was preferable to her being doubtful and sad. "Good enough. Rule two, I'm the one who does the talking during these interviews. You just need to listen, and later on, when we're far, far away from the stadium, you can give me your opinion on what was said."

Jazz paused by the front door. "No talking at all?"

"*Hello, thank you*, and *my what an impressive trophy* are all acceptable," Cappy said, ticking them off on her fingers. "And rule three, remember that this is just a conversation with these men. We're not accusing them of anything or sharing our conspiracy theory that this was a homicide. We're just trying to get to know Brian a little better."

"And you think we can learn this from them?" Jazz asked as they walked down the steps and headed into the tunnel formed by the Allen Library building, with clear skepticism in her voice.

"Do I think these people who spent hours a day with Brian over the past three and a half years might know him well enough to judge how he's been feeling lately? Yes, I do."

"We'll see," Jazz said. "I agree that they might...oh dear."

Cappy followed Jazz's gaze to the HUB, the Husky Union Building. Tig and another woman had just come out of the building and were heading toward them. They were a study in contrasts, with Tig in don't-notice-me brown and her companion in a bright pantsuit in shades of yellow and orange, with a green headscarf. "You don't seem happy to see them," Cappy said in a low voice as they approached. "Isn't Tig a friend of yours? And the one who is currently dating my sergeant?"

"Yes, and that's Professor Samiya Ayari with her. Sami. They are brilliant and lovely women, and I'm quite fond of them. Individually. But they're both obsessed with the new Mediterranean Studies program they're designing, and when you get them together, they meld into a Med Studies hive mind. If you say it looks like it might rain, you're likely to get a half-hour lecture comparing weather patterns in the 3rd century BCE Mediterranean basin."

Cappy laughed. "You're exaggerating."

"I don't exaggerate," Jazz said. "Go ahead, try it."

"I will," Cappy said, continuing to whisper. "You know, they look like one of the autumn trees on campus. Tig is the bark and Sami's the leaves."

Jazz laughed out loud just as the two groups met up. She gave Cappy a shove with her shoulder and controlled her voice enough to introduce her to Sami. Cappy grinned, proud of herself for breaking Jazz's characteristic composure, and shook hands with her.

"Antigone has told me that you were a friend of the young man who passed recently," Sami said, reaching for Jazz's hand and giving it a squeeze. "I am very sorry about this loss."

Jazz thanked her with the sort of shaky look she got when Brian's death was mentioned. Cappy quickly jumped into the conversation, steering it away from Jazz.

"We're on our way to the stadium to talk to his coaches," she said, searching for a reason why the two of them would be going there, as well as a way to refute Jazz's theory about their hive mind. "A welfare check of sorts, to make sure everyone is doing okay. So, are either of you football fans?"

"Not really," Tig said, which Cappy interpreted as *not at all*.

"Not American football," Sami said with a shrug. "Although…"

She looked at Tig, who nodded as if agreeing with something unspoken.

"You're right, Sami. What a great idea for a special topics seminar."

"A comparative study of games and sports in ancient Mediterranean cultures. Thank you, Officer Flannery."

"Nice one, Cappy," Tig added, patting her on the shoulder as the two women walked away, talking rapidly about this new idea.

"Anytime," Cappy called after them with a wave. "What do you know," she said as they left. "I'm an influencer."

"Really. An influencer," Jazz said, minus the eye roll, but barely.

"On a campus level, at least," Cappy amended as they started walking along the path again. "I've influenced their curriculum, haven't I?"

"Ridiculous. They just use any excuse to turn the conversation to their department, like I told you."

Cappy smiled and bumped Jazz with her elbow. "Uh-oh," she said in a singsong voice. "Someone sounds jealous. What happened? Did you suggest a course on libraries of the Mediterranean basin, and they turned you down?"

"They didn't turn me down," Jazz said in a haughty tone but then she paused. "They said they'd think about it."

Cappy laughed. "Ouch. They'd *think* about it? Honey, don't waste your time waiting by the phone for that call. It ain't coming."

"Well, who needs them, anyway," Jazz said, still trying to look stern, but one side of her mouth quirked up in a smile.

"That's the spirit," Cappy cheered her on. "There are plenty of other departments in the sea."

"Bigger ones, too," Jazz added with a full smile.

"That's right," Cappy said, turning back to face the path in front of them because Jazz's smile threatened her emotional stability. "You'll find yourself a bigger, better department that won't take you for granted like they do."

Jazz laughed, too, then they fell silent as they weaved among the buildings that housed the Engineering and Computer Sciences Departments. Cappy had to remind herself that Jazz was a burden. This case was stressful and unpleasant. She was supposed to be getting through the interviews with all haste, not enjoying herself and feeling like she had won a prize when she made Jazz smile, with bonus points if she laughed.

They came out of the trees and the entire UW sports complex opened up before them, with the Hec Edmundson Pavilion directly in front of them, and baseball and soccer stadiums to their left. Cappy loved this view, and it was the reason why she had wanted them to walk to the stadium instead of taking a patrol car, or even one of the golf carts the officers sometimes used to get around campus more quickly. She loved the moment when Lake Washington and the massive walls of Husky Stadium appeared, and today was no exception. Even though Mount Rainier was hidden from view by clouds, the area was gorgeous.

They crossed Montlake Boulevard on an overpass and headed toward the stadium. "Do you remember the rules?" Cappy asked.

"Yes, but when you ask questions like that, I have a difficult time obeying rule one."

Cappy glanced at her. "Well, at least you're making an effort. Sort of."

"I still don't understand why I'm not supposed to talk. What if I think of a question to ask? Should I mime it, or write it on a piece of paper and hold it up?"

Cappy broke rule one, but luckily it didn't apply to her. "Bring it up after we leave. If I think it was a good question, I'll call the coach later and ask. We're going to mainly talk about Brian's football career, I'm guessing, just to get a feel for how the coaches think he was handling the accident. Do you even know anything about football?"

Jazz shrugged. "It's a game with a ball. One team is trying to get it over, into, or through something, and the other one is trying to stop them."

"Let me guess. You're not a fan of team sports."

"There are too many variables to track. I prefer less chaotic sports like archery or tennis. Plus, I disagree with the inordinate amount of value our society puts on the elite players of these sports. We're defunding libraries far too frequently, while a handful of people in sports are paid enough money to rebuild the Library of Alexandria." She paused and bit her lip before continuing. "I suppose what we need to do is put something at library circulation desks for patrons to get a ball over, into, or through before they can check out a book. Maybe then they'll put more value on reading."

She laughed, but it wasn't the kind of laugh that earned bonus points. Cappy waited a few seconds, but Jazz remained silent.

"Well?" Cappy asked.

"Well what?"

Cappy shrugged. "This is obviously a topic you care about. I was expecting you to say more about it."

"Damn, she was right," Jazz muttered. "Libby," she said to Cappy who had frowned in confusion. "She told me that when conversations turn to subjects I'm emotional about, I make a joke, then go silent until the subject is changed."

"Ah. So, what other subjects turn you into a comedian?"

Jazz gestured vaguely. "Oh, there are these operas. And…other things."

Cappy thought she saw a slight flush on Jazz's cheeks, and she really wanted to know what the *other things* were. "Are you blushing," she asked, "or are you being overtaken by some sort of Viking battle rage?"

Jazz laughed again—a good one this time—and put the back of her hand against her cheek. "Battle rage. But back to the topic at hand, I do understand the basic rules of football, at least enough to take part in this conversation."

"Take part by listening," Cappy said, aiming toward one of the security guards near the front of the stadium and giving her name.

She was definitely bringing this conversation up again when they weren't about to interview someone. The guard pointed her toward a stairwell that would lead to the locker rooms, and she and Jazz walked away from the busy street and sidewalk and entered the relative quiet of the stadium.

The team was out on the turf in practice uniforms, running drills and scrimmaging. Cappy wanted to settle in the stands and watch, perhaps yelling a few pointers as they occurred to her, but she turned away from the field and aimed toward the head coach's office. She'd get her chance to see a little of the practice session when they went onto the field to talk to the offensive coordinator. She had spotted him on the sidelines, surrounded by a group of players.

When they got to Coach Moran's office, she gave Jazz what she hoped was a very stern shushing look—she was a librarian, after all, so she should understand that kind of look—and knocked on the partially open door.

Wayne Moran called for them to come in, and Cappy introduced the two of them, shaking his hand and thanking him for taking the time to talk to them. Wayne had sandy brown hair and a youthful face. From a distance, he would easily look as young as his players, but up close, Cappy could see the stress lines on his face. He was a man whose career hinged on the team's performance every week, the same as his players. UW had a strong base of fans and alumni, and they didn't accept losing particularly well. The head coach's reputation rose and fell along with the numbers on the scoreboard at every game.

"We saw the team out on the field," Cappy said as a casual opener to their conversation. "Getting ready for the game against Penn?"

He gave her one of those smiles he wore for sideline reporters. "Yes, ma'am. Penn's a tough team, a worthy opponent, but my men have been working hard and they're ready to fight for victory."

A vague and predictable answer. "You realize that Penn's relying heavily on their long-range receivers this year, don't you? Are you planning to switch to zone defense so we can get better deep coverage than you did in the game against Michigan?"

He seemed to barely keep hold of his camera-ready smile. "Is the police department sending officers here to tell me how to run my team?"

Cappy laughed, ignoring Jazz's laser-like gaze. She could feel it focused on her, likely transmitting the question *Tell me again why you get to talk, and I don't?* "Of course not, Coach. You're the expert here, and your record speaks for itself."

Okay, maybe not the best comeback, especially since his team had been taking a beating in the conference standings since losing Brian. Oh well, she was on the subject, so she'd have to continue.

"I know it's been hard for you, not only losing a star player like Brian Keyes to an accident but then losing him as a friend and former player. We're here as representatives of the department to offer our condolences and to let you know that we're prepared to assist any of your staff or players who might need help dealing with this loss. Ms. Harald has compiled a packet of community resources, and these are available at the station or at Suzzallo Library."

He softened again at the mention of Brian's name. She hadn't started the interview with much tact—and she still wanted to know how he was preparing to handle those Penn receivers—but she felt as if she'd pulled them back from the brink of being tossed out of the office.

"It has been a very difficult time," he said, and this time his emotions seemed to match his words. "Brian was a great kid, even beyond his undisputed talent on the field. He will be missed by all of us, coaches and players."

Cappy nodded. "Had you seen him much since the accident? Did he still come to watch practices, or was that too sad for him?"

Wayne frowned. "All the coaches visited him in the hospital, of course. He came by a couple of times after, but...well, it was difficult for all of us. The visits were awkward, I'm ashamed to say. I wish I could have done more."

Cappy wanted to ask what, exactly, had been difficult for the coach. Losing his star player? That should have taken a back seat to the one person actually facing the difficulty in life—Brian himself. She read between the lines and saw a boy whose life had been football, and when he lost the ability to play, he had still tried to connect with those people he had known through the sport, and the result had been awkward. Awkward? Cappy was surprised by the anger she felt at his words, and his vague wish that he had done more. He damned well should have. He should have brought Brian back into the fold and found some way to make him feel like he was still part of the team. Instead, had Brian come here and watched his coaches act as if they were mourning him before he was dead?

Unfortunately, and Cappy was about to regret this, her anger left enough of a silence for Jazz to decide to fill it.

"Coach, Brian was apparently in possession of performance enhancing drugs. Do you or your staff know how he got hold of these?"

CHAPTER NINE

The look the coach gave Jazz surely screamed battle rage far more than her little blush had. Cappy was staring at her with a shocked expression on her face. Neither spoke, and Jazz considered filling the silence again, this time with an apology, but she didn't. She really wanted to know the answer to her question.

"Are you accusing me of giving this young man drugs?" Coach Moran asked, his voice sounding barely controlled. "Or of being complicit in his suicide?"

Jazz had a brief moment when she thought she had caught him in a confession of sorts. She hadn't said Brian had overdosed on those drugs, merely that he had been in possession of them. Had the cause of his death even been released yet? Unfortunately, the realization that, if that was the case, she shouldn't have mentioned it to anyone outside the police department came hard on the heels of her momentary hope that she had discovered both proof of murder and a guilty suspect in one fell swoop.

"Of course not," Cappy said, stretching her arm in front of Jazz as if she was creating a barrier of silence around her. "It's a fair question for the man who coached Brian for nearly four years. Ms. Harald was merely asking if you were aware of any history of substance abuse in Brian's past."

That hadn't been what she was asking, but she had to admit it sounded more tactful than the words that had actually come out of her mouth.

Coach Moran shook his head sharply. "Brian Keyes was as clean as they come. He had far too much at stake to risk getting caught with drugs, and far too much natural talent to need them. If I had seen any sign of...well, I'd have put a stop to it immediately."

His hesitation had been brief, less than a second, and Jazz wondered if she had imagined it. Cappy, though, pounced on him like a panther that had spotted a juicy looking rabbit.

"Any sign," she repeated. "You did see a sign, didn't you? What was it, erratic behavior, changes in performance, money problems... ah, money problems," she said with a nod, apparently reading some slight change in the coach's demeanor. "He was on a full scholarship with a stipend and free room and board. Yet he still had financial trouble?"

Jazz had seen Cappy as a reluctant participant in this case, as a funny and playful conversationalist, and as a sympathetic person when Jazz was having her moments of sadness. Now she was seeing Cappy the cop, and she realized how lucky she and Brian were to have her on their side.

Coach Moran scowled at Cappy. "I would have noticed if he was on drugs. He blew through his stipend some months, and I helped him out now and then. Probably buying presents for his girlfriend or making payments on a sports car. He was going to be making a fortune soon, and who could blame him for taking an advance on the lifestyle? But drugs? No way."

Cappy nodded, writing in her notebook. "His girlfriend's name?"

The coach sighed. "Ex, I think, but her name is Justine Hillman. This is no secret. She was the one driving the car when he had his accident."

Cappy flipped her notebook closed and tucked it away again. "We've taken up too much of your time, and I need to get back to the station. Thank you for meeting with us, and again, I'm sorry for your loss."

The coach gave them a curt wave as they left, not bothering to stand or shake their hands. Cappy grabbed Jazz's sleeve as soon as they were back in the cement tunnel and towed her along the echoing path.

"What the fuck was that? How could you possibly interpret the rule not to speak as a request for you to accuse him of giving his players drugs?"

"I thought it was a reasonable question," Jazz said weakly, hurrying to keep up with Cappy's fast pace. Was she going to drag Jazz all the way back to her library? "I wasn't supposed to mention it, was I? Have they even released the cause of death?"

As soon as Cappy deposited her back at Suzzallo, she needed to research the penalty for sharing undisclosed police information. She was quite sure she wasn't going to be happy with the results.

"Not officially, no," Cappy said. "But it's been leaked, so it's common knowledge. I wouldn't have told you the forensics results in the first place if it hadn't been. That's beside the point, though. Probation is over. You were supposed to add value, not enrage the person we were interviewing."

"At least I didn't try to tell him how to coach his team," Jazz muttered.

Cappy stopped in the tunnel and faced her, hands on her hips. "Penn's receivers are beasts," she said, "and their quarterback has an arm like a catapult. We need to be prepared to…oh, fine. I shouldn't have said what I did, either. Still, you're back to doing research in the library. No more fieldwork."

Jazz frowned. She wanted to argue more, but Cappy was right. She had asked Jazz not to interfere, and she had gone ahead and done so. She didn't regret asking the question—after all, they had gotten valuable information as a result of it—but she was worried by the lack of control that had led her to ask it. She had wanted to fling the accusation at him, had wanted him to admit to being a murderer. Not because she had anything against him or because she actually believed he was the guilty party here—if there even was one—but because she was angry and sad and frustrated that no one truly believed her about Brian. She had wanted someone, anyone, to be guilty.

If she couldn't get through a ten-minute interview without losing control, Cappy was right to keep her away from them.

Cappy grabbed her sleeve again and continued towing her down the tunnel, breaking into a jog. "Hurry," she said. "We need to get to Pryce Walker before anyone else does."

Who? Oh, the offensive something…coordinator? "I thought I failed probation," Jazz said, running alongside Cappy.

"You did. Miserably. But it doesn't take effect until after we talk to Pryce, and that needs to happen before Moran alerts the entire coaching staff that the police are making accusations about drugs. We won't get anything more than soundbites out of them after that happens."

"And I get to come with you?" Jazz asked, although Cappy's grip on her shirt seemed to indicate the affirmative.

"I am not leaving you alone in this stadium. You can come this time, but please, please let me do the talking."

"Okay?" Cappy prompted when Jazz didn't respond.

"Yes, okay," Jazz said. "I thought you wanted me to start right away. Letting you do the talking, that is."

Cappy muttered something under her breath that might have been an insult to librarians everywhere, but Jazz couldn't afford to spend energy trying to figure out what Cappy had said and how to respond to it. She was too busy trying to keep up as they ran up the stairs, along a concrete plaza, and down yet more stairs to the field. She worked out regularly and had thought she was fairly fit, but she was apparently in good enough shape for wandering around a library and reading, not racing through a massive, labyrinthine stadium. When they finally got near enough to Pryce for Cappy to let go of her arm and slow to a walk, Jazz felt winded while Cappy looked as fresh as if she was out for a leisurely stroll. Cappy didn't need to worry about Jazz interrupting this interview because she was putting all her effort into looking composed and not shoving the players aside to get to their Gatorade.

"Jog much?" Cappy asked sweetly.

"Shut up," said Jazz. Not her cleverest retort, but it was all she could manage.

Cappy laughed as they paused for a moment and waited for Pryce to finish talking to one of his players. "He was a talented receiver in college," she said quietly. "Ohio State. Went pro for a few years but didn't get much playing time and never really distinguished himself at that level. He's been a decent coach, though, and should be next in line if Moran ever decides to leave. Or is let go. Job security isn't great in this business."

She raised her voice as the player trotted back onto the field, greeting Pryce and going through her introductions and story about why they were here just as she had with the head coach. Pryce was wearing a headset, which he slid off his ear and let drape around his neck while he talked to them. He didn't look much older than Moran, but his dark hair was thinning, and he kept it long and swept to the side in what seemed to be the early stages of a bad comb-over. He was leaner than the coach and had on a bright white polo shirt that had *Coaching Staff* in purple and gold letters on the chest pocket.

"Damned shame," he said. "I loved that kid. Love all of them, you know, they're like sons to me, but he was something special."

"I heard that he came back to visit a couple of times after his accident," Cappy said. "I know it must have been a struggle for him to accept the loss of his career as a player, but did you notice anything unusual about his mood or attitude, aside from the expected disappointment?"

Pryce shook his head. "He put on a cheerful face, but we were all still in shock. It was good to see him up and around, but they were real somber visits. I never knew quite what to say."

His words echoed what Moran had said. Jazz couldn't help but wonder how painful those visits had been for Brian. His coaches seemed focused on how hard it had been for them to talk to him but didn't seem to put much thought into how Brian had been feeling.

"He lost more than his career in that accident," Cappy said, and Jazz thought she detected a hint of icy disdain in her voice. "He lost his team—his coaches and his teammates. I'm sorry it was uncomfortable when he came to visit, but maybe he came back here because he was trying to keep some aspect of these connections. Do you know if he had many friends outside of football?"

Pryce shrugged, seemingly indifferent to what Cappy was saying. Jazz heard the censure in her words, but he acted oblivious to it. "Brian was set apart from the beginning," he said with a shrug. "Between school and football activities, whether they were practices, games, or team social events, he didn't seem to have time for much else. Some of our players are more involved with campus life, but he had been on track for going pro since before high school. He was very driven and focused on succeeding, and that didn't leave room for much else." He paused and gave a derisive laugh. "He had that girlfriend, though. And look where that got him."

Cappy glanced at Jazz as if worried she might say something insulting to Pryce, but she kept her silence. She wouldn't have minded punching him in the gut, but she guessed that might have been an unspoken rule four: Don't turn the interview into a boxing match.

"Had you heard about any trouble he was having before the accident?" Cappy asked. "Issues with drugs or money?"

He shrugged. "I loaned him money a few times, but that was it. Some of these kids go a little crazy first time away from home, being a big deal on campus. High-maintenance girlfriend, you know. Drugs, though? Not a chance. He was a stickler for the rules. Why do you ask about that?"

Cappy echoed his shrug. "You've heard rumors about how he died, I'm sure."

Pryce nodded. "Those things are around. If the kids really want them, they'll find them. But while he was playing? Not a chance."

Cappy thanked him and reiterated the offer of community resources for the grieving teammates, then she and Jazz walked along the edge of the field. Jazz glanced back and saw Pryce watching them leave. He had his headset on again and was talking into the mouthpiece. To Coach Moran, most likely. She turned away again and followed Cappy until they reached the shadow of the tunnel leading back the way they had come.

Cappy turned and watched the players running around on the field. She pointed at one of them. "Greg Masters," she said. "He replaced Brian as running back."

Jazz had no idea how she knew which player was which, since they all looked similar in their helmets and practice uniforms. "Is he any good?" she asked.

"He sucks," Cappy said. "The team was built around Brian, capitalizing on his strengths and designed to support him. These coaches started mourning Brian over a month ago, when he had his accident. I can't imagine how he felt, coming back here and seeing the disappointment in their eyes." She looked at Jazz. "You saw a future for him. I really don't think anyone else did."

Cappy sighed and continued walking out of the stadium. Jazz trailed after, thinking about the ramifications of what Cappy had said. She might have had a small impact on Brian's life, encouraging his rediscovered passion for old dinosaur bones, but was Cappy correct that no one else did? Were ten minutes a night in the library enough to make up for the loss of his career, his teammates and coaches, and even his girlfriend?

"Today made you even more sure he died by suicide, didn't it?" Jazz asked.

Cappy shrugged. "Look, I want to believe you, but I think you're seeing a small part of the picture. Maybe the Brian you knew in the library wouldn't have felt enough despair and pain to decide to end his life, but the Brian everyone else knew would have. It sounds like he didn't have many friends outside of football. He didn't have a roommate, or even a girlfriend anymore. He was facing a very lonely life, and he would have been starting over in a new academic department, not knowing anyone and not having the same background in the subject as everyone else. And this is a boy who was accustomed to being the best, to winning, to being the star of the team. He would have gone from that life to being just one of a crowd of students. Mediocre at best, low tier at worst."

Cappy sighed and ran her hand through her hair as they climbed the stairs to the overpass. "And the money. Whether he was buying drugs for himself or jewelry for his girlfriend, he was borrowing from at least two of his coaches. He was probably expecting to pay them back in a big way someday, with a car or a house or some other grand gesture, but suddenly money is even tighter than before, and he has no likelihood of making much for at least, what, six years or so more school, including graduate work? His scholarship would have ended with the school year, and there goes his stipend and his housing."

Cappy shook her head. "The interview with Moran was a bit of a fiasco, but it was good you were there today. You needed to hear this for yourself, and not just get it secondhand from me. I'm sorry that we didn't learn anything that would support your homicide thesis, but that proof you're looking for doesn't exist. Everything points to Brian being a very lonely young man who was facing loss and a future full of hardships."

Jazz stopped on the side of the path and faced Cappy, ignoring the drops of rain she was starting to feel on her face and shoulders. "So that's it? You're done?"

"No. I have a couple more people to talk to first. I want to be confident that the report I give Kent is thorough and conclusive. Even more than that, I want to be able to look you in the eye and say I did my best and that I took you seriously."

Jazz nodded, not trusting herself to speak. She needed to make a joke, then climb into a shell of silence. Or find a way to stop caring about why and how Brian died and simply let herself mourn the boy she had known. She wasn't sure she could do either one, but she was out of options.

"You tried," she said. "Thank you for that. You'll let me know how the other interviews go?"

"Of course. And I'm sorry."

Jazz waved off to the right. "I'm going to head back to Suzzallo now."

"And I need to get back to the station." Cappy pointed slightly to the left of where Jazz had indicated. They were actually going in basically the same direction, but Jazz was glad that Cappy was accepting this attempt at parting and not dragging on their conversation halfway across campus.

She was about five yards away when she halted on the path, even though the rain was coming harder now. She had just remembered that Libby's party was tomorrow night. Damn it. The party Cappy and her grandmother would be attending. So much for their dignified and dramatic parting, when they wouldn't even go a day without being in forced proximity at a small get-together. Jazz considered declining the invitation, but her friends would show up on her doorstep, concerned about what was wrong. And if she said she didn't want to see Cappy, she knew exactly what conclusions they'd reach.

Incorrectly, of course. This had nothing to do with a romance gone wrong. Romance hadn't even had a chance to go right for the two of them. Not that Jazz wanted it to, but still…her friends would be even more difficult to convince than she herself was.

If she said she was sick, they'd bring chicken soup. She considered claiming she had an emergency at work, but even she had trouble coming up with a plausible library emergency that couldn't be easily verified or refuted by her friends. Misshelved books in the biography section? An urgent need to resharpen all the tiny pencils next to the catalog computers? No. She'd just have to go to the party and stay as far away from Cappy as was possible in a two-bedroom apartment. Not a problem. Jazz reached into her bag and pulled out a black umbrella, opening it over her head even though it was too late. She was already soaked.

CHAPTER TEN

Cappy came around the corner of Odegaard early the next day and paused on the edge of Red Square. There were only a few people walking across the large expanse of red brick at seven in the morning, but Cappy would have had no trouble spotting Jazz even if she had been buried in the midday crowds of students and staff. She was facing her library, sitting on one of the benches surrounding the square's large sculpture, a long geometric form with a pointed end balancing on a triangular base. Cappy wasn't able to distinguish Jazz's features from this distance, but something in her posture spoke of the emotions she was facing. She wasn't hunched over and rocking back and forth with grief, but somehow her careful, erect posture revealed a sense of fragility and pain to Cappy.

She hadn't been expecting Jazz's call yesterday, after they finished their dubiously successful interviews, but Cappy hadn't hesitated to agree to meet her this morning, without even bothering to ask what Jazz wanted. Maybe she was going to argue her case for remaining on the investigation, or maybe she had some new piece of evidence to share about Brian. Or maybe she was going to give Cappy a lecture about the Dewey Decimal System. Cappy didn't care. She would have come no matter what the reason. Jazz had asked—she had said yes. No question, no logic, no common sense. Just yes.

She sighed and walked out of the shadows, crossing the square and stopping when she reached Jazz. She looked over her shoulder, following her gaze to Suzzallo. The sun was beginning to rise behind the library, and a diffused light was shining through the tall stained-glass windows. The early morning haze was ambiguous, just as likely to turn into rain as to dissipate and leave them with a clear fall day, but for the moment it blanketed the campus in a hushed, enveloping fog.

"It's beautiful," Cappy said when Jazz turned to look at her, her expression somehow managing to seem both confident and vulnerable at the same time. She was careful not to slip and say *You're beautiful* instead. She would allow herself to think it, but not say it out loud.

Jazz nodded in agreement, angling her body so she was facing Cappy when she sat next to her on the bench. "The library is austere during the day, and elegant all lit up at night, but I like it best in the morning when it's mysterious and timeless."

Cappy smiled. "Sounds like you spend a lot of time standing outside and admiring the building."

"Please," Jazz scoffed. "I have a full life which leaves very little time for that. For example, I spend about ten hours a day standing *inside* the library and admiring it. And sometimes I go to dinner with my friends and annoy them by talking about how much I admire it."

"I'm honored that you made time in that busy schedule of yours to meet with me," Cappy said, laughing. She waved her hand up and down her body. "Even with my disappointing lack of Gothic elements."

"I admire beauty in all forms, and you're certainly not a disappointment in that regard." Jazz winced and shook her head. "Wow. I'm usually better at keeping those sorts of comments unspoken. My filters aren't operating at full capacity."

Cappy stared at her for a moment. This was the perfect opportunity to gently inform Jazz that she didn't date civilians, and to move the conversation off the subject of beauty. Instead, she mumbled some combination of *it's okay* and *thank you* and felt her cheeks grow warm, which wasn't the same thing at all.

Jazz grinned and bumped her shoulder against Cappy's. "Sorry. I didn't ask you to meet me here so I could hit on you. My filters might be misfiring, but my sense of appropriate timing is still functioning just fine. I wanted to talk about Brian."

"Well, that's a relief," Cappy said with an exaggerated sigh to let Jazz know she was teasing. "Because having a gorgeous woman like you hit on me would be the absolute worst way to start my day. I was either going to run away or ask you about that sculpture behind us to distract you."

Cappy pointed over her shoulder at the metal form looming over them, and Jazz brightened. "Oh, that would have worked. It's called *Broken Obelisk* by Barnett Newman, and it was donated to the university in 1971. There are also copies of it in MOMA and in Houston. It was removed in 2008 so they could correct an old repair job that made it look a little different from the other two."

Cappy laughed, feeling the awkwardness of their conversation sliding away. "I thought my question might be distracting because you'd have to run into Suzzallo in search of a reference book. I didn't realize you'd be able to give an impromptu lecture."

"Please," Jazz said, waving her off. "A lot of people know about the obelisk. Besides, it's right outside my building, so of course I learned some basic information about it. It's not like I can recite details about every sculpture on campus."

"Of course not," Cappy said, not missing the slightly suspicious look on Jazz's face when she made that claim. "So if I were to mention the big bronze bowling pin near the astronomy building, would you feel compelled as a librarian to tell me what it's really called?"

"I feel absolutely zero compulsion to tell you that it's *Everything that Rises* by Martin Puryear," Jazz said in a haughty tone, then laughed. "All right, I can name all the sculptures on campus. And all the buildings, street names, and faculty members. I belong to this school, and I feel like it's my responsibility to learn as much about it as I can."

Cappy nodded, feeling a small thrill at the way her interactions with Jazz seemed to change tone with ease, from a little embarrassing flirting to joking around to a sense of seriousness. They seemed to match each other as the topics and tenor of the discussion flowed and changed. She cleared her throat and got back to the topic at hand.

"Brian falls into that category, too, doesn't he? And all your library regulars? You want to feel like you really know them."

"Yes," Jazz admitted with a thoughtful frown. "But it's not as if I see them as encyclopedia entries to study and memorize. They're real people, and I want to understand them as well as I can." She shrugged. "In some ways, I think you knew Brian better than I did, even though you never met him. You saw him play before his accident, and you are more familiar with the world he was part of. You saw him playing football, and in his element. I was hoping you could tell me about him."

Cappy sighed, resting her palm on the bench between them and leaning slightly toward Jazz. "He was a great running back," she said. "I think there can be a tendency when a player is lost at a young age to exaggerate how good they were, but he really was one of the most exceptional college players I've ever seen. My gramps was a massive football fan, especially at the collegiate level, and I grew up immersed in Pac-12 stats. I didn't see Gramps often, so I'd memorize details about every game, and we'd spend hours discussing them on the phone. We never lost the habit, and over the past couple of years, Brian's name came up in most of our conversations. Gramps was a big fan of his playing."

She paused and glanced back at the library, giving herself a moment to ease past the painful loss of her grandfather and trying to figure out how to bring Brian's playing to life for Jazz, who had only seen him in the more static context of the library.

"A running back has to be versatile," she continued. "He has to be agile because once he gets the ball handed to him, he needs to break through a wall of defensive linemen. He has to be quick-thinking, because no matter how carefully they map out a route during practice, they can never predict where all the players will actually be once the ball is snapped. And he has to be strong, because if he isn't getting the handoff, he has to switch gears and protect the quarterback. Brian had all three qualities, but he really came to life when he'd run with the ball. It was like the football gods themselves were laying out a path for him to run, and he was simply following it."

Okay, it was a bit dramatic, but still true. Besides, it made Jazz smile.

"Thank you," Jazz said, nudging Cappy's foot with hers. "I can picture him out on the field. I suppose those qualities wouldn't have been transferrable to paleobiology, although he'd have needed to be quick-thinking in case those fossils shifted an inch over a thousand years."

Cappy laughed. "Maybe not directly transferrable, but he was disciplined and focused. He likely was a natural problem-solver. Not to give you false hope, but he had skills that would have helped him succeed in any area, as long as he felt as passionate about it as he did football."

Jazz nodded. "No false hope taken. I don't have an agenda with this. I really just want to know him better."

"Glad to help," Cappy said. She looked up and realized with some surprise that their peaceful morning oasis was rapidly changing. Campus residents were stirring to life, and Cappy saw a couple of students sitting on the steps of Suzzallo next to heavy-looking backpacks, apparently waiting for the doors to open. The haze had lifted, leaving them with a layer of gray clouds covering the sky—still thin enough to let the bright light of the morning sun illuminate them, but dense enough to promise rain later in the day.

"Well, I need to get to the station," she said, standing and reaching out a hand to pull Jazz to her feet. "And you need to get inside. Your library isn't going to admire itself." She looked at Suzzallo, then back at Jazz. "Although maybe it will. It seems like a very self-satisfied building."

"Wouldn't you be?" Jazz asked, giving the library an indulgent smile. "All those lovely arches and books. It has every right to feel smug."

Cappy laughed and gave Jazz's hand a squeeze before letting her go.

"Thank you, again," Jazz said. "For talking to me about him."

"Anytime," Cappy said, wishing she didn't mean it as thoroughly as she did. Her feelings for Jazz were moving dangerously close to feeling like something real. She could still classify this meeting as connected to the case, so it was permissible, but she'd have to make sure their relationship didn't morph into anything more sociable and romantic than official.

"See you tonight," Jazz said with a sad smile as she turned away and headed to her library.

Cappy sighed. Well, except for tonight at Clare and Libby's pizza party. After that, definitely no socializing with Jazz. She headed toward the station, trying to ignore how their friends and colleagues were becoming more intertwined, threatening to draw her and Jazz into closer proximity in the future. If it weren't for all of them, she wouldn't have any trouble keeping her distance, both emotionally and physically, from Jazz. She gave a short, humorless laugh, startling the student who was passing her. Yeah, right. No trouble at all.

CHAPTER ELEVEN

A ren't we supposed to be getting ready for company?" Clare asked in a sleepy voice. She knew the answer was yes, but she didn't make any move to dislodge Libby, who was draped across her, the sheets tangled around their bare legs.

"We were, but then you lured me into the bedroom," Libby said, snuggling closer, her head resting on Clare's chest.

Clare grinned. "I called out to you and asked if you knew where my blue shirt was. I don't think that counts as luring."

Libby laughed, her breath soft and warm against Clare's breast. "Oh, please. Everyone knows that's code for *Come in here and have sex with me*."

"Everyone knows this?" Clare asked, sifting her fingers through Libby's hair and watching it drift back onto her skin. "If I knew that, I'd have nothing but blue shirts in the closet."

Libby rested her hand on Clare's sternum and propped her chin on it, meeting her eyes. "Well, anything you say from the bedroom is code for sex. Or if you're standing by the couch. Anywhere in the apartment, really."

Clare laughed and stretched forward to kiss Libby's mouth, lingering for a moment before dropping her head back on the pillow. "I love you, Professor Hart."

"I know you do. And I love you, too, Officer Sawyer, and not just because you have a pass card to the police station." She paused and sighed. "To be honest, I'm feeling a little anxious about tonight, and I never feel that way when we're having our friends over. I might have been more susceptible than usual to your wanton, come-hither-and-find-my-shirt ways."

Clare groaned. "It's Jazz and Cappy, isn't it? Please tell me you're not going to play matchmaker tonight with those two."

Libby playfully smacked her on the shoulder. "No, of course not. Although, wow, they'd be a striking couple, wouldn't they? Romance aside, though, I think the two of them have the potential to be amazing friends with each other. They're both so clever, and they share that dry, understated sense of humor, but at their cores, I think the two of them are the most deeply caring and empathetic people I know. I worry that the emotional baggage of this case will always be between them, and they'll never be able to get past it and just enjoy each other's company."

"If we're talking about a core of kindness, you have everyone I know beat," Clare said, kissing Libby's forehead. She sighed. "But I know exactly what you mean. Cappy came back to so many changes with Kent and the department and me. Even though she wasn't gone long, it's been an adjustment coming back, and I don't know if this case is making it better since it's occupying a lot of her time and attention, or if it's making it worse since it's stressful for her."

Libby just nodded, not asking Clare to explain herself more fully. That was one of the things—one of the many, many things—that Clare loved about her. Libby hadn't known Cappy long, and she only had the bare details about her life and her past, but she would never pry into the stories that were Cappy's to tell, not Clare's. She might be relentless in her demands to know about all aspects of Clare's life as a cop, but she respected people and their privacy.

"And Jazz is sad," Libby said, after a pause. "I don't think she's very good at being sad."

"Who is, really?" Clare asked, wrapping her arms around Libby and holding her even closer. "But maybe, instead of being a wedge between them, this case will bring them closer. Maybe they'll find a way to help each other through it."

Libby nodded, her hair sliding across Clare's breast and making her breath hitch. "I hope so. But that won't happen if Jazz is on the sidelines, not feeling like she's part of the investigation. Being sad and helpless is even worse."

"I know. I'll talk to Cappy, even though I doubt I need to. She'll come to that same conclusion herself, I'll bet." Clare ran her hand down the length of Libby's back. "Everyone will be here in a little over an hour. I suppose we should get up."

Libby shifted a little, trailing her fingers across Clare's belly and down to her inner thigh, leaving a lingering warmth everywhere she touched. "We could," she said with a shrug. "But the apartment is clean, Jazz will be bringing something fancy for dessert, and we're ordering pizza. Really, what more do we need to do?"

Clare pretended to think for a second. "Well, we could always look for my shirt again," she suggested hopefully.

Libby laughed and pushed herself up, straddling Clare's hips and leaning down to kiss her. "That sounds like the perfect use of our time."

CHAPTER TWELVE

Jazz locked her office and went into the staff breakroom, opened the fridge, and pulled out a large domed carrier. She set it on the table and stood there for a moment, contemplating how best to balance the carrier, her leather messenger bag, a heavy canvas library tote full of books, and her laptop case. Was having too much to carry a reasonable excuse for missing tonight? She wasn't sure how she felt about seeing Cappy again. Their first parting, after the interviews, had had a sense of finality to it, until she had remembered the party. Later last night, she had decided that since they were going to be seeing each other anyway, she might as well ask Cappy for a peek into Brian's world—the world he had known before his accident, and one she had briefly spent time in during their interviews. All very logical, but when she added her ridiculous flirting and the disconcerting comfort and ease she felt when simply hanging out with Cappy and talking to her, well, avoidance was looking like her best option for handling Cappy.

"I'll take that one," Tig said, pointing at the plastic dome as she appeared in Jazz's doorway and put an end to her hopes of getting out of the party. "It looks like food."

"Thank you," Jazz said with a sigh as Tig slung the laptop case over her shoulder alongside her own satchel and picked up the carrier. "I underestimated how many arms I was going to need today when I left for work this morning."

She hefted the tote and her bag, and they headed out the door. "So, are you here to check on me, or were you sent to make sure I didn't back out of movie night?"

Tig shrugged the arm with the bags, making her wobble for a few steps before she got back on course. "Both, I suppose. Kent told me about your interviews, and Libby called, asking if I'd heard from you. I guess—"

"Yes, yes," Jazz interrupted. "Cappy told Clare who told Libby who told you. Does anyone realize how annoying it is to have my personal experiences filtered through the police department and distributed to all my friends?"

"Yeah, we all find it annoying, except maybe Libby. Ari said that even if she walks into her classroom one day and finds all her students murdered, she's just going to give her lecture like normal, then leave for the day, rather than getting involved with the cops."

"She always has been the smart one of the group." Jazz had been the one to march herself down to the station voluntarily. Libby had been called in for an interview, and Tig had managed to draw the cops to Denny Hall by getting in the middle of a brawl. If Jazz had known how the look into her allegations would turn out, would she still have gone down there? Damn it, yes. Her conscience wouldn't have let her do otherwise.

They took the elevator downstairs, then Jazz led them to the back exit. Libby's apartment was only a couple blocks from campus, but if she drove there, she wouldn't have to walk back to campus for her car. Besides, they had too much to carry for it to be a pleasant walk in the rain.

"So, are you ready to go back to being group leader, now that your involvement with the case is done?" Tig asked, standing next to Jazz and holding the umbrella over her head while she stowed her bags in the trunk.

Jazz considered that for a moment. Aside from the silliness of the made-up title, was she ready to go back to her normal life? Could she let go of her convictions about Brian's death, mourn him as a student who had been part of her library life, and then move on? Not yet. Cappy and the rest of the world might be ready to accept his suicide, but she still had her doubts. Would she ever have peace about this? She hoped so.

"Soon," she assured Tig. She waited until Tig was settled in the passenger seat and then handed her the domed carrier. "Cappy is still interviewing some more people, so maybe one of them will have information that convinces me to let this go. Until then, I'm too emotionally compromised to be the detached, robotic leader this group needs."

Tig laughed. "I don't think I qualify as robotic any more than you do, but I'm willing to remain leader pro tem, especially since I haven't had to do anything for the job. Well, I did feed Libby a chocolate croissant this afternoon, but I don't know if it counts since it was mine, and I didn't get it for her on purpose. She came into my office and looked hungry."

"That's basically what I do," Jazz said. "You're fulfilling your responsibilities very well."

Jazz parked on the street near Libby's apartment. She shut off the ignition but didn't make a move to open her door. "Is Kent coming tonight?" she asked.

Tig shook her head and gave a particularly lovesick sigh. "No. She tries to be careful about how much time she spends socially with Clare, and dinner and a movie at her apartment is too much. A casual dinner in public now and then is okay, but not this."

Jazz laughed. "So she and Clare are sharing custody of our friend group now? I'll have to create a schedule for them once I'm leader again, so I know whom to expect at our dinners."

"Just don't assign that task to me, or we'll never see Clare."

Jazz smiled, then leaned forward against her steering wheel, peering through the droplet-covered windshield. "It's raining harder. Maybe we should give it a few minutes before we go in."

"Sure. Look, if we're going to sit out here and avoid Cappy for a while, I'm eating one of whatever is in this box."

"Chestnut cream profiteroles. And I am not avoiding Cappy."

"Whatever you say." Tig unsnapped the domed lid and pulled out a small round chocolate-iced pastry. She took a bite and then licked cream off her fingers. "Wow. Good thing you didn't add group pastry chef to my list of duties as leader. We would have been stuck with a store-bought box of doughnuts instead of these little chunks of heaven."

"Group pastry chef and group leader are two different roles," Jazz said, watching the door to Libby's apartment building.

"I was blissfully unaware of the complex political structure that underlies our friendships," Tig said as she popped the last bite of profiterole in her mouth. "Are you in love with her?"

"What? Love? Why would you…Are you kidding? There's no way…" Jazz finally managed to stop sputtering and take a deep breath. "The answer is a simple no," she said much more calmly. "I barely know her. I mean, she's nice enough. Sort of pretty if you like that Celtic warrior-woman type. Really clever."

Jazz sighed. She really needed to make a joke and then let silence descend instead of prattling on about Cappy. She tried to salvage her dignity by redirecting the conversation. "See? This is why I'm not fit to lead. I'm not in love, but I'll admit I might possibly be avoiding her, just a little. I messed up yesterday on the interview, and I'm embarrassed about it. I'm not accustomed to being embarrassed, or to speaking without thinking, or to failing *anything*, let alone a made-up probationary period for attending interviews."

"Was she mean to you? I can beat her up if you want."

Jazz laughed. "You? Didn't you get your nose broken in your one and only fistfight? And weren't you not even meant to be part of it?"

"Bruised, not broken, and you know it," Tig said. "And I'm taking another pastry because of that rude comment."

"Cappy wasn't being mean, just sensible," Jazz said, leaving the teasing and returning to the uncomfortable topic at hand. And she had been understanding, too, especially this morning. Jazz decided not to mention their early meeting, when Cappy had also been compassionate and kind. There was always the possibility, though, that Libby had her bugged and had texted a transcript of the conversation to everyone.

"I know how important this investigation is to you, Jazz," Tig said, the teasing tone gone from her voice. "Tell her you want a second chance to take part in the interviews, and I'm sure she'll come around. You're the one who knew Brian, and you're the one who has this instinct about how he died, so you should be involved. Not that I don't believe that Cappy will be thorough, but you might notice something she doesn't."

Jazz nodded. Tig was right. Jazz didn't know Cappy well, but she trusted her to keep her word and look carefully into Brian's death. But no matter how many interviews she did and questions she asked, she might miss something Jazz would have noticed, especially with her bias toward this case being a suicide. Jazz had to admit that Cappy's bias was seeming more and more justified, but that didn't mean it was correct.

"Okay, I'll talk to her," Jazz said, swatting at Tig's hand as she was reaching for another pastry. "And my ill-advised warrior-woman comment does not leave this car."

"I promise," said Tig. "I'll only tell Kent, who will tell Clare, who will tell Libby, who will tell Ari, who will tell Officer Keaton, who will tell her dentist, who will…"

Jazz got out of the car and slammed the door on Tig's phone tree, which was unfortunately only a slight exaggeration of the one her friends used in real life. When they got inside Libby's building, Jazz closed her umbrella and left it in the stand near the front door before they climbed the stairs to her apartment.

They entered to a chorus of greetings, and Jazz paused to take off her jacket and give herself a moment to regain her usual composure— or at least a vague facsimile of it. She was unsettled by how she was immediately aware of where Cappy was in the room, even before she had taken more than a cursory glance. She hadn't seen Cappy out of uniform before—had she really expected her to wear her uniform to a pizza party?—and the sight of her, especially after Tig's ridiculous question in the car, made her want to march back downstairs and stand outside in the rain until she was cool and in control again.

Before she could run away, though, Libby took her arm and towed her into the living room to meet Cappy's grandmother, who Libby introduced as Edith Flannery. Jazz managed somehow to look away from Cappy, who was wearing slim, dark blue jeans and a simple red T-shirt whose sole purpose in life seemed to be showing off the curves of Cappy's breasts and biceps. It was fulfilling its destiny quite masterfully.

Edith, standing next to her granddaughter, might have been shorter and older than Cappy, but their resemblance was startling, as if someone had computer-generated a senior version from Cappy herself.

"I'm so pleased to meet you, Jazz," Edith said, taking her arm. "My Cappy has told me so much about you. Come sit down and keep an old woman company for a bit."

"Shit," Cappy said. "Gran, you can't—"

"Language, dear," Edith interrupted before turning back to Jazz. "She gets that from me, I'm ashamed to say."

Cappy rubbed her forehead. "Gran, I'm sure Jazz has plenty of things to do without needing to keep you company."

"Things to do? At a party?"

"She probably has a full agenda of things to do," Libby chimed in. "And the first on it will be rearranging my books until I can't find anything. I'm begging you, Edith, monopolize all her time."

"It's called an alphabet, Libby," Jazz said over her shoulder as Edith led her to the couch. "You might want to try using it sometime."

Jazz took one more glance at Cappy, who didn't looked pleased about being left behind.

"She's kind of bossy," Jazz said as the two of them sat on Libby's comfortable couch.

"Tell me about it," Edith said with a sigh. "She's worried that I'll tell you embarrassing stories about her."

Jazz settled back. "I hope she's right to worry."

"Oh, she is. She speaks very highly of you, you know. And she doesn't impress easily."

"Well, I...thank you. I mean, I think she's...um..." She looked over at Cappy, who had her arms crossed over her chest as she leaned against the fireplace. She looked every bit the relaxed partygoer as Jazz felt.

Edith chuckled and patted her on the knee, looking far too perceptive for Jazz's comfort. "Have the two of you always been close?" Jazz asked, moving the conversation in a direction that wouldn't include her.

Edith frowned. "In a way. The weeks she spent with me and Rog, her grandfather, made for some of the best memories in my life. She was such a bright little girl, very inquisitive and kind. But her father—my son—is a very proud man. He was determined to take care of her, especially after Cappy's mother left them, and he didn't like having her away from him for very long. We would have loved to have been more a part of her life, but we didn't always have the chance." She smiled in Cappy's direction, which only made Cappy scowl a little deeper.

"That's why I was so willing to move up here after Rog passed. It's coming a little late in life, but I'm not passing up the chance to know her better."

Jazz absorbed the information, setting it aside to ponder later. When Cappy had mentioned not seeing her grandfather often, Jazz had assumed distance or other practical issues had been the reason why. Now, Edith had shrewdly given her hints about Cappy's childhood—with an absent mother and a father who sounded controlling to Jazz—and she didn't believe Edith was sharing the story by accident. Neither in the words she'd used or the person she'd chosen to hear them. Jazz wasn't sure how she felt about that part, but she'd put it aside for later, too.

"Clare said the two of you are living together in a one-bedroom apartment. I suppose you're getting to know her quite well in such a small space."

"Yes," Edith agreed, her voice wry. "I'm looking forward to knowing her a little less well once I move out." She paused, then gestured around the room. "You're lucky to have friends like these," she said. "My Rog was sick for several years before he passed, and I spent so much time taking care of him that I lost track of the friendships I had. I have Cappy up here, of course, but she has all of you, plus her career. I'd love to start making some connections of my own, so she doesn't feel the burden of being my entire social life. It's not easy to start over at my age, though."

Jazz looked around the room. Clare was standing behind Libby with her arms wrapped around her waist as they chatted to Cappy, somehow managing to make her laugh even though she kept glancing in her grandmother's direction. Or Jazz's direction? Hard to tell. Tig was in the recliner with Ari perched on the arm, and the two of them seemed determined to finish the plate of profiteroles before anyone noticed.

She smiled at Edith. "I'd give you some advice on how to make friends like these, but I honestly have no idea how I managed to get so lucky and find them. Or they found me, I suppose. Do you like reading, or have any other hobbies? That's a good way to connect with other people."

"I love mysteries," Edith said. "I was in a book club years ago, but it was the kind that was more about drinking wine and socializing than talking about the books. I loved it."

Jazz smiled, resting her elbow on the back of the couch and resting her head on her palm. They talked about books and authors, crocheting and cooking. Edith was easier to talk to than Cappy, in some ways—maybe less closed off and with softer edges—but she and her granddaughter shared a sharp sense of humor and a natural confidence that Jazz enjoyed. Edith was telling her about a birdwatching trip she had taken when she was about Cappy's age when Ari interrupted.

"Edith, didn't Libby tell me you were bringing some embarrassing old photos of Cappy? I'll save you one of these profiteroles if you let me see them."

"Of course, dear," Edith said. "Would you get my purse for me?"

Ari bounced off the recliner and retrieved the purse, coming to perch on the arm of the sofa next to Edith.

"How about we don't do this," Cappy said in what she might have thought was a stern cop voice, guaranteed to intimidate them into listening to her. It didn't work. Jazz felt a little sorry for her, but not enough to step in and stop the picture show.

"Here she is in the bathtub," Edith said, handing her a photo of a curly-headed, naked little Cappy. "She was four years old."

Clare leaned over Jazz's shoulder from behind the couch. "I've seen her in the locker room, and I've got to say, she's really let herself go."

Cappy walked over to the coffee table and picked up Ari's glass. "Is this Scotch? I'm confiscating it."

Ari laughed. "Go ahead, but if you want to get drunk enough that you don't care about these adorable photos, then you need to skip the little glass and go directly to the bottle. And it's watered down Diet Coke, not Scotch. The ice melted about an hour ago."

Jazz was watching Cappy as Ari spoke and saw the change in her expression. One moment she was smiling at Ari's joke about the bottle, and the next she was holding herself very still, as if lost in thought. She shook her head slightly and set the glass back on its coaster. "On second thought, I'll grab a beer instead. Hey, Lib, I need to make a quick call. Mind if I use your office?"

"Not at all," Libby said, passing a picture of Cappy dressed in a pirate costume to Tig. "Boots is in there, so she can keep you company."

Cappy smiled, but Jazz thought it seemed forced, and suddenly she had the feeling that Cappy's distracted air didn't have anything to do with her childhood photos. Cappy crossed behind the couch to where her jacket was hanging on the coatrack and took her phone out of the pocket. She gave Jazz's shoulder a quick squeeze as she walked by, but in an absent-minded way, as if she didn't realize she had touched her.

Cappy disappeared into the second bedroom that Clare and Libby used as a library and office, and Jazz glanced at the others in the room. They were laughing together and didn't seem to have noticed anything unusual in Cappy's behavior, except for Clare. She looked away from the office door, which was slightly open, and made eye contact with Jazz, giving her a slight shrug.

"I'll check on her," Clare murmured to Jazz, before trailing after Cappy.

Jazz was pulled back into the general conversation by Edith, who asked her how she had made the pastry cream for the profiteroles, and Jazz did her best to answer even though she wished she had been the one to follow Cappy out of the room.

Chapter Thirteen

"Hello, Detective Ellingsen? This is Cappy Flannery from the UW campus police. Yes, from Brian's apartment. Sure, I can wait."

Cappy looked up and noticed Clare hovering in the doorway. She motioned for her to come in and shut the door, and Clare silently entered and walked over to lean against Libby's stone gargoyle, Pierre. He was wearing a feather boa and a fedora—probably Clare's doing, Cappy assumed—and her gray-and-white cat, Boots, was curled in a sleepy ball on his lap. Or at least what passed for a lap on a crouching demon creature.

Cappy had expected either Clare or Jazz to follow her back here and had left the door partially open for them. She wasn't surprised that it was Clare who came, and it was for the best, given the call Cappy was about to make, but she found herself wishing she and Jazz were shut in this room together. She hadn't had a chance to talk to her before her grandmother and those damned photos had captured Jazz's attention, but now, while she was merely following a hunch, she didn't want to risk raising Jazz's hopes.

"Yes, I'm still here. I just had a question about the report you sent to the station. It said there were alcohol and pill bottles that were removed before we got there, and there was also a glass?" She hesitated, having second thoughts now that she was on the phone with the brisk-sounding detective, but Ari's comment had struck home, and she needed to follow through.

"Are we talking a big water glass or stein?" She paused, then pushed on. "Just…I mean, put yourself in his place. You're about to overdose. You've worked up the nerve to do this, so do you really get a little juice glass out of the cupboard and keep pouring yourself small drinks? How long can you continue before you're incapacitated and can't accurately pour anymore? Was there alcohol sloshed around on the floor? It just doesn't seem to make sense to me."

Out of the corner of her eye, Cappy saw Clare push herself off Pierre and into an upright position. She trusted Clare to grab the phone and apologize to Ellingsen if she thought Cappy was making a mistake here, but she remained silent. Listening.

"Yes, but were there other glasses in the apartment? In the kitchen? All I'm asking is that you check those for prints before releasing the keys to his family. Just…maybe someone else was there. Yes…yes, fine…okay, thank you."

She ended the call and gave Clare a shrug. "She's going over there right now to check. This might be a colossal waste of her time, severing our working relationship with the Seattle PD."

"You followed a good hunch, in my opinion," Clare said. "Kent wanted you to look into this death, and you're doing just that. If you had ignored your instincts, I think you'd have always regretted it. Always wondered."

Cappy nodded and perched on Pierre's knee, scratching Boots under her chin. "Does what I told her make sense to you?"

Clare shrugged. "Logically, yes. I think he would have gotten a punchbowl and mixed everything together and chugged it down, rather than daintily sipping from a little glass, but who knows where his mind was at when this happened. Maybe this made sense to him, somehow." She hesitated, then continued. "Still, even though I think the question was worth asking, I'm not sure what you hope this will accomplish. If there are glasses in the kitchen with other prints, then they could have been left at any time. This won't prove foul play."

"No, I know," Cappy said. She wasn't sure what her end goal was either. Maybe, selfishly, her own peace of mind. She had said she wanted to be able to look Jazz in the eye and say she had done her best to investigate. If she had ignored her reaction to Ari's words, she wouldn't have been able to do so with a clear conscience. "And that's why we can't tell Jazz about this right now. She'll be too disappointed if this leads nowhere, which is likely what it will do."

"Deal," Clare said. "On one condition."

Cappy ran her hand through her hair. She had a feeling she knew what Clare was going to propose, and she had already anticipated it. "Let me guess. The entire gang out there believes Jazz deserves another chance and should be allowed to stay on the case with me."

Clare grinned. "See? That's why we make such good partners. You're almost as smart as I am."

"Careful with the praise or I might nominate myself for Cop of the Year. And I was already going to give her a second chance." She made a sheepish grimace. "After all, I'm the one who tried to tell the coach how to run his defense. I was right, though."

"Maybe she was, too," Clare said with a shrug. "I'll admit it wasn't the time or place for a comment like that, but those drugs came from somewhere. Unfortunately, sometimes they come from coaches. I can guarantee that this won't be the end of that particular investigation, because of the death of a player being connected to drugs, but it'll be out of our jurisdiction."

"Thank goodness for that," Cappy said. She had enough on her plate with this unofficial investigation. She wasn't ready to take on corruption and drug use in the collegiate football world.

"Come on," Clare said. "They'll be wondering if something's wrong." They went back into the living room, where everyone was talking and laughing the same as before. "Or maybe not," Clare added with a shrug. She walked over and sat next to Libby on the floor by the couch. Boots followed them into the room and jumped on Edith's lap.

Jazz was the only one who seemed to be paying attention to them as they came out of the office, and Cappy only hesitated for a second before going over and stepping past Libby and Clare to sit next to her.

"Is everything all right?" Jazz asked.

Cappy nodded, not wanting to lie, but also not ready to share this with Jazz. "I just had to call in something about work."

Jazz nodded, obviously aware that Cappy was being evasive, but she didn't pry. "Okay," she said.

Cappy raised her eyebrows. "Really? That's it? No weeping and wailing, begging me to tell you every last detail from every case the department is working on?"

"Please," Jazz scoffed. "Do I look like Libby?"

Cappy laughed, and Libby, who was leaning against her shin, smacked her in the leg. "I did not weep when I was working with Clare on Turnbow's murder. Or beg."

"*Well*," Clare said, drawing out the word. "There was some wailing. And you did threaten me."

"I remember that," Libby said. "I threatened to walk away from the case and out of your life, and you *still* didn't tell me everything that was going on."

Clare shrugged. "I called your bluff. I knew you weren't going anywhere."

"See? I'm above all that," Jazz said in a low voice, meant only for Cappy, as Clare and Libby continued their playful bantering without them. She hesitated. "I might not, however, be above negotiating with you."

Cappy looked at her for a moment. Jazz was so close, with her lips curving in a slow smile as she seemed to recognize from Cappy's expression that she had the upper hand here.

"I'm open to negotiations," Cappy said as soon as she was fairly certain she could control her voice. "Although I'm probably undermining my position by letting you know that I've already decided to let you come to the next interview."

Jazz's smile widened. "Good. Then I'll tell you what I learned today about Greg Masters. Is he the one we're interviewing?"

"Greg? Brian's replacement on the team?" Cappy asked, twisting her upper body toward Jazz and resting her arm on the back of the couch. "He wasn't even on my radar for an interview." She shrugged, which brought her shoulder into contact with Jazz's arm and momentarily made her lose her train of thought. "I mean, if we were investigating Brian's accident, I might have considered it, since that's how he got his big break. Not that he's taken advantage of it, unfortunately."

"I don't think he's a suspect," Jazz said. "But Greg might have more insight into Brian's life. Did you know they went to high school together? Apparently they were close friends even then, although reading between the lines in articles, it's obvious that Brian always outshone him."

"Greg went to Canterwood Heights?" Cappy asked, and Jazz nodded. The Heights was a fairly new private school in the posh Canterwood community in Gig Harbor, across the Sound from Tacoma. Their football team had been getting a lot of attention, even breaking into national rankings, and they had been producing some of the latest and greatest college stars, with Brian as one of the elite.

"I didn't bother learning about Greg's past as a player since I didn't think he'd be the first-string running back for much longer. I figured he'd be replaced as soon as they found someone faster, like maybe a turtle or a slug, whichever one looks best in the uniform. Did Brian tell you this?"

Jazz shook her head. "Research. I needed to find something today to convince you that I'm adding enough value to the case to get a second chance. The local newsfeeds were full of praise for Greg when he was a high school sophomore, but then Brian's family moved to Gig Harbor from Longview, and he became their big star."

"What do you want to bet that they moved there just to get him on that team?" Cappy said. "That must have been devastating for Greg, to lose his chance at glory, when their school was starting to attract national attention." She shrugged. "You've got a good point, though. I'll give him a call and set something up. It won't hurt to get more insight into Brian's past. But if I start lecturing him on how to take a handoff without dropping the ball, give me a kick under the table."

"Gladly," Jazz said.

"Hey, you don't have to sound so enthusiastic. I'm letting you back on not one, but two interviews now."

"Yes, but you said I failed probation, so you deserve at least one good kick. Do you know the last time I failed anything?"

"I'm guessing never?" Cappy ventured, judging by the indignant look on Jazz's face.

"Correct. And do you know how much I enjoyed the experience of failing?"

"More than you expected?"

Jazz elbowed her in the ribs, but Cappy had managed to make her laugh, so she would accept the prodding without complaint. She had been making Jazz frown more than smile during this investigation, but maybe after it was over and Jazz found some peace with the answers she had received, Cappy might have a chance to bring more laughter into her life.

For now, though, she was committed to a different path, but one almost as important—doing her job well enough to pass Jazz's high standards of research. Nothing less would satisfy her.

She looked around the room, wishing she could give up tonight's plans and stay here. The others were arguing over which movie to watch, and Libby sounded dangerously close to winning with her choice of a documentary on some sort of architecture. Her advantage was mostly due to her control of the remote, and she was defending her position of power by using Cappy's shins as a shield from Clare. Jazz was sitting close to Cappy, not quite near enough to touch, but Cappy felt the warmth of her from her shoulder to her thigh.

Yes, she would gladly have stayed in the same position for another few hours, learning about roofs and walls or whatever, but Miles was working the late shift, and he had promised to help Cappy. Besides, her gran was definitely looking worn out from the evening. Happy, but exhausted. After the past weeks of grief and hectic packing and moving, this brief foray into a place of laughter and friendship seemed to have been very good for her. Even the embarrassing photo show was worth it.

Cappy leaned closer to Jazz. "I need to get to the station to go over some footage with Miles," she said quietly. "Can you come by there tomorrow morning at nine? We can talk to Brian's tutor."

"Oh, I knew he was working with someone, but I didn't have any details about it. How did you find them?"

"Her name was in Brian's planner," Cappy said. "In his apartment."

Jazz nodded, her eyes sad. "Do you need any help tonight?"

She was tempted, but it wasn't worth dragging Jazz away from her friends to sit in front of a laptop screen for hours. "Nah, it'll be very dull. Well, marginally more boring than Libby's choice of show, at least."

"Hey!" protested Libby, whacking her in the knee with the remote.

Cappy laughed and leaned toward her grandmother. "Ready to go, Gran?"

Edith transferred Boots to Jazz's lap, and with one last pat for the cat and one of farewell on Jazz's knee, she stood up. They worked their way toward the door amid good-byes and thank-yous, and Cappy shared one last look with Jazz before giving her a little wave and heading into the hallway.

"She's lovely, dear," her grandmother said as Cappy shut the door behind them. "I approve."

"I agree, Boots is a great cat," Cappy said with a shrug. "But I doubt Libby would part with her."

Her grandmother laughed at her intentional misunderstanding and let the subject drop as they walked out to Cappy's car.

Cappy took her grandmother back to her apartment, then returned to the police station, still in her civilian clothes. Miles was behind the desk looking drowsy as he tapped away on his keyboard when she came in out of the rain, shaking water from her hair.

"Hey, Cap," he said, looking glad to have some company. Some of these night shifts on the desk were painfully boring, with hardly any civilians coming in and needing help. And then one would come in needing help, and you'd wish you were alone again. Cappy had pulled her share of desk duty.

"Hey, Miles. Got anything for me?"

He nodded and buzzed her through the door leading from the foyer. He handed her a small stack of papers.

"You were right about the regularity of the deposits," he said. "They were varying amounts, but always about a thousand. He'd withdraw five grand from the ATM at the HUB the next day, eating into his stipend for the balance, I guess. Like clockwork. Crazy money for a kid to have, isn't it? I checked a couple of the dates real quick, and he went directly back to the apartment after getting the cash." He waved at the small desk behind him. "I have you set up there, with the camera footage from outside his apartment building, starting about an hour after one of the withdrawals. Let me know when you want me to track him."

Cappy thanked him and sat in front of the screen, starting the playback, then speeding it up until she had it going at a comfortable pace. Then all she had to do was sit and watch. Of course, there was a chance someone was coming to the apartment to get the cash for whatever reason Brian had it ready each month, but she hoped he would take it somewhere instead, so they could find out why he needed the money. A legitimate payment for a car or diamonds for his girlfriend wouldn't have commonly been made in cash.

The monotony of the recorded footage gave her plenty of time to think, which of course meant she had plenty of time to think about Jazz. She liked her, there was no doubt about that. She had no problem with it either—she liked a lot of people, including Clare and Libby and all their friends. Her concern was liking Jazz too much. Looking forward to seeing her, hoping to make her smile. Was it really Jazz herself, or was Cappy just automatically following the lead of Clare and Kent with their civilian assistant–detectives? Was there some clause in the campus police handbook that she had failed to read, mandating that all officers solve a murder with help from someone on campus, and then kiss them as a thank-you?

Okay, her physical reaction to the thought of kissing Jazz's lips as they curved in a smile had nothing to do with the precedent her friend and her sergeant had set, and everything to do with Cappy's attraction to Jazz. That was scary. She'd rather be mindlessly doing whatever her friends did, like a sheep, than be having real feelings for someone she had only known for a couple of days. She had been concerned from the start that the emotions associated with this case would damage her shields, and the fact that she couldn't stop thinking of kissing Jazz was proof that she—

Cappy sat up and rewound the recording, moving it forward again in real time. She called Miles over, and together they watched Brian leave his apartment, clutching his jacket around himself and looking around furtively. She knew she was looking at old footage, but the sight of him alive and without crutches caught her by surprise anyway and made her heart ache.

"The kid does not know how to look innocent and casual," Miles said, keeping his eyes on the screen and pushing at Cappy's shoulder until she got out of the chair. He sat down and started clicking through different screens, tracking Brian until he disappeared into a blind spot near the Life Sciences Building. Miles stayed on the same camera, and moments later Brian emerged from the dead zone and hurried back toward his apartment building.

Miles was busy taking time stamps on each camera's recording, and then he brought up four screens at once, surrounding the blind spot.

"Yep," he said, when a few minutes later a tall man in jeans went into the same blind spot and came back out quickly. "Here's our guy. Amos. He's one of Miko's. Now *he* knows how to look casual."

"Miko," Cappy repeated. "The bookie?" Cappy had been assuming Brian's trail would lead them to either drugs or gambling, and she wasn't sure which would have been the more favorable outcome. Neither, really, but here they were. "How do you know these people?"

"I know a guy at SPD who's been monitoring them, so I'll send him this info. It's unusual for them to be so blatant on campus, but Brian was a good mark. With his stipend, ridiculous as it was for a college kid, he'd provide a steady source of income." Miles continued scribbling notes, muttering to himself as he documented what they had seen. "We're probably talking fifty grand if he was paying ten percent, but that'll be compounded every month. Likely off the books, since they haven't made any claim on his estate like they would have for a legitimate debt. I'm sure the interest rate was exorbitant, so he might have been making these payments for the next thirty years."

Cappy sighed. "Or for the next few months, until he got an NFL deal and made enough to pay it off."

"Yeah," Miles said. "That would have solved all his problems."

Chapter Fourteen

Cappy didn't want to go back to her apartment in the middle of the night and wake up her grandmother, so she took a nap in one of the meeting rooms until it was close to time for Jazz to arrive. She took a shower and then changed into one of the uniforms she kept in her locker. She wasn't technically on duty today, but she always felt more comfortable in uniform and not in her civilian clothes when she was doing an interview.

She was also hoping this outfit would help her keep her distance from Jazz. Last night she had foolishly let herself imagine continuing to see Jazz after this case was over. She knew better, and she was angry with herself for even letting the thought form in her mind. She was a cop. Hers was a dangerous job, not only because of the physical risk to her while on duty, but also because of the emotional toll it could take on partners and families. Some people seemed to make it work, like Clare and Kent with their relationships, but Cappy had seen firsthand what could happen at the other extreme. If she cared for Jazz at all, she wouldn't take a chance on hurting her.

Of course, her good intentions seemed to dissipate the moment she saw Jazz through the foyer's glass front, approaching the station. She looked stylish and classy as always, in slim black trousers and a fitted emerald-green sweater. Cappy needed more than a uniform to protect herself from her growing feelings for Jazz. She should have checked out some riot gear to wear instead.

She met Jazz in the lobby, trying to match Jazz's bright smile, but probably failing. She knew this day was going to be difficult for

Jazz, with the information about Brian's debt and the two interviews ahead of them. Every step in this investigation stacked more weight on the side of this being a suicide, and Cappy was concerned about how Jazz would handle it when she finally accepted the evidence they were accumulating. She'd be there for Jazz, help her through as well as she could, then hand her off to her friends. They would take care of her better than Cappy ever could.

She led Jazz into the same meeting room they had used the first night she had come to the station. Cappy already had her notepad and pens there, and Liam, who was on the front desk this morning, was ready to activate the recording equipment once Brian's tutor arrived.

"How was the documentary last night?" Cappy asked, avoiding the topic of Brian as long as she could.

"We watched some cop movie that Clare picked instead. Tig and Ari joined forces with her, and they got the remote away from Libby." Jazz laughed. "Libby was the only one who paid much attention to it, though. She seemed to treat it like a training video she was required to watch, while the rest of us ate pizza and talked."

Cappy smiled. "I'll bet Clare wished she had gone with the architecture show."

"Definitely. When we left, Libby was practicing securing the apartment. Boots was supposed to pretend to be a suspect who was hiding from her, but she didn't cooperate and just sat in the middle of the hallway and cleaned herself."

"That's why we never used cats during our practice scenarios in the academy," Cappy said. "They weren't interested in acting. Those guinea pigs, though. They always threw themselves into the parts."

Jazz laughed, then her humor faded away with a sigh. "You're trying to cheer me up, which is thoughtful of you, but go ahead and tell me what's on your mind. I can take it."

"Can you?" Cappy asked.

Jazz shrugged. "I'm really not sure, but I'll try."

Cappy told her how they had tracked Brian from old footage. "We checked two different months, and each time the same thing happened. Later in the day when he had withdrawn the money, he took it to what was likely a drop point, and after he left, one of Miko's guys would go to the same place and pick up the cash. We're assuming, at least, since it's a blind spot for the campus security cameras. Miles and I walked over there at about two this morning, and it's just a dirt patch with a few tall trees around it. Clever spot, though."

Jazz was sitting very still, except for one finger tapping on the metal table. "So, a gambling debt."

"A big one. We don't have any concrete proof of this, though. Miles is turning the information we gathered last night over to SPD, and they'll dig deeper. For us, though, I think what we observed is sufficient as more evidence that Brian's financial situation was devastating. He was barely scraping by with his stipend and the loans from his coaches and possibly some other sources, and as soon as this school year ended, those would have been gone. Gambling debts aren't like student loans—you can't defer them because you're staying in school to study dinosaurs."

Jazz closed her eyes. "I didn't realize. Here I was encouraging him to stay in school for another few years when he probably had no idea how he'd survive past next June."

Cappy reached across the table and put her hand over Jazz's, stilling her tapping fingers and making Jazz open her eyes and look at Cappy. "Don't blame yourself for that. There's a good chance no one knew about this debt. It's not the type of news you share with everyone. It's the kind you hide from as many people as possible. You gave him a chance to dream, and you can't feel guilty about that because you weren't aware of his financial situation. If money had been tight in a normal way, he could have taken out loans or applied for scholarships to pursue his dream. Who would have guessed this went beyond that?"

Jazz looked away but nodded. Cappy wasn't convinced that she wasn't still blaming herself, somehow, but they'd have to let it go for now because there was a knock on the door that most likely meant Brian's tutor had arrived. She probably should let go of Jazz's hand now. When had she laced their fingers together? She couldn't remember doing that, but she was reluctant to let go. She sighed and pulled back, motioning for Jazz to come around to her side of the table.

She went to the door and opened it to find Liam on the other side. He gestured toward a young woman who was standing behind him in the hallway, and Cappy thanked him before approaching her. She looked like a typical student, wearing jeans and a light blue turtleneck sweater, with her dark hair pulled back in a ponytail. She seemed a little nervous, her brown eyes wide as she looked around the station, but otherwise she was…well, very normal.

"Mia Wallace?" she asked. "This way, please. Have a seat."

She closed the door behind them. "I'm Officer Flannery, and this is Director Harald from Suzzallo Library."

"Oh yes. Hello," Mia said to Jazz, predictably seeming to recognize her. She looked a little confused, though, and was probably racking her brain to remember if she had any overdue library books.

"You were Brian Keyes's tutor, is that correct?"

Her response to his name was immediate, and Cappy quickly handed her the box of tissues she had placed beside her notebook.

"I'm sorry to bring up a painful subject," she said. "But it would help us if we could ask you a few questions."

"Yes, but why…I mean, I thought he…"

"It's standard procedure," Cappy smoothly inserted into Mia's broken queries. "Just a formality."

She glanced at Jazz, who seemed distracted. She apparently hadn't needed to worry that Jazz might say something inappropriate in this interview since she seemed disinclined to say anything, or even to look at Cappy or Mia.

She turned back to Mia. "What subject were you working on with him?"

"Biology," Mia said, wiping at her eyes with a tissue, but sounding more in control. "He was interested in paleobiology, but he only had a three-point-oh in his intro class. He didn't want to repeat, so he was hoping to get ready to move to the next level instead."

"How was he doing? Did he seem motivated to study hard?"

Mia smiled—well, more accurately, she glowed. Yep, Cappy nodded to herself. She had been in love with him.

"He did great. He's…he was very smart and dedicated. He would have done so well…"

She sniffed and swiped at her eyes again with the wadded-up tissue, and Cappy gently moved them past the moment.

"Are you a paleobiology student, as well?"

"No, that's not my specialty. I'll be starting the PhD program next year, with a focus on environmental biology. Most of the students I tutor are studying basic biology and chemistry."

"Does it pay well?" Cappy asked. "Do you mind me asking that?"

Mia shrugged. "Not at all. It pays better than working in retail or in a restaurant, plus it looked good on my application for grad school. Tutoring and a couple of small scholarships got me through undergrad without any loans."

Cappy nodded. "That's impressive," she said. She paused for a moment, figuring out how to phrase her next query. "I suppose it was easy for Brian to afford extra tutoring. I mean, with his football scholarship and all the perks that came with it."

Cappy was able to read Mia's awkward expression well enough to surmise that she was at least partially aware of Brian's money issues.

"I sort of helped him out, I guess," she said. "Maybe before the accident it would have been, but after, well, the scholarship wasn't going to get him a biology degree. He had to be careful with money, so I gave him a discount."

"That was very kind of you," Cappy said. She was starting to feel anxious and wanted to wrap up the interview soon. Jazz's silence was worrying her. "Were you romantically involved with him?"

Mia looked startled by the abrupt question, and Jazz shifted as well, moving her attention off the fascinating table surface and back to the interview.

"We were friends," she said, although Cappy was worried that the heat from her bright red cheeks might set off the room's sprinkler system. "I mean, we barely knew each other." She sighed, and a dreamy expression replaced her embarrassed one. "I guess it doesn't hurt to tell you now, does it? I mean, it's not like…and we weren't together until after he broke up with his old girlfriend. We were just…I don't know how to describe it."

"Meant to be?" Cappy offered.

"Yes. He felt it, too. I know he did. We just didn't have enough time."

Okay, crying again. Cappy wondered how much of their relationship was in Mia's imagination and how much in real life. Given the suddenness of his death, she figured those lines had been blurred even more than they had been when he was still alive.

Mia blew her nose, then turned to Jazz. "He talked about you a lot," she said. "He told me you were the one who helped him figure out what he wanted to do with his life, and I know he liked spending time in the library."

Jazz was silent for a moment, before replying, "I liked having him there, too. Thank you for telling me that, Mia."

Her smile was kind, and her words sounded genuine, but Cappy wasn't fooled into thinking there wasn't pain under Jazz's surface composure.

"I was supposed to meet him there that night. He wanted to show me something, but then in the morning I heard…I heard he was gone."

Cappy leaned forward. "Show you something? Did you have any idea what it was?"

Mia blushed again and looked down at her hands, which were twisting the tissue into oblivion. "It was a special place for him, you know? For starting over. I just thought…" She met Cappy's gaze. "Did you find anything in his apartment? Maybe a ring?"

Cappy had not been expecting that, but force of habit kept her from revealing her thoughts in her expression. Mia's expectation was ridiculous, given what Cappy knew about Brian's life. He was going through a tremendous loss of his career, he possibly owed a huge sum of money to a bookie, and he had only known Mia for, what, a few weeks? Yes, a marriage proposal would really have simplified his life. Mia's earnest expression kept her from launching into a lecture about making good choices in life.

Cappy looked at Jazz, who was still being quiet but was now looking fully engaged in the conversation.

"The Seattle Police Department is currently in possession of his belongings," Cappy said. "They'll eventually be released to his family. I'm afraid I can't tell you more than that."

Mia nodded, tearing up again, and Cappy thanked her again for coming in, giving her a card and asking her to call if she thought of any other information.

She dropped into the chair next to Jazz, exhausted by a night of little sleep and what had turned out to be an emotionally challenging interview.

"That poor girl," Jazz said. "Did she honestly believe he was going to propose to her?"

Cappy shook her head. "She might have hoped for that when he asked her to meet him there, but probably not with as much conviction as she showed today. She's grieving now and focused on what might have been, so her grasp of reality might be a little shaky."

"Do you have any idea what he wanted to show her?"

"Probably something simple like the answers to some study questions," Cappy said with a shrug. "Did you ever see him with anything besides the usual study paraphernalia?"

"No. Books and his laptop. If he had anything special on that, he could have shown her anywhere."

"You were very quiet," Cappy said. "I felt like I had accidentally left you at Libby's and brought Pierre to the interview today instead."

Jazz sniffed. "I didn't want to get in trouble again," she said. Cappy raised her eyebrows, and Jazz sighed. "I guess I was still processing what you said about his debt, and it wasn't easy to get out of my head and concentrate on anything else. Once I did, though, the interview with Mia felt different than yesterday's. I was angry with the coach for seeming untouched by Brian's death, beyond what it meant to him and his team, so it felt natural to speak out. But she seemed fragile. I was almost afraid to say anything and take a chance on breaking her." Jazz reached over and brushed her hand over Cappy's, pulling it away again quickly. "You were very respectful with her. It would have been easy to treat her like a foolish little girl, but you didn't."

Cappy shrugged, awkward with the compliment but appreciating it. "She seems like a good kid. If she can just keep herself from marrying someone she hasn't known for at least a full month, she might go far in life."

"Maybe sometimes it doesn't take a month to know," Jazz said quietly.

Cappy was internally debating whether she should pursue that comment and the feelings behind it when—thank God—Liam knocked on the door again.

"Kent wants to see you in her office after your next interview," he said, the verbal equivalent of a cold shower.

"This can't be good," she muttered. The only thing worse than being called in was having to wait and stew about it for an hour.

"Have you done something wrong?" Jazz asked, looking amused at Cappy's discomfort.

"Nothing comes to mind, but I'm sure she unearthed something from my past. Or she's just in the mood to yell, so she'll make something up. Kent should have exhausted her vocal cords by dinnertime, though, so I should still make it home in time to eat."

Jazz laughed, and Cappy felt a startling sense of relief to see her looking less preoccupied than before. Even getting called into Kent's office was welcome if it led to Jazz smiling again.

CHAPTER FIFTEEN

Jazz was relieved to have the distraction of Kent's summons, otherwise she might have tried to explain that she hadn't been talking about her and Cappy, or her and anyone in her past, falling in love so quickly. And if she had started to explain herself, she likely wouldn't have known where to stop and would have ended up in the dangerous realm of overexplaining, where suddenly the original words were far too present in the room.

All she had meant was that it didn't need to take months and months to be able to discern someone's character, or to recognize an attraction that might be more than a mere physical pull toward a stranger. Or to acknowledge that maybe this other person was the missing piece.

Yes, she had definitely been fortunate that the other officer had interrupted them. Jazz suddenly realized just how perceptive Cappy had been in her observation about Mia, when she said that lines got blurry and emotions got tangled when someone was dealing with an enormous grief.

She was grieving for Brian—both the boy she thought she had known so well and the young man who, in reality, had the weight of the world on his shoulders. She had been so certain about what he would or wouldn't have done, when she only had a fraction of the details about his life. The enormity of her arrogance rocked her, but at the same time she didn't have any regrets for coming to the station the other night and starting on this journey with Cappy. If nothing else was accomplished here, at least a fuller version of Brian's story was becoming known.

Maybe it was time to let go. Let Brian have his rest, and let the campus mourn him and move on. Let Cappy get back to the important job she had, which she was setting aside to investigate Jazz's allegations. Even though Cappy didn't believe Brian was murdered, she had been thorough and caring in the effort to make sure they had the correct answers.

And what would Jazz do with herself once she walked away from this? She wasn't sure. She thought life might seem different from now on, but would the work she did here on campus evolve as well? Was it even possible? She could make more of an effort to get to know the students who frequented her library better, but what was she going to do besides ask about their studies and their goals, the same way she always had? The same way she had done with Brian. What was her big plan, anyway—to ask them to bring in their bank statements and IOUs from bookies, or hound them about their personal lives and ask if any coaches had been unkind to them? No. Unless they willingly shared bigger issues, her sphere was the world of books and academia. She just didn't know if that was enough anymore.

Cappy reached over and softly brushed her temple, before sliding her fingers lower and tucking Jazz's hair behind her ear. "You have a lot going on in there, don't you," she said, as more of a statement than a question.

Jazz nodded, taking a deep breath to steady her voice before she spoke. "I'm wondering if it's time for me to let this go. To accept that I was wrong, and he did take his own life. Could the hope of potentially studying dinosaurs sometime in the future possibly have been enough to give him strength to bear all of this?" She shook her head, answering her own question.

"You can let it go," Cappy said softly. "I still have work to do on this case, and I won't stop until my job is done. But it's *my* job. Give yourself permission to walk away, and trust that I'll see this through."

Jazz nodded, not necessarily agreeing that she was ready to give up, but acknowledging that she knew Cappy wouldn't stop until she had explored every other option.

"It was nice, what Mia said to you. About how much you and the library meant to Brian. I think you gave him an island where he could get away from some of his troubles, at least for a little while."

"I've always wanted my libraries to be a haven for the people who use them, especially children, when I was working in public libraries, and my students now." She hesitated before continuing, making a conscious choice to open the subject enough for her to talk about her past. Somewhere along the way she had decided to trust Cappy, and she wanted her to understand more completely the kind of haven she had been trying to create for Brian and her other students. "I guess it's because that's what libraries always were for me."

"Did you need to get away from trouble at home?" Cappy asked, her voice casual but with an undercurrent of anger to it, as if she'd go back in time to punish anyone who had been mean to Jazz.

"Not trouble. Just loneliness," Jazz said. She pulled Cappy's notebook closer to her and riffled the corner of the pages with her thumb, over and over. "My parents moved to America from Norway when Mom was pregnant with me, and my sisters were two and four. Dad left us when I was very young, but she wouldn't talk about him, so I never knew why. Another woman? Too many fights? Whatever the reason, I know she was angry with him for leaving, and resentful that she had left her family behind to follow him here, but she shut it away inside."

"Did you see much of your dad after that?" Cappy asked. She had one foot on the rung of Jazz's chair, and she leaned her elbow on the table, resting her head on her palm, giving Jazz the feeling that she was curling around her, trying to protect her from her past. Those were just her cop instincts probably—sensing pain and doing her best to protect others against it. Jazz felt the shelter of her, the sense of Cappy giving her space to talk but staying close enough to lend comfort.

"No. My mom didn't want anything to do with him, so she wouldn't accept any child support or let him spend time with us. He could have fought for us, I suppose, but I don't even know if he tried." She shrugged. She had never felt overly emotional about him since he simply hadn't existed to her child self. "My mom was the one I really missed, even though she was the one who stayed. She wanted us to be strong, never relying on anyone else for support, and she did her best to be an example of independence for us. I appreciated the message, but it also meant she had to work hard to support a family of four, always having at least two jobs and taking on extra work during the holidays or when we needed new clothes or things for school."

"Ah," said Cappy. "Librarians to the rescue?"

Jazz laughed at the phrase, impressed again by the way Cappy's mind leaped agilely from connection to connection. "Exactly. The library was my home when my own was empty. I was technically too young to be there without a parent when I first started hiding away in the children's room, tucking myself in a corner with a pile of books, but the librarians sort of adopted me. I'm sure they recognized my loneliness, and they made an effort to fill the void of an absent parent. So did my books. Given my childhood, I don't think I could have become anything other than a librarian."

Cappy was upright and a respectable distance away from Jazz before she had quite finished her last sentence. She only had a moment to wonder why, and to recognize the loss of warmth from her close presence, when there was a knock on the door and she understood why Cappy had moved so quickly.

"Cop ears," Cappy said with a smile, apparently reading Jazz's confusion at her sudden shift away from her. She rested her hand briefly on Jazz's thigh, as if reassuring her that she wasn't intentionally moving herself out of the little bubble of intimacy they had created, before she got up to answer the door, returning in a few moments with Greg Masters.

Greg followed Cappy into the room with the cocky stride of a kid who knew he was a big deal on campus. Jazz had seen the same swagger in Brian before his accident. It wasn't necessarily arrogance, just a sureness of his place within the small universe of the university. Where Brian had been darker and good-looking in a more understated way, Greg had the Golden Boy look to him. He had fashionably long blond bangs that he regularly swiped to the side, only to have them drift back over his forehead. After the third time he made the same move, Jazz wanted to reach across the table and cut them off. Annoying as the habit was, though, she could picture him after a game, pulling off his helmet and running a hand through his hair while smiling for the cameras and his adoring fans. He looked like a star, although according to Cappy, he didn't play like one.

Jazz sat back and remained quiet while Cappy went through the same introductions and reasons why they were talking to him as she had with Mia. She was relieved to have a chance to shut herself up and let someone else talk for the next hour, or the next week. She didn't think she had ever in her life said so many words about herself and her past in one fell swoop as she had done today with Cappy. Her friends most likely knew the full story she had just recounted, but they had gotten it in snippets over the course of a few years. Jazz waited for the twinge of regret, the feeling that she had overshared and should now feel awkward or annoyed at herself, but those feelings didn't come. She had talked, and Cappy had listened. She was glad, in a way, that Cappy now possessed her story. It seemed fitting in this process of unearthing Brian's history that Jazz also bring hers out of hiding.

But still—she was quite happy to be done with the autobiographical session of the afternoon, and to listen to Cappy and Greg's conversation.

Which was apparently about the team's chances against Penn next weekend. Jazz figured Cappy was establishing a rapport with Greg as they had an animated discussion about the other team's strengths and weaknesses, and she could feel the shift in Cappy's demeanor as she changed from *Hey, I'm your buddy so let's talk football* to cop mode.

"You know, I have a good feeling that this is going to be your breakout game," Cappy said, and Jazz would have bet her car that Cappy didn't really believe Greg had a chance of playing spectacularly well. "You have big shoes to fill, but you can do it."

Greg nodded as if accepting the segue to talking about Brian. "He was a great player. We have different styles, so I don't ever try to play the way he did. I don't want people to think of me as his replacement, but as a great player in my own right." He rested his hands on the table, fingers clasped together, and looked solemnly at Cappy, then at Jazz. "I won't lie and say I'm not thrilled to have a chance to play first-string, but I really hate the reason it happened. The accident. But he was still there, ready to cheer us on at the games. Losing him just…it really hurts."

He wasn't as weepy as Mia had been, but he looked sincere. Jazz couldn't read him clearly, but she was too caught up in her own pain, and too aware of how poorly she had read Brian, so she just listened and left the analysis to Cappy.

"I understand the two of you have been friends for a long time now," Cappy said. "Didn't you go to Canterwood Heights together?"

"We did. He moved just three blocks away from me in our sophomore year. Since we were both running backs, we always practiced together, so I saw him more than I saw my own family." He brushed the heel of his hand over his eyes. "He was my brother. We say that a lot on the team, but with some guys it just means more. I want to honor his memory by playing well."

"That would be a meaningful tribute to him," Cappy said. "Like I said, this conversation is just a formality we follow after a loss like this, but we'd appreciate it if you could give us an idea of what Brian was like off the field and in high school. You're one of the people who knew him best."

"Like I said, he was a great player. Football was all that mattered to him. Well, maybe not the game itself as much as winning. He had dreams, and he was willing to do anything to make them come true."

"Anything?" Cappy prompted.

Greg shrugged. "I heard rumors about drugs, but after what we got him through in high school, I hope they were wrong. He was fast and very strong. Was that natural, or did he have some help? It's hard to say."

Jazz thought he was finding it all too easy to say, actually. Cappy shifted slightly and stepped on her foot. Not too hard, but enough to make her realize she had gotten tense. She took a slow breath and relaxed again. Well, as much as she could.

"You think he would have risked his career for a little enhancement? He could have lost everything if he got caught."

"Yeah, probably not. Like I said, these are just rumors you hear around the locker room."

Cappy nodded, flipping through the pages of her notepad. "And his girlfriend, Justine. Did you know her very well?"

Greg snorted. "Not her in particular, but I know her type."

"Her type?" Cappy repeated.

"Well, she broke up with him right after his accident, didn't she? Not hard to figure out why she was with him in the first place. He was her ticket to being an NFL wife, and he was broken up after she dumped him. Brian was like that. Kind of naive sometimes. He wanted the fame and the pro football lifestyle, but did he realize she wanted that, too, and that was the only reason why she was with him? No. He thought they were in love."

He leaned forward conspiratorially. "And guess who she hit on the very next weekend, just before the game? Go on, guess," he said when Cappy and Jazz both remained silent, assuming it was a rhetorical question.

"You?" Cappy offered.

"Yes," he said with a delighted laugh, then he became serious again. "I told her no, of course. I wouldn't do that to Brian."

"Did you tell him about this?"

"No way. He'd have lost it." He paused and swiped at his hair before sighing and shaking his head sadly. "He lost everything, though, didn't he."

And Greg had gained all of it, Jazz thought. Cappy was right. If they were investigating the accident and not Brian's death, Greg would have been her prime suspect. Every move he made seemed carefully crafted, as if he was doing a postgame interview. Jazz figured he had practiced plenty of those in his mirror at home.

Cappy seemed to sense that they weren't going to get any further with Greg, and she wrapped up the interview, escorting him out before coming back into the room and flopping down in her chair. "He's exhausting," she said. She sighed. "I need to answer Kent's summons, but briefly, what are your thoughts?"

"He comes across as shallow," Jazz said. "He acts confident, but his insecurities came out, especially when he felt the need to belittle Brian after every positive thing he said about him."

Cappy nodded. "I agree. He's under a lot of stress because I'll bet the coaches will replace him if he doesn't perform well in the next game, so he's on the brink of losing everything just like Brian did. He's brittle. And if he and Brian were like brothers, they were probably the kind who can't sit next to each other at family holidays."

"Exactly. And why is everyone hating on this Justine girl?"

"Well, Mia was jealous of her. The coaches were angry with her because she was the driver when Brian was hurt. And she never hit on Greg, or my instincts are way off. I'm thinking it was probably the opposite, and she turned him down. We'll have a chance to talk to her tomorrow, and it will be interesting to hear her side of the story."

Cappy paused and rested her hand on Jazz's shoulder. "Or I can talk to her. Take some time to decide if you want to keep putting yourself through these interviews, okay?"

Jazz nodded. Part of her wanted to walk away from the case, and another, less rational part wanted Cappy to ask her to stay because she wanted her around. Come to think of it, that second part offered a very strong argument for Jazz getting the hell out of this investigation. She was already too emotionally close to all aspects of it, including Cappy.

"I promise I'll think about it," she said. "And you need to stop stalling and go see Kent before she calls Tig who will call Libby who will call me and tell me to send you in there."

Cappy laughed and stood up. "With any luck, Kent will be finished yelling at me before the calls get all the way to you." She opened the door again and led them out of the room.

"She'd better hurry, then. They've gotten very efficient at spreading the news," Jazz said as they parted ways in the lobby. She left the station and headed to Suzzallo. If she was going to do some serious thinking, she needed to be in her library.

Chapter Sixteen

Cappy heard laughter and voices coming from Kent's office as she walked down the hall. She wasn't sure if that was a good sign or not, and when she reached the open door, she saw Detective Ellingsen sitting in the chair across from Kent. She still wasn't sure if this was a good sign.

"Come in and shut the door behind you," Kent said in her customary curt tone. "I believe you've met Ellingsen already and apparently know her well enough to call in favors on her day off."

"Oh, well, I just had a thought about the case," Cappy said. "I didn't mean to—"

Ellingsen waved off her apology. "Don't let her scare you," she said. "She's grouchy on the outside, but cuddly as a teddy bear on the inside."

"Is that teddy bear filled with dynamite instead of stuffing?" Cappy asked. "Because then I'd believe you."

"That's it, Flannery. You're fired. For real this time," Kent said while Ellingsen laughed at her joke.

"I like this one," Ellingsen said to Kent. "She reminds me of you when you were younger." She turned back to Cappy. "We went to the academy together, about a hundred years ago. Buy me a drink sometime, and I'll tell you stories about her from the old days."

"I'll buy you an entire bar if the stories are really embarrassing," Cappy offered, bemused as her sergeant joined in Ellingsen's laughter. Neither of them could have more than a decade on her. Who was this woman, laughing with an old friend and mooning over a new girlfriend? Kent had certainly loosened up in the short time Cappy was out of state. It looked good on her.

"Sit," Kent said to Cappy as the laughter died down. She pointed at the desk. "Or perch. Whatever. I really need to get another chair in here. So, JC told me what bothered you about the glass they found next to those liquor bottles in Brian's apartment. Good thinking on your part. I'm interested to hear what came of it, but we've been waiting for you."

"Thank you," Cappy said, resting her hip awkwardly on the edge of Kent's desk. Her heavy duty belt, with its numerous bulky pockets, made perching a precarious activity.

The detective sighed and leaned back in her chair, all business now. "Kent told me you were looking into this possibly being a homicide, based on a civilian's allegations. I'm sorry that I don't have anything conclusive for you, but your observation has at least raised some questions. Last night we went back there and found several more glasses of the same type in his kitchen, along with assorted other mugs and pint glasses. We dusted all of them for prints, and only his showed up, which isn't unusual since he has a dishwasher and would have been the one to put them in the cupboard. Except for one of the small glasses."

"You found another person's prints?" Cappy asked when Ellingsen paused.

"We found no prints at all," she said. She shrugged. "Like I said, this doesn't lead to anything definitive. Brian could have wiped the glass with a towel and put it away while still holding it that way, so his fingers never touched the surface. Or someone else used it and wiped it down thoroughly and intentionally before putting it away. I'm inclined to believe the former, although this irritated my brain enough for me to go back early this morning to go over the scene one more time before we released it."

"Yes, yes," Kent said with an impatient wave when Ellingsen remained silent for a few seconds. "Dramatic pause. Now go on. What did you find?"

"I found the lock broken. Someone had kicked their way in overnight, and apparently searched the apartment."

"Looking for the glasses?" Cappy asked, still stuck on that part of the detective's story.

"Doubtful. Like I said, there's nothing overly suspicious about a really clean glass, aside from the fact that it was in a student housing room. This person was mainly looking through books and Brian's desk. According to our inventory, nothing was taken. When I was there last night, some of the tenants were having a loud party on the floor below, which likely concealed the sound of the door. The lights were broken out in the hallway, and people were in and out all night, most of them wearing coats and hoodies, so we can't separate the one intruder from the rest of the crowds."

Cappy had a brief and somewhat silly vision of Mia breaking in and searching for her mythical engagement ring. She shook her head, replacing that thought with a more reasonable one. She quickly told Kent and Ellingsen about her research with Miles the night before.

Ellingsen nodded. "I wouldn't be surprised if one of Miko's guys went over there, hoping to find some cash for one last payment. They'd probably feel it was their right, if he still owed them money."

"Fits the entry method, too," Kent added. "Careful and professional enough to choose a party night to mask the break-in, but gutsy enough to break through the lock instead of trying to pick it."

Ellingsen stood up. "I'm going back to the station to track down the footage Officer Larson sent over," she said. She handed Cappy her card. "I'll want details about the interviews you've done, so go ahead and email that to me. I'll keep you apprised if we learn anything new. Call me anytime you have another hunch. See ya, Kent."

"Bye, JC."

"It's still messy," Kent said to her once they were alone. "None of what the two of you have turned up fully convinces me that this is anything other than a suicide, but I don't want you to stop until we feel certain."

Cappy nodded. She felt the same. She had enough doubt in her mind now that she didn't feel ready to walk away from the case, even if she didn't factor in her desire to bring Jazz the peace that would come with knowing the truth—or as close to the truth as they could come. They might never find closure. "He had a more complicated life than I anticipated."

"He did. Probably more than he felt he could handle. More than I'd expect anyone to be able to handle, whether a young man or an adult. He was faced with a lot of pain and loss, along with the life-threatening stress of being indebted to a non-legitimate bookie. And who had anything to gain by killing him?"

Cappy couldn't think of anyone. None of the football players or coaches, since Brian was already moving out of their lives. Certainly not Mia, and definitely not Miko. Brian's funds were going to dry up eventually, but they hadn't yet. Why not get as much from him as possible? Of course, there were other reasons to want someone dead, aside from personal gain.

She rubbed the heels of her hands over her eyes, feeling the weight of the case and her restless night catching up to her.

"You're not even supposed to be here," Kent said. "Isn't this your day off? Go home. Say hi to your gran and take a nap. This will all be waiting for you when you get back."

Cappy nodded, standing up and saying good-bye to her sergeant. She changed back into last night's clothes and aimed toward her car, her apartment, and a fresh pot of coffee.

Cappy got her nap and her coffee. What she didn't expect was to get company, too. She answered a knock on the door in the afternoon and opened it to find Jazz in her apartment hallway. She hesitated, holding the edge of the door and staring at Jazz—not because the visit was unwelcome, but because it was unexpected. In fact, it was very welcome, and she felt the urge to grab Jazz's shirt and pull her inside, while her common sense recommended slamming the door in her face.

Her compromise was to stand in the doorway, unmoving, for an awkward length of time before she managed to find her voice.

"Jazz, hi." She finally stepped out of the way. "Come in."

Jazz stepped past her—quite close, since Cappy was still partially blocking the entrance—and stopped once she was over the threshold.

"I should have called first," she said, sounding as surprised to be there as Cappy was to see her. "If you're busy, I can go. We can talk later."

"No, it's fine. I wasn't doing anything." Yes, that was the way to impress a competent woman like Jazz, to admit you were lounging around doing nothing. Not that she wanted to impress Jazz for any reason, but still. She looked around the small apartment, seeing it through the eyes of a visitor, and winced. The floor was covered with her gran's boxes and, unfortunately, some of Cappy's clothes. She had been sleeping on the couch, so it was covered with bedding that was rumpled from her nap. A football game from six years ago was playing on the television.

"I suppose I should have been cleaning," she said, taking the remote off the coffee table and turning off the TV.

Jazz held up both hands. "Please. You should see my place."

Of course, she didn't say that her place was a mess as well. Cappy raised her eyebrows. "That's a very tactful thing to say. Now, tell me one similarity between my apartment and yours."

Jazz bit her lip, hiding a smile as she looked around. "Well, we both chose the option of walls. Oh, and I have windows, too, just like you."

Cappy laughed, feeling the awkwardness of Jazz's unexpected appearance starting to ease, and Jazz's relaxed smile seemed to indicate that she felt the same way.

"Let me just make my bed, and we can sit down," Cappy said, grabbing the blankets and pillow off the sofa in a huge armload and dumping them on a chair. "Did Clare tell you where I live?"

Jazz gave her a look that clearly said *Come on, use your brain*, and Cappy nodded. "Oh, that's right. I forgot that you have an advanced degree in nosiness. You seem to be walking a fine line between being a librarian and being a stalker, you know."

"Please. The two are completely different," Jazz said, sitting on the couch. "I keep my notes in file cabinets, not thumbtacked all over my walls."

Cappy laughed and was about to offer a retort when her grandmother came out of the bedroom. She was relieved to have a reason not to get cozy on the couch with Jazz, but at the same time, she wanted to get cozy on the couch with Jazz. It was the setting, she decided. Even though she had been around Jazz at Libby's, there had been other people there. This was her own apartment, and the sense of intimacy was overwhelming, especially since she hadn't had any time to mentally prepare for the visit.

"Oh, I didn't realize you had company," her gran said. "I thought I was hearing the TV. Why don't I just go out for a nice walk and let the two of you have some space."

"No," Cappy said at the same time as Jazz. They looked at each other, and Gran laughed.

"Don't trust yourselves to be alone with each other?"

Cappy sputtered as she searched for a way to explain her hasty response without admitting that her grandmother was correct. Luckily, Jazz interrupted her half-formed words.

"Actually, I came to see you, Edith. Well, both of you." She went over to the dining room area and took a folder out of her bag, moving a box of cereal and some puzzle books aside so she could set it on the table.

Cappy shrugged at her gran. "Probably a dossier on you, with all the details of your employment history, your social security number, and your ties to the San Bernardino crocheting society."

"Very funny," Jazz said sarcastically, but then she gave Cappy a sheepish-looking grin. "But not too far off."

Cappy was intrigued, curious to find out what this complicated woman had been up to in the—what was it, only five hours?—since they had last seen each other. They joined her at the table and she started pulling out stapled packets of paper.

"I know you've been planning to look for a place of your own, Edith, so I did a little preliminary research for you. I focused on senior living apartments and retirement communities, ones that are within walking distance of this apartment building, or an easy bus ride away."

She handed Edith a map with the various addresses marked on it, surrounding a starred address that was Cappy's place. Cappy leaned over her grandmother's shoulder and looked at the color-coded dots. She had been feeling overwhelmed at the prospect of finding a new home for her gran, and she didn't trust herself to speak for a moment as she took in the amount of legwork Jazz had already done for them.

"What are the different colors?" her grandmother asked.

Jazz slid one of the packets in front of her. The front page had a printed photo of the apartment building with an orange dot in the top corner of the paper. As she flipped through, Cappy saw pages with details about amenities and prices.

"The orange ones have more options for socializing that fit your interests. See? This one has wine tastings and book clubs and classes on crochet and knitting." She gave Cappy a quick shrug and a grin. "You guessed that one right. Anyway, the ones with blue dots have fewer social offerings and are basically just nice places to live. The yellow ones are lower tier, either really close or inexpensive, but without much else to recommend them. The ones with an extra green dot next to them allow cats."

"Cats?" Cappy repeated.

"Cats. Small furry animals with pointy ears and sharp claws. People keep them as pets."

"Thanks," Cappy said with a shake of her head. "I'm familiar with the concept. I was just curious why they got their own dot."

Jazz shrugged and addressed Edith. "You seemed to like having Boots in your lap when we were at Libby's. Plus, some of the photos you showed us had a cat in them."

"Oh," said Edith with a fond smile. "Mr. Kibble. Cappy named him."

"Of course she did," Jazz said wryly. "So, I thought you might want the option of getting one."

Aside from the fact that Jazz didn't seem impressed by her pet-naming skills, Cappy was stunned by the effort Jazz had put into her research. Not only because she had provided such detailed information, but mainly because she had clearly listened to Gran and tailored her results specifically to her interests and to the desire they both had to have her close to Cappy.

"I don't know what to say, Jazz. This is an incredible help. I was worried about just picking places at random."

"It's what I do," Jazz said dismissively, but her smile showed she was pleased with Cappy's words. She put her hands on the table and stood up. "I'll leave you two to look through these. I don't mean to rush in and out, but I need to get back to campus for a library event, and I wanted to get these to you right away."

"I'll walk you to your car," Cappy said, getting up and pulling on a sweatshirt while Jazz said good-bye to her gran.

"I've been thinking about tomorrow's interview," Jazz said as they took the elevator down to the ground floor. "I have to admit I'm curious about her, this person Brian was dating. The way the other people we've talked to have described her…well, that just doesn't sound like the type of person that would attract him. Still, I've been wrong about so many things connected to this case."

Cappy thought back to her first impression of Jazz based on Clare's description of the frightening, axe-wielding Viking woman. Jazz's friends—and now Cappy, too—saw how much depth there was beyond that image, but Cappy wondered how many other people saw past Jazz's austere surface and recognized the empathetic and passionate woman she really was.

"She reminds you of yourself, doesn't she?" Cappy asked. "Someone who is noticed, who attracts attention, but is rarely truly seen?"

Jazz shrugged, bumping Cappy's shoulder. "Maybe, a little. I might be reading more into her than will really be there, though. My instincts seem off lately, and it makes me wonder if they were ever as sharp and intuitive as I thought they were. I might be reading everyone the wrong way."

"Justine is coming to the station after her morning cheerleading practice," Cappy said, holding the building's glass door open for Jazz and following her out onto the sidewalk. "I have to admit that the first picture that came to mind was of a girl with a pleated skirt and a bow in her hair, doing backflips across the station's lobby. Stereotypes. We're constantly running up against them in this case, it seems."

Jazz nodded. "I was proud of myself for seeing more to Brian than just a football player, or then just an injured ex-player, but I think that what I was imagining beneath that surface was maybe what I wanted or expected to find there. I didn't realize how far off I was until we started investigating." She stopped by her car. "Like I said, if you'll still have me, I'll come tomorrow, but after that I'm going to leave the detective work to the professionals. You'll be able to wrap this case up more quickly without me there."

Cappy shook her head and was about to protest, but Jazz held up her hand. "Don't, please. It's kind of you to try to make me feel like I've been helpful, but I haven't contributed anything worthwhile. I was inappropriate in the interview with the coach, and silent for all the others. The only insight I've provided into Brian's emotional state was wrong, based on faulty assumptions. My only role in this has been to force you into an investigation you didn't want to do in the first place."

"That's because..." Cappy said, nearly letting her personal reasons for wanting to avoid this case spill out. This wasn't the right moment for that. Mostly because she really didn't like sharing her life story, but also because this moment was about Jazz and how she was feeling, not about Cappy.

"That's because I saw it as a closed case, and I accepted the simple conclusion along with everyone else. You made me look deeper."

Jazz laughed without humor. "Yeah, you looked deeper and found no evidence to contradict the original determination of suicide. It's been a waste of your time."

"There's more to this story than anyone realized," Cappy said. She quickly recapped Detective Ellingsen's visit and the new information she had turned up.

Jazz took it all in and came to the same conclusion Cappy had. "Do you think the break-in was the bookie, looking for money? If they knew Brian routinely had large sums of cash on hand, they might have hoped some was lying around while the cops waited for the autopsy. Or maybe a student just wanted to poke around a crime scene. Maybe take something to sell later on, or keep as a ghoulish kind of souvenir."

Okay, Cappy's mind hadn't gone there, but she had to admit it made sense. She could picture a student breaking in on a dare, or because of the fascination some people had for high-profile—locally, at least—cases like this.

"You agree, don't you," Jazz said, correctly reading Cappy's thoughts. "Those are the likely scenarios, not a murderer returning to the scene to smuggle out a too-clean glass."

Cappy shook her head, resting her hand on Jazz's shoulder. "They might be likely, but they might also be incorrect. Every time I learn something new about Brian or about the events in his life, I feel the need to push a little more, explore a little deeper. I'm not sure what my next step will be after talking to Justine tomorrow, but I'll let you know when I think of one. Then you can decide if you want to join me or not. No matter the outcome, it's never a waste of time to try to learn all the dimensions of a person."

She moved her hand from Jazz's shoulder and cupped her cheek before leaning forward and giving her a brief kiss on the lips. She brushed Jazz's cheekbone with her thumb before dropping her hand and stepping back.

"Thank you," she said. "For what you did for me and Gran. And for caring so much about your students that you'll fight to protect and support them, even when they're no longer alive. You're an amazing woman." She shrugged. "Nosy, but amazing."

Jazz smiled, still lacking the forceful confidence Cappy had seen in her when she first came to the station, but Cappy hoped she would be able to reclaim that unwavering belief in herself and her convictions. She waved as Jazz got in her car and drove away, frightened by how much she wanted to stick around and help Jazz find her way back to herself.

CHAPTER SEVENTEEN

Jazz's thoughts were still churning when she arrived at the station the next day. She had been trying to come up with some useful questions to ask during the interview, wanting to participate more and not just sit there in silence, but she couldn't think of anything. It seemed that every time they talked to another person who had known Brian, they learned more about his life that led to the same sad conclusion. She was hesitant to contribute to the questioning because any answers she heard would only bring them closer to the conclusion that he really had died by suicide, and that she had read him wrong and hadn't been there to help him.

Unfortunately, her inability to come up with interview questions left a void in her internal reflection that was immediately filled by Cappy and that kiss. Jazz wasn't sure how she felt about it. Well, she was quite sure that it had felt wonderful. More natural and comfortable than she would have expected after having known Cappy for such a short time, but with an undercurrent of potential passion that had remained latent—Cappy had simply been trying to comfort and thank her, after all—but that was definitely present. Jazz wasn't sure how she wanted to handle the situation, and her own indecision was unfamiliar to her. She wasn't accustomed to being thrown off-kilter by a kiss, especially from a woman to whom she was attracted. And unlike the women she had dated in the past, she knew that Cappy would match her in mental and emotional strength, while at the same time allowing her moments like yesterday when she felt weak and uncertain. Jazz hadn't minded letting Cappy see her that way, when she normally would have struggled to hide those feelings from anyone else.

She walked into the station's lobby, alternating between wanting to see Cappy and talk about that kiss and wanting both of them to pretend it hadn't happened. Her uncertainty about Brian and how she had thought she'd known him was seeping into her personal life as well. Maybe she should appoint Tig as her romantic liaison along with being group leader. She could make these decisions for Jazz until she felt ready to handle them on her own again.

On second thought, that wasn't a good idea. Tig was so lovesick over Kent that she'd have a bias toward romance and would push Jazz into something before she was ready. Or she'd just give her a lecture on love in the ancient Mediterranean region. Even in her more chaotic state, Jazz was better off making decisions on her own.

Rather than Cappy, though, Jazz saw Clare standing by the station's desk. She grinned and came over to Jazz as soon as she spotted her.

"Morning, Jazz. What brings you down here?"

"Cappy and I are interviewing Brian's ex-girlfriend today," she said. "Well, Cappy is interviewing her. I'm just observing."

"Ah," Clare said. She leaned closer. "Word of advice? You might want to get that blush under control. You get a little pink around the gills every time you say her name. Libby would notice that from across campus."

Jazz resisted the urge to feel her cheek for telltale warmth. "I don't blush. I just got overheated on the walk here from Suzzallo."

"Yeah, fifty degrees and raining. I'm surprised you didn't get sunstroke." Clare glanced across the lobby and grabbed Jazz's arm. "Oh, look, there she is, looking all sexy in her uniform." She spoke like a giddy schoolgirl, then burst out laughing. "Sorry, I can't keep a straight face when I say that. She's too much like a sister to me."

Jazz relaxed and laughed along with Clare. With her here to ease the tension, she felt more in control when Cappy spotted them and came over.

"You," Cappy said to her in a stern voice. Jazz hadn't expected her to bring up the kiss with Clare standing next to them, but she had expected maybe a certain softness from her. Instead she sounded cranky. "Guess where Gran and I went after you left yesterday."

"Oh, to see one of the apartments?" Jazz asked, brightening at the thought.

"That would have been sensible, right?" Cappy responded, her hands on her hips. "But no. We went to an animal shelter because *someone* reminded her of Mr. Kibble, and suddenly she needed to get a cat. She couldn't possibly wait to get her own apartment first. You owe me a thousand dollars."

She poked Jazz in the ribs, and she laughed, swatting at Cappy's jabbing finger. "You paid the shelter a thousand dollars? Just how fancy is this rescue cat?"

"No, that was for the nonrefundable pet deposit and one month pet rent for my place."

"For one cat?" Clare chimed in. "And who is Mr. Kibble?"

Cappy sighed and shook her head. "Two cats. Apparently they're a bonded pair, which is shelter speak for *Hey, sucker, you know that one cat you didn't want? Well, we're going to guilt you into buying two instead.*" Cappy ran both hands through her hair, bypassing slightly tousled and going directly to standing on end. "I don't have floor space in my apartment for two cats and two litter boxes. Two! My gran and I manage with one bathroom, but no, it's cruel to only have one box. If they're really so bonded, you wouldn't think they'd mind sharing."

"Oh no," Jazz said in a sympathetic voice, putting her hand on Cappy's shoulder. "Does this mean you have to put your clothes in the closet? That's horrible." Clare laughed along with her, but Cappy seemed determined to ignore their wisecracks.

"That's not the worst of it. Guess what she named them?" She paused, as if for dramatic effect. "Cougar and Apple. Can you believe it?"

Even Jazz knew enough about football to catch the reference to UW's local rivals, the Washington State Cougars who played against them in the Apple Cup every year.

Clare was bent over with her hands on her knees, trying to catch her breath. "Oh, Cap, I love your gran. And now I see where you got your sense of humor."

"Well, the joke's on her. I'm calling them Kibble One and Kibble Two."

Jazz turned to Clare. "A hundred dollars says she won't let her grandmother take them when she moves out."

Clare nodded and shook her hand. "It's a bet. I say she'll let them go, but another fifty says she cries when they leave."

"I'm giving each of you one for Christmas," Cappy said. She looked over Jazz's shoulder at the door and her demeanor changed in an instant. "Justine is here."

"I'll let you get to it," Clare said. "And fix your hair."

As Clare walked away, Jazz caught herself reaching to smooth down Cappy's disheveled hair but managed to stop in time to let Cappy do it herself.

"Do I look okay?" Cappy asked.

Jazz smiled. "*Okay* isn't the first word that comes to mind, but it'll do."

Cappy winked at her. "I'm going to bring that up again later. Come on."

They walked over to where Justine was standing at the desk, talking to Lea. Lea gestured at Cappy, and Brian's ex-girlfriend turned to face them.

No bows or backflips. She was wearing a purple track suit with a Husky logo on the back of the jacket, and she looked slightly sweaty and red in the cheeks, like any athlete coming directly from practice. Jazz thought she was lovely, with red hair that leaned more toward auburn than ginger and light green eyes. She didn't recall seeing her in the library before, but it wasn't uncommon for undergrads to stick to Odegaard. She was certain she had never seen her in Suzzallo with Brian.

They went back into the interview room. Jazz was getting familiar with it by now. She knew Libby would have thrived on this series of interviews, interjecting with her own insightful comments and questions, but Jazz merely felt out of place. She preferred talking to her students in the library, where the warm atmosphere invited confidences, as opposed to these cold rooms full of metal and plastic. They invited shields and carefully crafted responses. And there were no books.

Cappy gave Justine the spiel about their standard-procedure questioning, then jumped into personal questions more quickly than she had during the other interviews.

"You were dating Brian until the accident," she said, not asking but making a statement. "Rumor has it you broke up with him after because he was no longer destined for the NFL. I'd like to hear your side."

Jazz had seen Cappy in five interviews now, and she suddenly realized what a chameleon she was. She had been gentle with Mia, buddy-buddy with Greg, and now she was being almost forcefully up-front with Justine. Justine seemed to relax after hearing the direct question, and Jazz thought again that she likely had people judging her without really seeing her. Cappy was letting her know she wasn't swayed by rumors and was giving her a chance to tell her side. Although Cappy had said she had made a mistake telling Coach Moran how to run his team, Jazz wondered if she had intentionally wanted to put him in a defensive position.

Justine nodded and rested her folded arms on the table. "You want the truth? He broke up with me. He was very angry..." She paused, and her eyes filled with tears, but she closed them tightly for a moment, then looked at Cappy again and continued. "Who could blame him? He lost everything, and it was my fault. I was angry with myself, too. I still am."

"You were hit by a driver who ran a red light. The accident was not your fault," Cappy said, leaning forward and speaking with intensity.

Justine shrugged as if she was beyond being convinced of that. "We were fighting, and I wasn't paying attention like I should have been. Yes, they ran the light, but I might have been able to stop in time if I had been more focused on the road."

"Maybe, but also maybe not. That car was going well over the speed limit, and it might have happened too fast for you to respond, even if you had been staring directly to your right with total concentration. What were you fighting about?"

"Stupid things," Justine said with a bitter shake of her head. "My birthday was coming up, and I wanted to go out to dinner somewhere nice. Brian had a game the day after and didn't want to go out the night before, so he said he'd take me to the Burke to celebrate the day after his game. The museum, can you believe it? I hated that dusty old place."

She looked down at her arms, then up at Jazz, then Cappy. "When the chance is gone, suddenly being at the museum with him seems like it would have been the best date ever. But at the time...I mean, how ridiculous is it to have been jealous of a bunch of bones?"

"So, he told you he blamed you for the accident?" Cappy asked.

"Not in those words, but I could feel it. He just said he needed time." She shrugged. "It's funny, but when I first started dating him, I liked him for all the reasons people think. Everyone knew who he was, and just walking around campus with him was exciting. He was going to be rich and famous, and I wanted all of that. I felt like I was somebody, too, when I was with him."

"And that changed?" Cappy prompted when Justine grew quiet.

"Yes. At some point I realized that I felt good about myself with him because he really liked me, not because other people thought we were special. When I finally had the chance to show him that, after the accident when he was just Brian again, he pushed me away."

She didn't say *Like I deserved*, but Jazz thought she heard it in her voice.

"Did you see him again after that?" Cappy asked.

Justine nodded. "I went over to his place one night, just a few days before he...before he died. I told him I loved him and still wanted to be with him. I think he felt the same way, but he said he was seeing someone else. He said he needed time to decide what to do."

"But you believe he was going to pick you, deep down, don't you?"

"Yes," she whispered. "We had a history together. I know he loved me, too."

Cappy nodded and wrote down some notes, letting the silence stretch for a few seconds.

"What can you tell me about his friend Greg? Do you know him very well?"

Jazz didn't need to be an expert in reading facial expressions to interpret Justine's distaste for him. "I knew him. He was always around at parties and things, or if I'd go watch Brian practice. Brian would have done anything for him, but he wasn't the great guy Brian thought he was. He asked me out not long after the accident, acting like I would be thrilled to date another football player. Like they were interchangeable."

"Do you know much about his friendship with Brian from before coming here? Maybe Brian felt like he owed Greg something, and that's why he was willing to do anything for him?"

Justine shrugged. "When Brian talked about high school, it was mostly old football stories. I always figured he felt guilty about being so good while Greg sat on the bench."

Cappy glanced at Jazz, but she just shrugged. She didn't have anything to add, of course. She could at least have offered to take notes during the interview, just to feel like she was taking part.

Cappy nodded and ended the interview, walking Justine out to the door and coming back to sit by Jazz.

"What do you think?" she asked, kindly letting Jazz give her impressions first, as if she had real insight to offer.

"I think we can add relationship drama to the list of stressors in Brian's world," she said. "He didn't seem to have anything stable and reliable in his life."

"Except you and the library," Cappy said. She shook her head, looking over her notes. "Both Justine and Mia seemed to believe he was going to choose them, but maybe he did make his decision. Maybe he told one of them he was going to date the other, and she killed him in a jealous rage. Could have gone either way, but these two are the only ones we've found who might have had some motivation to murder him."

"If that's true, then I'm ready to completely give up on my insistence that Brian was killed and it wasn't suicide. Neither of these young women seemed like the type to turn to homicide to heal a broken heart."

"Huh," said Cappy. "Did you ever meet Libby's stalker, Angela? Quiet young student who spent her evenings studying architecture, fantasizing about Libby, and hacking up people with a knife?"

"You have a good point there," Jazz said, remembering those frightening days that led to Libby being held at gunpoint on a wooded trail and Clare getting shot in the stomach. "But she has to be an aberration, not the norm for brokenhearted coeds."

"Let's hope," Cappy said with feeling, and Jazz saw a haunted shadow pass over her face.

"I know how terrifying that day was for them, but it must have been horrible for you, too, watching and waiting for a chance to rescue them."

Cappy nodded, not trying to make a joke or shrug it off, which let Jazz know how much that day had truly affected her. "I have never in my life been so scared. If I had lost either of them...well, I'm not sure how I would have handled it."

Jazz wanted to touch her, to offer some comfort, but the door leading to the lobby was partially open. She settled for shifting slightly until her leg was pressed against Cappy's. She heard Cappy's sigh as she leaned into Jazz.

"Thank you," she said quietly. She flipped through her notepad again. "I've been to the Burke Museum on calls before, but I've never made it past the foyer. I remember seeing posters about exhibits in Brian's room. Care to go there with me now? I'd like to see what the appeal was for him, plus I hear it's the campus's romantic hotspot."

Jazz pretended to swoon. "Wow," she said in a breathless voice. "And it's not even my birthday."

Cappy stood up and reached out to pull Jazz to her feet, letting go as soon as Jazz was standing. The touch was brief, but Jazz missed the contact when it was gone. "Never let it be said that I don't know how to show a woman a good time," she said as they walked out of the room. "Provided she likes dusty old dinosaur bones, of course."

CHAPTER EIGHTEEN

Cappy went into the locker room and changed out of her uniform and into a pair of faded jeans and a cream-colored Aran sweater. She wanted to experience the museum as Brian would have, not as a cop who drew attention everywhere she went. Although, he probably drew his own crowd of fans wherever he went on campus, especially after those Rose Bowl wins. Still, she wanted to blend in and observe.

She returned to the lobby and found Jazz sitting on one of the padded benches by the windows, reading a book. She was an islet of elegance in a bustling room full of officers at shift change, and Cappy forced herself to exhale slowly at the sight of her. She really was one of the most beautiful women Cappy had ever seen. Whether she was holding herself in that still, composed way or fretting about Brian and the investigation, she had an underlying intensity to everything she did. Not to mention she was brilliant, with a core of empathy that encompassed her friends and students, even Mia and Justine, whom she barely knew.

Yes, she was the type of woman who would constantly challenge, interest, and excite anyone fortunate enough to be connected to her, whether as a friend or a partner. Cappy had allowed herself to blur those roles last night, when she had ignored all logic and kissed Jazz, but she needed to keep her distance from now on. She wasn't doing a great job of it so far, especially since she had sort of asked her out on a date, in a weird, post-interview way. She could spend time with Jazz and still maintain an emotional distance, couldn't she?

Nope, she decided when Jazz looked up and saw her, giving her a crooked smile as if she was trying not to look too glad to see Cappy. Both Jazz and Cappy were all-in kind of people. Cappy needed to stay firmly on the friendship side of their relationship or she'd be lost. At least, more lost than she already was. As difficult as it would be for Cappy, she wanted to explain her past to Jazz, so she'd understand Cappy's decisions.

"You brought a book to an interview?" she asked as she approached the bench.

"I bring an emergency book everywhere," Jazz said, standing up and tucking the book into her bag. They went outside, where it was breezy but not raining for the moment. The museum was only six blocks from the station, so they crossed onto the campus and walked along the leaf-strewn paths.

"What kind of emergencies are you expecting to come across? Bookends with nothing in between them? A table with one short leg?"

Jazz laughed as they turned left and walked parallel to the western edge of campus. "You never know when you'll have to wait in line for your coffee, or when your friends will be running late—and they're always running late—or when you'll be sitting in a police station after an interview while a cop changes out of her uniform. The last one is new to me, but at least I was prepared."

"If you're ever stuck there without an emergency book, just ask at the desk. There are plenty of criminology handbooks for you to read while you wait."

Jazz shrugged. "As long as there are words, I'll be content."

They crossed the street and saw a line of people waiting to get into the museum, mostly families with children running and shrieking around them. "I wasn't expecting a crowd," Cappy said. "I probably should have kept my uniform on."

Jazz just shook her head in mock exasperation, leading Cappy down a ramp to the lower street level of the building, where a security guard was standing near the entrance.

"Hello, Ms. Harald," he said, unhooking a rope that cordoned off this doorway. "I haven't seen you in a while."

"It's been too long, Johnny. I brought…oh."

Cappy followed Jazz's gaze to the low black wall surrounding some shrubbery in front of the building. Someone had placed a framed photo of Brian there, wearing his uniform. There were flowers laid out as offerings, along with a couple of footballs and teddy bears wearing Husky uniforms.

"I heard that Brian really loved your museum," Cappy said to the guard, taking Jazz's elbow to steady her. "He must have come here often."

"All the time," Johnny said with a nod. "Even after the accident, he'd take the campus shuttle and come sit with the dinosaurs. We sure miss having him around."

Cappy made the appropriate sounds of sympathy as she moved Jazz past the memorial and into the building. She checked out a map etched on the wall and then led Jazz to the stairs.

The building was a slender rectangle, much longer than it was wide, with rooms on either end and an open center area and narrow hallway connecting them. It was far from the dusty old museum Justine had described. Instead it had an industrial feel to it, with metal and glass everywhere. The contrast with the displays of colorful textiles and plant life was fascinating. As they walked down the hall, Cappy saw public display rooms as well as glassed-in areas. They passed an alcove where a young woman in a bright red, embroidered dress was helping children weave tiny clay-colored baskets.

"Are you okay?" she whispered to Jazz as they walked past a gallery full of artifacts from Indigenous cultures. Most appeared to be from the Northwest, but Cappy saw some displays for other countries, as well.

Jazz nodded. "Yes. It just caught me by surprise, but I should have expected them to find a way to honor him."

They walked up the stairs to the second floor, and Cappy paused by one of the glassed-in rooms. She wanted to help Jazz past the shock of seeing the memorial and figured that getting her to take on the role of tour guide would be a good way to start. Plus, she wanted to know more about the museum, which was more interesting than she had anticipated. "This is an awesome place," she said. "What all goes on in here?"

"It's a working museum," Jazz said, slipping naturally into the role Cappy had offered. "There are labs, storage spaces, and artist workspaces in these rooms, alongside the public exhibits." She paused by a room with a couple of people hunched over a tall bench. A hand-lettered sign on a whiteboard was propped against the window, informing visitors that the students inside were prepping arachnid specimens for a future exhibit. "It's an opportunity for people not just to see static displays from the natural sciences, but to see scientists in action," Jazz continued, as they wound through some of the exhibits, pausing occasionally to read the display placards.

Eventually they headed up the stairs to the third floor and entered the paleontology room. There were fossils of all sizes, including a massive T. rex skull, as well as models of full dinosaur skeletons. Jazz sighed as they stepped into the space. "I failed him, Cappy."

Cappy spotted an empty bench on the far side of the room and took Jazz over to it. They sat down, and Cappy sat close to Jazz, giving her as much physical support as she could in the crowded, public place. Behind them were the massive glass windows, looking out over a parking lot and campus entrance. They were facing the displays of fossils, and Cappy wondered how many times Brian had sat in this same spot.

"How did you fail him?" she asked, certain that Jazz was picturing him here, as well.

"At first I thought it was because I couldn't make people understand why I didn't believe he died by suicide. But with all the stories about his life that we've uncovered, I think the real way I failed him happened earlier, when I didn't look hard enough to see how much he was hurting."

They lapsed into silence, and Cappy sat and watched the families and students moving through the exhibit. On the wall in front of them, across the tables full of fossils, colorful informational panels, and the T. rex skull, was a wall full of curved, fossilized shells. Today, she just wanted to be here and see the big picture, but she'd definitely come back and spend time looking around in more detail. She made a silent bet with herself and gave Jazz a nudge.

"I like those curvy shells," she said, pointing at the wall across from them. "Do you know what they are?"

"Mesozoic ammonites," said Jazz in a distracted voice, and Cappy laughed.

"I owe myself twenty dollars," she said. "I made a bet that you'd know what they were. Unfortunately, I can't afford to pay myself because now I have cats."

Jazz smiled. "You're not fooling anyone with the cranky act. You know you love them."

"Meh. They're okay. I still haven't forgiven you for putting the idea of them into Gran's head, but I think you're truly amazing. Everyone else was laughing at the silly photos of me, but you really looked at them. You noticed Mr. Kibble, figured out how much he meant to my gran, and even looked for places where she could live with a cat again. Or two. You're something special, Jazz, so please don't sell yourself short because you didn't see something Brian was trying so hard to hide."

Jazz sighed and settled closer to her. "Edith told me that you weren't able to spend much time with them, only a couple of weeks a year. Judging by those photos, she and your grandfather did their best to cram a childhood worth of memories and experiences into the short time they had with you."

Cappy stared at the T. rex skull, breathing slowly until she felt more in control of her emotions. Jazz somehow knew how to hit at the very heart of the matter, and Cappy wasn't used to having other people see that deeply into her life.

"Did she tell you why I wasn't there often?" she asked, turning her head to look at Jazz.

"She just said your father was proud and wanted to take care of you himself after your mom left."

Cappy nodded, aware that Jazz had been able to discern some of the negative implications of those innocent-sounding statements.

Only Kent and Clare and a few other officers Cappy had known were aware of her family history, and even they didn't know everything. She wanted Jazz to know why this case was hard for her, too. And for her to accept that Cappy understood some of what she was experiencing.

She exhaled and looked away again, out toward the bones and fossils. "My father was a police officer, too. There was always a lot of alcohol in the house, for him to use as a way to unwind after work and for my mom, I think to help her deal with the stress of marriage to a man with a dangerous profession. He was a sad drunk, but she was an angry one. She got mad and slapped me a couple of times, and he warned her to stop. But one night she hit me too hard, and I fell down the stairs and broke my collarbone."

"Oh, Cappy," Jazz said softly as she paused in her story.

"I was five," Cappy said with a shrug. She pointed at her shoulder, trying to lighten the mood even though she knew it wouldn't work given the story she was telling. "See? All healed now. But my dad was furious, and he did what he thought he had to do to protect me. He took me to the hospital and turned her in to social services. He made her move out, and they were divorced within the year. I had monitored visits with her, so I saw her fairly regularly, but she...well, the drinking got worse, and I think something broke inside. She died by suicide two years later."

She had been seven, nearly eight, and her father hadn't shielded her from any of the details from her mother's departure to her death. Some might fault him for that, but Cappy didn't regret her understanding of the situation. Would it have been easier to be babied and protected, hearing only euphemisms and carefully crafted, simplified versions of events? Maybe. But she wouldn't be the same person she was now.

"He never touched a drop of alcohol after she left. He did his best to be both mother and father, somehow not fulfilling either role very well. But I was all he had, and he didn't like me being away from home. His parents—my grandparents—did what they could, but he didn't allow them much."

"Do you still see him?" Jazz asked.

"Sometimes. He came up when I graduated from college, and then from the police academy. We talk on the phone sometimes. And I saw him at Gramps's funeral. I guess you could say we have a strained relationship. It's not like we had major fights or anything, but the past is heavily in the room whenever we're together. We can't get beyond it to really connect to each other."

Cappy sighed and leaned back against the window, feeling drained. "I'm telling you this delightful story because I want you to know that I understand just a little bit how you and the others are feeling right now, after losing Brian, even though the situations are very different. I also hope it lets you know that I'm taking his death very seriously, no matter if it was a suicide or a homicide. He matters. You matter. And so do all the people he left behind. I'm here to protect all of you, as much as I can."

Jazz put her arm around Cappy's shoulders and drew her close, kissing her temple, and then just sitting in silence with her. "I'm glad she's here with you now," Jazz said. "Edith, I mean. And the little Kibbles."

Cappy laughed, resting her head on Jazz's shoulder and letting her be the rock for the moment. "I'm glad, too. This case is difficult to bear, but we'll get through it. We'll do this right, for Brian."

Jazz snorted softly. "You will, that is. I've done nothing besides barging into the station and rallying everyone to arms, probably for no reason."

Cappy sat up, reluctantly pulling out of Jazz's embrace and shifting on the bench so she was facing her. "You've lost yourself in this," she said. "Remember that night, when you were so certain that you knew Brian, knew his state of mind, his hopes and dreams well enough to be sure that he hadn't harmed himself? Even Kent respected your intuition enough to assign me to this case. But as we've gone along, you turned all your focus to the things you didn't know about him. He lived a whole life before meeting you, so of course you won't know every detail. But maybe you should put your attention back where it belongs, on the boy who came into your library and talked to you about dinosaurs."

Jazz frowned. "I don't know if I can. I lost my faith in all that."

"Please try," Cappy said. She looked around her, at all the different specimens, from tiny plants and insects to massive dinosaurs. "What do you think caught his attention most when he sat here?"

Jazz didn't hesitate but pointed to the two glassed-in paleo workspaces on either side of the ammonite display. "I think he pictured himself in one of those labs, working with those other students."

Cappy nodded silently. She thought so, too.

An hour later, Jazz slowly made her way upstairs to her office. Cappy had seemed understandably worn out after talking about such a painful past, and Jazz had been struggling to process what she had heard, connecting those events to the Cappy she knew today. They had wandered through the museum's rooms, leaving the dinosaurs behind and going instead to the cultural and environmental exhibits, talking about recyclable materials and native plant species because there wasn't energy for anything more personal. Jazz had shared her own story the day before, and Cappy today. Jazz sensed that it was as unusual and unexpected for Cappy to show another person these old wounds, but she hoped Cappy felt as little regret as she did. She had no idea where they'd go from here, but at the very least, she had found someone who had the potential to be a close friend, maybe more. Jazz would never take that kind of connection lightly.

She decided that if she was going to trust Cappy with her childhood, she also needed to trust her advice. Instead of going to her office, she walked over to Brian's carrel and sat next to it. The area was quiet, with only a couple of students occupying desks at the end of the row. This had always been Brian's place, and he had filled the space with his presence.

Jazz thought back to when she and Cappy had first sat here, talking about him across the span of his carrel. And further back, to when he would come up here and rest his crutches next to him, fighting his way here rather than choosing an easier place to sit because he wanted to prove he was still capable.

She looked over at the elevators, which were only a few yards away. For someone taking the stairs, this would have been more of a trek from the front door, but Brian always took the elevator. He actually would have had less ground to cover getting here than if he went into the large study hall on the main floor, so coming up here wasn't an act of defiance in the face of his injury. Besides, like Johnny had said, Brian had been using the campus shuttle system since his accident, getting rides to his classes, the library, the museum. He wasn't above accepting help.

Why had he come up here? To see Jazz? Although she'd like to have been the reason for any of his actions, she didn't believe it in this instance. Besides, she regularly walked around the entire library, and she would have sought him out if he had moved downstairs.

So, he liked sitting here. Jazz wasn't sure why she had suddenly fixated on this, but it had to do with Cappy's admonishment to pay attention to what she knew about him, not bemoan everything she didn't. There was a nice view, and it was a quiet place to be. It was his place, and even during the day it was extremely rare to see anyone else sitting here. He was a campus figure, and if he had staked a claim to this carrel, then who was going to argue?

He had even wanted Mia to come up here, to show her something. He could have done that anywhere, including wherever they were when they had their tutoring sessions. Then why here? Unless whatever he wanted to show her already was here, and he didn't want to move it.

She switched to his chair, sitting at the desk for a long moment and glancing around to make sure no one was watching before she dropped off the chair and onto her knees. She pulled out her phone and used it as a flashlight to light up the underside of the desk.

Where a slim brown envelope was taped.

The phone slipped out of her hand and went dark.

She quickly got back in the chair and picked up her phone again, calling Cappy with suddenly shaking fingers.

CHAPTER NINETEEN

Cappy was on I-5, about to take a downtown Seattle exit on her way home, when she got Jazz's call. As soon as she saw her name on the screen, she put the call on speaker. She followed a hunch and turned left instead of right, crossing over the freeway and taking the northbound on-ramp, heading back to campus.

"What's up, Jazz?" she asked, carefully merging into traffic. "Are you okay?"

"I'm fine. I just…I need you to come to the library."

"Already on my way," Cappy assured her, trying to assess the situation while maneuvering through commuters. "What happened?"

"I found an envelope under Brian's desk. I'm not sure what to do with this."

"Leave it where it is," Cappy said. "I'll be there in ten minutes, and I'm calling Clare, too. Don't touch it or open it."

There was a brief silence on Jazz's end of the line. "Well, but I already read what was inside, then posted copies in the main study room, near the front door. Wasn't that all right?"

Cappy smirked. "Of course. Just don't show anyone besides the entire student body. Now sit your smart ass in his chair, and wait for us to get there."

"You probably should hurry. I already called Channel 5, and I have an interview about this in half an hour."

"I'm hanging up now so I don't get in a wreck."

Cappy shook her head at Jazz's comments. She really could have just said *Good idea. I won't tell anyone about what I found.* Of course, Cappy would have responded the same way if someone had given her such obvious information. She called Clare and told her to meet them in the library, then took the exit to the U District and parked just a few spots from where she had been fifteen minutes ago. She ran across campus until she reached Red Square, then slowed to a walk so she didn't draw attention to herself entering Suzzallo.

She reached Brian's carrel and found Jazz sitting in the chair next to it. For all her sarcasm on the phone, she looked pale and anxious. Cappy crouched down next to Jazz, resting her hand on the arm of her chair.

"Hey. You got here quickly," Jazz said, reaching out to briefly touch Cappy's hair. Her fingers were featherlight, but the contact plus the slight easing of tension in Jazz's expression when she'd first seen Cappy walking across the library seemed monumental. Cappy was accustomed to making a difference in people's lives—whether negative or positive, depending on the situation—but for this one moment she felt as if she really mattered to Jazz.

"I drove fast," she said as soon as she had control over her voice again. She glanced around the quiet area, then looked back at Jazz. "It's under there?" she asked, gesturing with her head toward the desk. Jazz nodded. "Okay, then you be lookout. I'm sure Libby's gone over this as part of your Crime Fighters Club training."

"Of course," said Jazz. "My job is to kick you really hard if I see someone coming."

Cappy laughed and pulled on the gloves she had brought from her car before she dropped to a seated position and wormed her way ungracefully into the tight space under the row of desks. She used her phone to scan the area under his desk and the adjacent ones—finding far too much gum and other clumps of goo for her comfort—then snapped some photos of the envelope. She was about to reach for it when Jazz kicked her in the side.

"Ouch!" She jumped, bumping her head on the underside of the desk, hoping she had missed all the goo.

Jazz lowered her head and peeked under the desk, grinning at her. "Sorry, it was just Clare."

Cappy shook her head, then returned to the job of carefully detaching the envelope, leaving most of the tape in place. She scooted out from under the desk and stood up, coming face-to-face with Clare. And Libby.

"Jeez, Sawyer. I said Jazz might have found some evidence about Brian. I didn't ask you here on a double date."

"I know," Clare said, gesturing at Libby. "She was next to me on the couch when you called. You try to tell her to leave."

"I'm here to provide moral support for Jazz," Libby said, tagging along with them as they hurried to Jazz's office, "not to intrude on your investigation. But a double date sounds fun—we should do that sometime."

Cappy sighed, setting the envelope on the desk. "Can we just close the door and see what Jazz found? And maybe have her tell us why she was crawling under his desk in the first place."

Clare shut the door and came to stand next to Cappy while Jazz and Libby sat in the chairs on either side of Jazz's desk.

"I was trying to figure out why he kept coming upstairs to study, since it didn't make sense that he was trying to prove he could still get around like before. Plus, he said he wanted Mia to come up here and see something, so I guessed that what he wanted to show her might already be here. If people saw him switching to a downstairs seat, this carrel would have become public again, and not Brian's unspoken territory."

"Good instincts," said Clare. She pulled on a pair of gloves identical to Cappy's and poked at the envelope. "It's not sealed, so there's no reason why we can't look inside." She carefully unfolded the flap and pulled out a handful of papers, spreading them on the desk and adding a thumb drive to the pile.

Cappy pointed at the drive. "Can we use your laptop, Jazz?"

"Of course," said Jazz. "I'll log on to my Instagram account, so I can post whatever we find on there. I hope that isn't against police procedures or anything."

Clare looked confused, and Cappy shook her head. "Sarcasm," she said briefly. "I told her not to show this to anyone before I got here, and I think she took the comment as a personal insult to her intelligence."

"Rookie mistake," Libby said, getting up on her knees in the chair so she could lean over the desk and look at the papers, carefully keeping her hands away from them. "What is all this?"

"Evidence of drug deals?" Clare asked.

Cappy noticed the initials *PW* on the pages, alongside a list of local parks and other areas around downtown, with dates and times next to each one. "Pryce Walker?" she guessed. "Brian may have been meeting him at these locations, but this isn't enough evidence to accuse Walker of anything. Let's see the drive."

She leaned across Jazz and inserted it into her laptop, swiveling the computer so the others could see the screen. Unfortunately for her composure, the action left her practically draped across Jazz's shoulder with her breast resting against Jazz's upper arm. She couldn't move away from the contact without bumping into Clare, and Jazz was effectively pinned against her desk. Cappy was just going to have to tolerate being so intimately close to Jazz and hope her voice didn't come out all squeaky the next time she talked.

"Play one of the video clips," Cappy suggested, scanning the contents of the drive.

They watched a short video of someone—presumably Brian—showing the door to Pryce's office, with his name clearly marked on it. The footage panned through the office and then zeroed in on a hand unlocking and opening one of his desk drawers, focusing on the small plastic bags and bottles of pills. Brian had possibly stolen the coach's keys to film the evidence, and the trembling quality of the film revealed his nervousness. Another clip showed Pryce entering the empty locker room and putting a bag in one of the lockers. When the person with the camera came out of hiding, Cappy could see they had been standing in the darkened shower area. They walked over to the locker and opened it, revealing the contents of the bag on film. There were also a dozen or so still shots of Pryce in locations that likely correlated to the list of presumed drug deals, handing or receiving packets from unknown people.

The room was silent after they had looked through all the contents of the thumb drive. Cappy stood upright, edging away from Jazz so she could think again, and ran her hands through her hair. This case had just jumped several levels in complexity, and her mind was working hard to catch up.

"Is this enough to convict Walker of anything?" Libby asked.

Clare shook her head. "There could be reasonable explanations for what the coach was doing. Or the bottles in his office could have been planted there."

"And maybe he was just hanging out in the park, sharing a falafel with his friend," Cappy added. "Not enough to convict on its own, but is it enough to open an investigation and possibly do enough damage to his career that he never works in collegiate football again?"

"Absolutely," she and Clare said at the same time.

"We have two questions to answer now," Cappy continued. "One, assuming that this envelope did belong to Brian and that he was the one collecting the evidence against the coach, what did he intend to do with it?"

Libby scanned one of the pages closest to her. "Some of these dates are from last year. He seemed to have enough evidence back then to bring to the authorities, if that was his goal. So why hadn't he done it yet?"

Clare shrugged. "Blackmail? Maybe he didn't want to get Pryce fired but just wanted to hold this over him."

"He had been giving Brian money for his gambling debts," Cappy agreed. "Perhaps Pryce wasn't the benevolent benefactor he wanted us to think he was. Blackmail makes sense. The dates on some of the pictures on the drive are from last year, as well. He went through the effort of collecting this evidence—and based on the shaky footage I'll bet he was scared out of his mind while doing it—but he didn't turn it over to Moran or campus authorities."

Clare nodded, and Cappy continued, "He might have been afraid of taking these films, but Miko would have been even more terrifying if Brian wasn't able to pay his debts. He might have felt like he had no other choice."

"And if Pryce was tired of paying…" Libby paused and looked at Jazz. "Maybe this wasn't a suicide after all. If any of this is true, then Pryce obviously had the drugs on hand for getting rid of him."

"But would Brian have trusted him enough to drink with him?" Jazz asked. "Especially if he thought he was engaged in illegal activity? There wasn't any evidence of force."

Cappy was irrationally proud of her in that moment. Here was the first glimmer of evidence that Brian's death might have been a homicide, and still, she was following logic and reason, asking intelligent questions instead of demanding they go arrest the coach immediately.

"He could have," Cappy answered. "The bond between a coach and a player is almost like a father and son sometimes. Maybe Pryce said he wanted to talk about this, or he was going to change his ways, or something. Just enough to get Brian to take those first few drinks and become more susceptible to the offer of more."

Jazz nodded at her. "What was the second question?"

"What are *we* going to do with this evidence?"

"Don't you have to turn it in?" Libby asked.

"Yeah, of course," said Clare. "The question actually is *when*. Will it spook Pryce and keep us from finding out what happened to Brian? Are there other aspects of the case we need to investigate first?"

Cappy gathered the papers and thumb drive and slid them back into the envelope. "Right now, we need to take this to the station and lock it away. We can show Kent tomorrow and make some decisions then. But in the meantime—"

"Hurry down to the stadium and accuse the coaches of giving the players drugs?" Jazz asked. "Oh, wait. I already did that."

Cappy nudged Jazz's shoulder with her hip. "I was going to say that in the meantime, we should come up with a list of other leads that we want to follow before this becomes an official investigation."

Clare laughed. "No you weren't. You were going to say we shouldn't talk about this to anyone else. Good catch, Jazz. She does enjoy stating the obvious."

Cappy shook her head as the others laughed. "Well, whatever I was going to say, my advice about other leads holds true. I'm heading to the station now."

"We'll come with you," said Clare, and Libby grinned, probably hoping this would be the glorious day that the weapons lockers had been accidentally left unlocked.

"Are you coming, Jazz?" Cappy asked with an attempt at nonchalance. A failed one, judging by Clare's and Libby's snickering.

"I'm closing tonight, so I need to stay," Jazz said, looking as reluctant to part with them as Cappy felt about leaving her behind.

"You and I are working together tomorrow," Clare said, elbowing Cappy. She turned to Jazz. "We'll have you come to the station during our shift so the three of us can talk."

"Four of us," corrected Libby, mouthing *Call me* at Jazz.

Clare herded her out the door, giving Cappy and Jazz a moment of privacy. Once she had the moment, Cappy didn't know what to do with it. She gave Jazz an awkward pat on the shoulder.

"So, um, good night. I'll see you tomorrow."

She made it halfway to the door before turning around and walking back to Jazz. She put her hands on the arms of Jazz's chair, on either side of her, and leaned down to kiss her. She hadn't meant it to be, well, she hadn't meant to do it at all, but once she started she decided to give it her all. She had enjoyed the feel of Jazz's lips during their brief kiss outside her apartment building, but that was nothing, *nothing*, like this kiss. She pressed Jazz against the back of her chair, sliding her tongue along the curve of Jazz's mouth and dipping inside when Jazz's lips parted. While their tongues moved against each other, Jazz put her hands on Cappy's hips and guided her insistently until she was straddling Jazz's lap. Cappy relaxed into the kiss, reveling in the warmth of Jazz's hips and the feel of Jazz's hands as they moved up Cappy's back and tangled in her hair.

Cappy was close to losing all sense of the world around her, but a few words managed to penetrate her brain. Office. Library. Evidence. Clare and Libby. The last ones were enough to make her draw back, giving Jazz one last lingering—but relatively chaste—kiss and pushing herself back to standing.

Jazz leaned her elbow on the arm of her chair and rested her fingertips on her lips. "Well, that was…"

Cappy sighed. "Wasn't it, though?" She reached up to flatten her curls. "Does my hair look mussed up?"

Jazz laughed. "No more than usual. I find your tousled look very sexy."

"Useful information," said Cappy with a grin, using her hands to dishevel her hair. She backed toward the door. "I'll see you tomorrow. Good night."

"Well, it will certainly be a long one," Jazz said, barely loud enough for Cappy to hear.

Cappy met Clare and Libby at the end of the hallway. Clare took one look at her and turned away, making a gagging sound. Libby swatted her on the shoulder and looped her arm through Cappy's. "I want details," she said as they walked out of the staff area.

"I want absolutely no details," protested Clare from behind them.

"There's nothing to tell," Cappy said, which earned her exaggerated scoffing sounds from both of them. "Really. There's nothing going on between us, so don't try to make this into the Clare and Libby Saga part two."

"Part three," Libby said. "Don't forget Kent and Tig. I can't believe I tried to set Jazz up with Kent. Boy, was I wrong."

Cappy halted and looked at Libby. "Clare told me, but really? Those two?"

Clare shrugged. "Actually, on paper they make sense. In reality it was the most boring meet-cute in the history of matchmaking. I believe the word *efficient* was used. Maybe if Jazz had gotten punched in the nose like Tig did, it would have worked better."

Cappy shook her head and walked out of Suzzallo, aiming across campus toward the station. She didn't want to talk about her and Jazz, but even more, she didn't want to talk about Jazz and other women. At all. Which wasn't fair to Jazz in the least.

"Can you maybe wait until this case is over before you try setting her up with anyone else? We need her focused on the investigation."

"And once you're finished, you'll what? Just go your separate ways?" Clare asked. "Not that I want details about any of this, but the two of you seem good for each other. You fit."

"We don't fit. We just get along fairly well, in a noncommittal kind of way."

"Well, if that's not love, I don't know what is," Libby said wryly.

"It's not. I don't fall in love. I can't."

"Oh," Libby said. "Physically can't?"

Cappy halted on the path and looked at the two of them. "Emotionally. When I became a cop, I made this choice. Relationships with police officers can be destructive for civilians, and I don't want to take a chance on hurting anyone, especially someone I care about. Yes, I know. You two are making it work, and I couldn't be happier for you, but it's not for me. And I won't do anything to risk harming Jazz."

Except sitting on her lap and kissing her, then walking away and saying she couldn't handle a relationship with her. Cappy put her hands over her eyes, then dropped them to her sides. The kiss had felt good, but it hadn't been a good idea. She owed Jazz an apology for that. "I was selfish," she said.

Clare put her arm around Cappy's shoulders and gave her a squeeze, leading her down the path, with Libby taking her arm again on her other side. "Come on, partner," Clare said. "We'll help you haul that emotional baggage of yours down to the station. And maybe someday we can take it to the shooting range and blast the hell out of it."

Cappy gave a weak laugh. "I think I'd like that. Do they have any grenade launchers we can use?"

"Oh," said Libby with a big smile, "I am definitely coming along on that field trip."

Then they thankfully—and thoughtfully—changed the subject to one of Libby's classes, and Cappy let them carry the conversation while she wrestled with her own thoughts. Somehow, it was easier to do when she had the two of them by her side.

CHAPTER TWENTY

Jazz got a call from the circ desk the next morning and came downstairs to find Justine waiting for her in an alcove off the main reading room. She hesitated before joining her, watching her for a moment as she sat there fidgeting with the strap of her backpack. She was wearing a heavy knit sweater with *UW* in large letters across the front, and sweats with *HUSKIES* stenciled from ankle to hip on her left leg.

These kids and their uniforms. College almost demanded that they form a reductionist identity, tightening their focus onto a major, a career, or a high-profile activity like football or cheerleading. They came to college more multidimensional—in fact, needing to prove that in order to be accepted into the university—but then they gradually whittled themselves down to a narrower sense of self.

Jazz glanced down at her own outfit. Black pants, a wine-colored silk shirt. She sighed. These adults and their uniforms...

She walked over to the alcove and sat at the table. "Hello, Justine," she said. "Mr. Kincaid said you wanted to talk to me?"

"Hi, Ms. Harald. Yes, I...well, the officer said I should call if I thought of anything else about Brian, but I'm not sure if this counts. I hope it's all right that I came to you instead of calling her. I didn't want to waste her time if this wasn't important."

Her phrasing might have sounded as if she didn't care about wasting Jazz's time, but she doubted that was what Justine really meant. She was inclined to believe that she and the library were more approachable options for an uncertain young woman than an imposing police officer and the decidedly less warm station.

Jazz personally found imposing police officers in uniform to be very appealing, especially when they had soft hair and mesmerizing blue eyes…She cleared her throat and returned her focus to the matter at hand, and away from the woman who had been intimately at hand last night.

"This is fine," she said, impressed that her voice was steady and normal. "I can pass along the information to Officer Flannery if it's necessary, or we can go to the station together if you'd like."

Justine shrugged, settling her backpack on the ground next to her. "It's probably nothing."

Jazz crossed her legs and rested her forearm on the table. "Maybe, maybe not. What's on your mind?"

"It's Greg," Justine said with the same slightly cringing expression she had used during her interview when she had talked about him. It was clear she wasn't his biggest fan, and Jazz guessed that he had been an all-too-frequent presence in her life when she had been dating Brian. His world was football, and Greg had been a big part of that since high school. "He caught up to me on my way home from practice last night," Justine continued. "He seemed really on edge, and at first I was afraid he was going to ask me out again, but then he started talking about Brian. He said that the day before he died, Brian told him he was going to give me something, and Greg wanted to know if I had it."

"Give you something?" Jazz asked. "Do you know what he meant?"

Justine shrugged. "I don't know. I tried to ask Greg, but he wouldn't say."

"Did Brian ever mention something about this to you? That he had something for you?"

"No. But Greg really seemed upset about it. Or, well, I suppose he could have been upset about the game, and I only thought it was because of this."

Jazz frowned. "The game? The one against Penn?"

"Yes," Justine said, lowering her voice. "I'm not the only cheerleader who was dating someone on the team, you know, so we usually hear about the players even before some of them know what's going on. Anyway, one of the guys heard Coach Walker telling Greg he was off the starting roster for the next game. I guess Greg was really mad and was yelling at him for not letting him start. Football drama," she said with a dismissive shake of her head.

Yes, drama, but for Greg this could have been as significant as Brian's accident in terms of his career. Jazz wasn't as well-versed in the intricacies of the pro football world as Cappy—meaning she barely knew much at all—but she knew enough to realize that losing the starting position this late in his senior year could mean the loss of his dream of becoming a pro. "I suppose he had a lot riding on his performance," she said. "Now he won't have a chance to prove himself. It's understandable that he would be upset about that."

"He could have had a hundred chances, and he still never would have been the star Brian was."

"I never saw Brian play, unfortunately, but I heard he was something special." She could recall word for word what Cappy had said about the football gods laying out a path for him. Jazz wasn't even going to try to repeat that sentiment because there was no way it would sound as natural coming from her as it had from Cappy.

"He was amazing," Justine said, with a smile both fond and sad at the same time. "Really, really special." She picked up her backpack again. "That's all that happened. I know it isn't much, but it was kind of weird, so I wanted to tell someone."

"I'm glad you did. Thank you for coming to me about this, Justine. I'll let you know if Officer Flannery has any more questions, okay?"

Justine nodded and left the library. Jazz remained seated for a few minutes after Justine left. If the rumors about Greg's demotion were true, then Jazz thought it was likely that he'd seem angry no matter what the topic of conversation. This would be a big blow to his ego, after finally getting his chance to shine.

The topic of Brian giving something to Justine made the image of the envelope and its contents come to mind. Mia had talked about him showing her something in the library, which had led to Jazz's discovery of the evidence against Coach Walker. Maybe Greg misunderstood which of the girls Brian had meant?

She got up and headed up the stairs, pulling out her phone and calling Cappy as she walked, trying to ignore the memory of their kiss as she did so. Unsuccessfully.

"Good morning," she said when Cappy answered, trying to sound cheery and not at all hung up on that kiss. "How are you?"

"Spectacular. I happen to be enjoying a rather magnificent view right now."

Jazz's steps slowed and then stopped completely, as she turned around to see Cappy about ten steps below her. They both put their phones away as Cappy closed the distance between them. "I was just coming through the front door when my phone rang," she said. "I wanted to come by and talk to you before I start work."

"I'm glad," said Jazz, smiling as they continued up the stairs. "I needed to talk to you, too. Justine was just here."

"Interesting," Cappy said. "Let's talk about this in your office."

As soon as they were inside with the door shut, Jazz recounted Justine's story about Greg. Cappy gave a low whistle. "I'll bet Greg's devastated. I'm not surprised, though. If his performance wasn't improving during practice after the last couple of games, they really couldn't afford to let him start."

She tapped her fingers on the arm of her chair. "This mystery item Greg was looking for sure sounds like the packet of evidence against the coach. Your theory about the Justine and Mia mix-up makes sense. He might have said something vague, just using a pronoun, and Greg assumed that *she* meant Justine. I wonder why Brian was going to show it to Mia in the first place, if that's really what he had been referring to?"

Jazz shrugged. "She's very smart, and he was probably starting to trust her. Maybe he wanted to give it to her for safekeeping, instead of leaving it in the library. Or he might have wanted advice on what to do with it."

"He trusted you, too," said Cappy. "I'm surprised he didn't turn to you for help."

"No," Jazz said, dismissing that thought without any blow to her ego. "No matter how nice I might have seemed, I'm an adult and university staff. If he had shown me that packet, I wouldn't have had any choice. I would have confiscated it and turned it in. Mia wouldn't have been under the same obligation."

"True. He didn't seem ready for it to be public. If we assume Greg knew what was in there, then this was his chance to get revenge on Pryce, I suppose."

They fell silent, working through the questions this new evidence had raised. Or at least she figured that was what Cappy was thinking about. Jazz's traitorous mind was back on the kiss. Even now she could feel the weight of Cappy on her thighs, the taste of her tongue in—

"I owe you an apology," Cappy said, startling Jazz out of her memory.

"For what?"

"Last night. That kiss."

Oh. Apparently Cappy's mind hadn't been on the case, either.

"No need to apologize," said Jazz. "It was fine. I mean, there are some finer points of technique that could be improved, but on the whole it was quite…adequate." She laughed at Cappy's shocked expression. "I'm kidding. It was a wonderful kiss. I enjoyed it."

"So did I," said Cappy. "And I'm more than willing to put in the hours needed to improve my technique." She sighed and pressed the heels of her hands against her eyes. "That's what I'm sorry about. I keep saying things like that and kissing you, but I can't be in a relationship. I'm sending mixed signals."

"This case has been overwhelming and emotionally charged," Jazz said, wanting to put her at ease. She had no doubt in her mind about Cappy's attraction to her. She had felt hints of it before, but the mutual connection they had felt during last night's kiss was undeniable. Cappy's struggle seemed to be personal, and not necessarily about Jazz herself, and she wanted to allow her space if that's what she needed. "It's only natural that we've maybe, well, blurred some lines, like you said the other day. I don't think it's an unnatural reaction to us working together, and I'm not reading too much into it and expecting you to get down on one knee by the study carrels and propose. If we decide we want to explore what this relationship could be after we're untangled from the case, I'd like to give that a try. If you're not interested, that's okay, too."

Cappy shifted in her chair. "It's not that I'm not interested. I just don't think it's fair to expect anyone to be in a relationship with a cop."

"Oh, are you supposed to be celibate? You might want to let Kent and Clare know. They seemed to have missed that briefing."

"I didn't mean...of course, some are...just not me."

She seemed uncomfortable with the conversation, which oddly enough made Jazz feel more at ease. Not because she wanted Cappy to be miserable, but because she realized that this topic meant something significant to her. If Cappy simply wasn't interested in her, she would have had an easier time rejecting Jazz. As it was, she seemed to be struggling between wanting her and thinking she shouldn't.

"So, most cops can have relationships, but you can't. Is this a matter of preference, or a character flaw? Genetics?"

"I told you what happened to my mom," Cappy said, wincing a little, possibly at the memory of sharing her childhood story. "Starting the day she left, my dad told me over and over that if I wanted to follow in his footsteps and become a cop, I shouldn't put anyone through the pain of being married to that job. What happened with her, what he had to do to protect me—it changed him. It literally destroyed her. He's still alive, but it destroyed him in a lot of ways, too."

Jazz nodded, carefully searching for the right words. The pain on Cappy's face made her want to help her through this, whether Cappy ended up in a relationship with her or someone else. She deserved to be loved, simple as that. Her logic about why Clare could have a Libby or Kent a Tig but Cappy couldn't have anyone was clearly flawed, but Jazz knew firsthand how strong those messages could be when they were delivered routinely by a parent who was living with a type of pain no child in their formative years could fully understand. She could see the logical flaws in her mom's message about independence at all costs, but Jazz had battled with her difficulty in leaning on others her whole life. Her friends had helped her learn how to open herself a little to other people. She had a feeling Cappy might be able to batter down the rest of her walls, if given a chance.

"And you're sure your mother's anger issues and suicide were due to your father's job, and not exacerbated by other factors? There wasn't a chance your mother was living with untreated depression or a predisposition to alcoholism, for example?"

Cappy stared at her for a moment. "Yes, maybe. Those both seem likely. But I've tried to have relationships, even when I knew I shouldn't, and they always failed."

"Because of your job? How many relationships are we talking about?"

"Dozens," Cappy said. "And stop laughing. That was supposed to send you into a jealous rage."

"Oh, sorry." Jazz couldn't quite hide her smile. "I thought you were telling a joke to lighten the mood. So, dozens of women have stopped dating you as a direct result of your job."

"Yes. Okay, maybe not dozens. A few, or a couple, somewhere in there. A lot. And maybe not directly because of the job, but indirectly."

Jazz shrugged. "Have you ever considered that you might just be bad at relationships?"

Cappy opened and closed her mouth a couple of times, apparently startled by Jazz's question. "Is this meant to cheer me up?" she finally asked. "Because it's failing miserably."

"Really? I think it's good news. If you're a failure because of your job, you either quit or live alone for the rest of your life. If it's because you're bad at relationships, then you can always get better."

Cappy frowned at her in silence for a moment. "Actually, that's strangely comforting, I think."

"Of course it is. And why did you become a cop in the first place if it had so much misery attached to it?"

"Gramps was a cop, too. I wanted to be like him."

Jazz stared at her, waiting for her to make the connection, but Cappy seemed somehow oblivious to it. "By Gramps, do you mean the man in the longtime happy marriage to your gran?"

Cappy's brow furrowed. "Might be the same one. Might not. You're kind of a know-it-all, aren't you."

Jazz laughed and pointed at the diplomas on the wall next to her. "I am. That was the topic of my thesis. The burden of knowing it all when those around you don't have a clue."

Cappy laughed, her face releasing some of its tension. She stood up. "You have given me plenty to digest, Library Director Harald. I'm not going to kiss you right now because I want to think about all this before I do. But the next time..."

There was a hint of hope in her statement, that maybe she would be able to break away from her old ways of thinking, and that maybe there could be a future for them. And there was an unspoken promise, too, that she would never lead Jazz on if she wasn't going to be willing to follow through.

Jazz sighed as Cappy left her office. That had been the sexiest non-kiss she had ever had.

CHAPTER TWENTY-ONE

Cappy raced into the turnout room and flung herself into the chair next to Clare, bumping the table in front of them and making Clare startle.

"Whew, made it," she whispered.

Clare sighed audibly. "You have ten minutes to spare," she said in a normal voice.

Cappy looked around the room at the officers who were chatting and getting cups of coffee. "Huh. Force of habit, I guess."

Clare looked at her with a shrewd expression. "You look cheerful. What's wrong?"

"Nothing's wrong, and I'm definitely not cheerful," said Cappy, fighting the wide grin she could feel on her face. She gave up and shrugged. "I talked to Jazz this morning."

"Looks like it was the really good kind of talk that I do not want to hear about."

"A words kind of talk, not a smoochy one. She suggested that I might have failed relationships because I'm bad at them, and not because I'm a cop."

"Oh, well in that case..." Clare frowned. "You have to help me here. I'm not sure whether I'm supposed to congratulate you or offer to beat her up."

Cappy laughed. It was good to have Clare beside her again—it had been too many weeks since they had worked together. "Like she said, if it's because I'm bad, I can get better. If it's because I'm a cop, there's no hope."

Clare shook her head. "What an extremely Jazz thing to say to someone."

"I know, right? And actually, I think there's a chance I'm not bad at them, but I've just been with the wrong people. Maybe I could be very good at the right relationship."

"That's a very un-Cappy thing to say. And quite possibly the smartest comment I've ever heard you make. She's rubbing off on you."

"I'd like her to," Cappy said suggestively, laughing at Clare's groan.

"Don't you dare make me throw up in turnout," Clare whispered as Kent made her way to the front of the room. "I'd never live it down."

Cappy laughed, then settled in to listen to the usual morning spiel from her sergeant. She was still coming to terms not just with her conversation with Jazz, but the way it made her feel. Any discussion about romance in her past had been fraught with emotions and a somber pessimism. Jazz was one of the most serious and poised people she knew, but somehow her comments had made Cappy feel lighter, more hopeful. More like she was when with her friends and fellow officers, but with the added attraction that was more magnetic than anything Cappy had felt before.

She brought her mind back to the present as Kent wrapped up the meeting, trusting that Clare had paid attention to whatever information they might need on patrol today. She followed her out of the room, jostling with the other officers at the door, but then paused when Clare turned down the hallway instead of heading to the lobby.

"Where are you going?" she asked.

Clare turned to face her. "Did you hear anything that was said in that meeting?"

Cappy shrugged. "Nope."

"Kent wants to see us in her office. We didn't get a patrol assignment, so I'm assuming it's about the Keyes case."

They paused until Kent arrived and went into her office, gesturing for them to follow. They both rushed for the single chair and had a minor scuffle before Cappy claimed it. Kent gave them her usual look of mixed exasperation and a determination not to let them see her laugh.

"So, I talked to JC this morning about what you found under Brian's desk," she said.

"Who's JC?" asked Clare.

"Detective Ellingsen from SPD," Cappy said. "She and Sergeant Kent went to the academy together, and apparently she has some juicy stories about her."

"Oh," said Clare. "I met her when I worked there. We'll have to take her out for drinks sometime."

"That sounds like a great plan," said Kent, "as long as your goal is to get fired. Now, listen. I told her what you found, and she's coming over to get the envelope and its contents. Unfortunately, she has a significant backlog of work and won't be able to take any further steps with it until the day after tomorrow. You have two days, understand?"

Cappy nodded, sitting up in her chair, all humor and playfulness banished for the time being. Two days to try to uncover the truth about what happened to Brian—whether it was a suicide or a homicide—and then the case would no longer be theirs. It would belong to SPD, and likely the NCAA. It wasn't much time, but she understood that Ellingsen and Kent were going out on a limb and giving them a chance.

"Go," said Kent. "Make the most of this."

They nodded and left her office, stopping by the locker room to get uniform jackets and raincoats.

"What's the first stop?" asked Clare, giving Cappy the lead in this investigation since it had been hers from the start.

"Greg," she said without hesitation. She filled Clare in on Jazz's conversation with Justine this morning. "I want to ask him about that and find out how much he knows about Brian's evidence against Pryce, without letting him know that we've found it. It might be a tricky interview if we want to keep from tipping our hand. And after that, I want to talk to Jazz."

She paused while she organized her thoughts in her mind, and Clare patiently waited, not jumping in with a sly *I'll bet you do*. Cappy recognized how comforting it was to have a partner who matched her mood and appreciated the seriousness of what they were doing. It had been good when she and Jazz were working together, just the two of them, but now they needed Clare on their team. Cappy sighed, accepting the inevitable.

"If Libby happens to be there, too, I wouldn't kick her out," she said. She hesitated, then added, "If I did, she'd probably just listen at the door."

Clare laughed. "She likely has surveillance equipment set up in everyone's office. I found a book on that topic on her desk the other day. But I agree. She has good instincts, and she's up-to-date on what we've found, after last night. We don't have enough time to be picky about getting help."

Cappy pushed open the door and they walked out into the gray, drizzly day. They made a swooshing sound as they walked through the fallen leaves on the sidewalk. "We might want to talk to Justine and Mia again, but right now I don't have any specific questions to ask. We'll need to see if Pryce had an alibi for the night of Brian's death, but I don't want to spook him."

Clare pulled out her phone. "I'll call Miles. He should be able to access the team's calendar and find out if Pryce had any official business that night. If he either had no alibi or something personal, we'll have to find a way to ask him."

Cappy nodded, her mind turning through all the details of the case. She was looking forward to being with Jazz and Libby, laying out all the facts and looking for connections and missing information. Right now, everything was a confusing jumble in her mind. Last night had been the first time when she had seriously considered that this might be a homicide, and she wanted to move carefully from now on.

They walked toward Greg's building. He lived in one of the nicer student-housing apartment options, reserved for students with either the seniority or clout to be upgraded from the dorms. His building was nowhere near as new or fancy as Brian's, though.

"Hey, look," Clare said. "Isn't that him?" She increased her pace, moving to intercept Greg as he came down the brick staircase in front of the apartment building, but Cappy grabbed her arm, hauling her forcefully into a clump of rhododendron bushes along their path.

"Ow," Clare said, swatting aside a branch that had slapped her in the face. "What are you doing?"

She might not know why Cappy had done this, but she kept her voice low anyway. As Greg walked past their shrubbery, he was looking from side to side, but he didn't seem to have noticed their plunge into the greenery.

"Do you know what day it is?" Cappy asked as soon as he was out of earshot.

"Your birthday? Here. This is all I could find without more notice." She handed Cappy a leaf she had pulled out of her hair. Cappy dropped it.

"This was the day of the month that Brian made his gambling payments," she said. "According to his bank statements, it was a routine occurrence. I had forgotten, but something about the furtive way Greg was walking reminded me of Brian. Let's follow him."

They climbed out of the bushes, surprising a young woman who was walking past. "Just keeping the paths safe for our students," Clare said. "These bushes are all clear. Carry on."

She gave them a strange look, then hurried on her way while Cappy started walking in the direction Greg had gone. Clare caught up with her.

"What kind of hunch is this, Cap?" she asked. "Just a curious *Hmm, he kind of walks like Brian* one, or a *Please call Miles again and have him watching the drop spot* one?

Cappy considered that for a moment. She had no evidence to support the latter, but she was following her instincts right now. She didn't have enough time for second-guessing herself. "Call Miles," she said, ducking behind the corner of a building in what she hoped was a nonchalant, official police business kind of way. She was glad

Clare already knew about the gambling drops and the surveillance they had done because it would have been a pain to explain it all to her now. She hadn't even thought to keep a watch on this area since she had assumed the situation was concluded with Brian's death.

"Look, there he goes," she said as Greg glanced over both shoulders before walking into the tree-covered dead zone.

"We need to tell Kent about this spot," said Clare. "She'll be out here in the trees with a chainsaw."

They pulled back again as Greg walked out of the trees and down the path toward the humanities buildings. Then they split up, and Cappy waited until there was another building between him and the trees before she hurried to catch up to him.

"Greg, hi," she said with a smile, planting herself in front of him and making him stop. "Officer Flannery. We met at the station just the other day. This is Officer Sawyer," she added, gesturing toward Clare who was now standing behind him.

"Nice to meet you," she said, waving hello with an envelope in her gloved hand. He stared at her hand and she followed his gaze. "Oh, this? Just picking up some litter on campus." She opened it and peered at the contents. "Yep, lots of litter. It's strange what people will throw away around here."

"You can't..." he said, his face turning an interesting shade of ashy gray. "I need to..."

"Oh, a guessing game. Let me try," Cappy said. "You need to... hmm, pay Miko five thousand dollars for your gambling debts? Was I close?"

"Am I under arrest?" he asked in a quivering voice. He looked like he was going to be sick. "I was just...I must have dropped it."

"Oh, is this yours?" Clare asked. "Come on, then. We'll go to the station and have you fill out a missing items form. As long as you can identify the contents, you can claim it."

"You're not under arrest," Cappy added. "We just have a few questions for you, and then you can be on your way. With your, um, litter, if it really belongs to you."

They were positioned to stop him if he tried to run, but he seemed disinclined to do anything beyond follow them meekly to the station. Besides, she had seen his skills as he tried to evade tackles on the football field. They wouldn't even need to exert themselves to catch him. She kept those observations to herself, though. No need to rub salt in those wounds. At least not right now, as long as he was cooperating.

His anxiety increased as they walked, however, and by the time they had him in the interview room, he looked like a junkie looking for his next high. His eyes seemed clear, though, and his pupils normal. Miles had given them a knowing nod when they walked by, and Cappy could picture Miko's guy searching in vain for his cash. Greg's nervousness was easily attributable to his fear of what would happen since he had missed this drop. Cappy wasn't planning to drag out the interview, though, so he should be able to repair the damage they had done. She didn't want to get the kid hurt.

"Brian was paying your gambling debt, wasn't he," she said as soon as they were alone in the room. Clare had veered off to the desk to turn in the money and prepare to give it back to Greg.

The fear of an irate bookie was good incentive for him to answer her questions. He nodded. "He was helping me out."

"That's quite a friendship the two of you had if he was willing to pay that much money every month. He really was a good guy, wasn't he."

Greg snorted. "He owed me," he said. "After what I did for him in high school? He wouldn't have been where he was if I hadn't helped him get clean."

Cappy wasn't sure if he was being honest, or if it was just too painful for him to hear Brian being praised. "So those rumors you talked about, with Brian doing drugs, those were true?" she asked.

"They were. Like I told you, he'd do anything to get ahead. The drugs were messing with him, though, and I was there for him. So he was paying me back."

"Until he couldn't afford to anymore," Cappy said, "after his accident."

Greg shook his head. "He was planning to keep helping, but then…He can't pay if he's dead."

Cappy wasn't sure about the timeline. Had Brian told Greg he was on his own with money after the accident, or would he have been down there today on his crutches if he was still alive?

"One more question," she said. "You were looking for something Brian might have given one of his friends. What was it?"

He hesitated for about thirty seconds, long enough for her to guess that anything he said next would be a lie he had just fabricated. "His team ring. I asked Justine Hillman if Brian had given it to her. I kind of wanted to keep it, as a reminder of him, you know?"

She nodded as Clare came back in the room and sat at the table, sliding a form in front of him. She glanced at Cappy, who nodded for her to go ahead.

"What was in the envelope, Greg?" she asked.

He looked sullen, but he answered right away. "Five thousand dollars, all hundreds. I got it out of my bank account this morning if you need to check."

"No need. Just write a description of the envelope and its contents here, and we'll need your name, address, and signature over here."

As soon as he was finished, Clare checked the paper and handed him the envelope. He grabbed it and hurried out of the room without another word.

"Well, that was an interesting start to the shift," Clare said. "I'm going to make that dead zone a regular stop on patrol from now on. I might be able to retire early if I pick up enough trash in there."

Cappy smiled, but her mind was adding this new information to what they already knew in the case. They were silent for a while, and then Miles poked his head in the door.

"Your coach, Pryce Walker? He was in Southern Oregon the day Brian died. Scouting trip, so there will be tons of witnesses. He left that morning and flew back the next day. Want me to dig deeper, make sure?"

"Not right now," Cappy said with a sigh. "What about the head coach, Moran?"

"His personal calendar, and don't ask me how I know this, says he was at a Kiwanis Club meeting in Lynnwood. I have someone checking on that, but it looks legit."

"Thanks, Miles," Cappy said and pulled out her phone as he left. "I'll call Jazz," she said, "see if she can come down here, and we can go over everything we've learned so far. Do you want to call Libby, or do you just beam a Bat-Signal into the sky?"

"I'll call her," Clare said. "But I doubt it's necessary. She probably hasn't left Jazz's side all day, in case she misses something."

CHAPTER TWENTY-TWO

Jazz was trying to get some work done—as much as she could, with Libby sitting in the chair across from her hissing, "Is it Cappy? Or Clare?" every time her phone rang. She missed the good old days when everyone thought she was misguided for calling Brian's death a murder, and she'd actually been able to continue to run her library in between interviews. Libby was like an expectant father, anxiously awaiting news about her child's birth.

"Is it Cappy?" she asked again. Jazz shook her head, then finished the call with one of her vendors.

"I'm sure it will be hours yet," she said after she had hung up the phone. "Why don't you go back to your office and try to get some rest. Grade some papers. I'll call you as soon as I hear anything."

"No, I'd rather wait here," Libby said.

"Oh, goody," Jazz said quietly, although she secretly knew she'd be more edgy if she was here alone. The tone of the investigation had changed last night. She and Cappy had carried on a relatively normal conversation today—an unexpectedly intimate one, but at least not related to the case—but at that time there hadn't been anything new to discuss about Brian. Who knew what was going on at the station now that his notes about the offensive coordinator were in play? She either was picking up on Libby's instincts or developing some of her own, but she had a feeling they'd be seeing Cappy and Clare soon.

Libby sighed and scrunched her nose, looking up from her book and vaguely around the office. Jazz shook her head. Where was Tig when you needed her?

"Second shelf down in the fridge," Jazz said, pointing in that direction. Libby bounced off her chair and headed toward the break room, returning in seconds with a sandwich in her hands. "Want half?"

Jazz reached out and accepted the offering of half her own lunch. Roast beef with horseradish and avocado. One of her favorites, but she barely tasted it as she ate. "Maybe we should go for a walk after this," she said. "We have cell phones. It's not like we're going to miss an official police summons if we walk out of the office."

She had barely finished the sentence when her phone rang and Cappy's name appeared on the screen. "Hey," she said. "Wait…yes, Libby, it's Cappy…I'm back. Sorry about that. The vulture has been circling today."

Cappy's laughter came through the phone and eased Jazz's anxious feeling. "Can you come down to the station for an hour or so? We're going to review the case, and I'd like you here. And Libby, too. Oh, want to have some fun? Tell Libby that Clare says she can't come."

Jazz could hear Clare's panicked protest in the background. "You have a dangerous idea of fun, Cappy," she said. "I'd sooner go snatch a grizzly cub from its mother."

"Well, at least I had fun making the suggestion. You should see Clare's expression—it's hilarious. See you soon."

"See you," Jazz said, ending the call.

"We're going to the station?" Libby asked, shoving the rest of the sandwich in her mouth.

"Yes, and you could have eaten that on the way." She grabbed her bag, hastily checking to make sure she had her book and plenty of paper and pens for taking notes. Libby's anticipation was contagious, and Jazz let it fill her, pushing away the other emotions she had been feeling since Brian died. She had experienced too many highs and lows, when she normally was less extreme in her feelings. She had been moving swiftly through grief, anger that no one was taking her opinions about Brian seriously, and self-doubt about how well she had really known him. Adding her growing feelings for Cappy, and this had been one of the most volatile weeks of her life. She was determined to just let the day unfold without hope or despair, just acceptance. Would she be able to make that happen? Probably not, especially with Cappy involved, but it was a good goal to have.

They walked—well, she walked, while Libby kind of skipped— to the station, and Jazz headed without thinking to the room where she and Cappy had held all their interviews so far. Some couples had a special song or restaurant. She and Cappy had a special meeting room. How romantic.

Clare and Cappy were sitting at the metal table, and they had chairs for both Jazz and Libby. Jazz sat next to Cappy, returning her smile and feeling a sense that everything was going to be all right now. She was where she belonged. She sighed inwardly. So much for staying within reasonable emotional bounds.

Cappy gave them what Jazz could tell was a quick version of their encounter with Greg. "I'm really not sure where to go next," she said. "I thought we could go through each person we've interviewed and decide if there are follow-up questions we need to ask." She looked at Jazz and gave her knee a squeeze under the table. "We still don't have any evidence that this was a homicide, so we need to be open to both alternatives. Even though some of these people are guilty in their own ways, that doesn't mean they committed murder."

Jazz nodded. "I know. I'll be okay."

"Good. So, let's start with Brian. What do we know about him? Star football player, lost his chance to play in the NFL and have a lifetime of fame and money. He was borrowing money from his coaches to pay off Greg's debt."

"Maybe he told Greg he wasn't going to pay anymore, since he needed money for his new academic plans," Libby offered. "Or was he going to keep paying, but it stopped because he died?"

Cappy nodded. "It's a good question, but we can't know for sure. Greg was being evasive when he talked about this, and I doubt he's going to give us a straight answer. If Brian said he'd stop, then

Greg might have had a motive to kill him. If Brian was going to keep paying, he had incentive to want him alive."

"Back to Brian," Clare said, "he was also collecting evidence about his coach, for unknown reasons. Blackmail, which gives us another motive for murder, or because he was going to eventually turn him in. If he was, then what was he waiting for?"

"The end of the season," Jazz said. She cringed inside, about to play devil's advocate, but she couldn't ignore the possibility that Brian had been waiting due to selfish reasons. "They had a winning team, and he was set for a great future. If Pryce's skills as a coach were contributing to Brian's success, he might not have wanted to rock that particular boat until he was safely on shore."

"See?" Libby said to Cappy. "Beauty and brains. She's quite a catch."

"That's a given," Cappy said with a smile playing at the corners of her lips. Jazz managed to look away from those lips with what felt like a superhuman effort, scowling instead at Libby for turning a debriefing into a matchmaking session. Libby, of course, was unperturbed by her glare.

"Let's focus on what we don't know." Cappy cleared her throat and continued, "So, Brian has a new career goal, he gets a tutor and starts dating her, and then he tells her he wants to show her something in the library. Most likely, it was this evidence and not an engagement ring. Why? Jazz suggested he might be giving her the evidence for safekeeping, or he just wanted to share it with someone, figure out what to do."

"Or he knew he was in danger and wanted someone else to know where he had hidden this. It could have stayed under there for years," Libby said. Jazz was uncomfortable with the idea that Brian might have known something was going to happen to him. Of course, if he had been planning this, then he obviously had known. She hated thinking of how alone he must have felt, either way.

Cappy nodded at Libby. "Meanwhile, Brian breaks up with his girlfriend because he blames her for the accident, but then he might or might not have been planning to get back together with her."

"Leaving someone with a case of unrequited love," Libby said with a visible shudder, obviously reliving her own past experience with Angela. Clare shifted closer and draped her arm over Libby's shoulders.

Cappy reached across the table and gave Libby's hand a pat, where it was resting on one of the file folders. "This leads us to Greg. He either hit on Justine and was rejected, or vice versa. I'm inclined to believe her side, but that might just be my bias. Either way, there's another broken heart, or at least a case of wounded pride. Brian also could have found out and confronted one of them."

"And at some point, Brian told Greg he was giving the evidence about Pryce to his girlfriend," Jazz added, still unsure why Brian would have admitted this to Greg. What was his reasoning behind all the subterfuge and tracking he had been doing with Pryce? "Maybe he was vague enough that although he meant Mia, Greg assumed he was talking about Justine. It doesn't sound like either of the girls knew about this packet, or they might have reached the same conclusion we did about it being the mystery item."

Clare nodded. "But Greg apparently knew and was trying to find it. Why? To continue blackmailing the coach—or to start, if Brian hadn't already been doing that? He needed to pay those gambling debts, and I'm betting it was going to be a strain on him." She paused and looked sheepish, as if replaying her words in her mind. "Although, given the circumstances, maybe I should learn from their example and not gamble."

They laughed, easing the tension in the room, and then Cappy got them back on track. "Greg again. He knew Brian in high school, where he apparently helped him get away from drugs, which made him the player he was in college."

"Allegedly," Jazz amended, and Cappy nodded.

"True. But we don't have another reason to explain why he took on such a huge financial burden. Maybe Brian did feel he owed Greg for his success, and he took on this gambling debt as repayment, until he stopped, either intentionally or because he was gone."

"With the coaches helping," Clare put in. "Loaning him money. If Pryce was giving him money because of blackmail, he'd be a prime suspect, but his alibi is solid."

Cappy sighed. "Which leads us back to having no evidence of foul play, aside from the issue with the clean glass, which is flimsy. And no one with a solid motive except the man who wasn't in the state at the time."

"We're forgetting about Coach Moran," Jazz said, looking over the notes laid out on the table, sorting and categorizing the information. "He had a strong reaction when I mentioned drugs, and now we find out that one of his coaches was possibly providing them to players. What if he found out that Brian was collecting this evidence?"

Cappy jotted that down. "He was at a Kiwanis Club meeting, but he could have gotten over there in time."

"And who broke into Brian's apartment?" Clare wondered. "You were thinking it was the bookie looking for money, but it could have been any one of the people who were looking for this evidence."

Cappy nodded. "And casting the net wider, one of the players who was getting illegal drugs might have been willing to kill to stop Brian from removing their source. Whoever took the videos of Pryce seemed determined not to show any player names, unintentionally or in order to protect them, so we don't know their names."

"That narrows it down," said Libby dryly. "Should we add all the drug dealers in Seattle, just to make it more interesting? This would have been a lucrative gig."

Cappy threw her pen on the table and pressed the heels of her hands to her eyes, before sliding her fingers back through her hair. "I can't see what we've missed," she said. "Or maybe we have all the information, and the reason it doesn't lead to a murder suspect is because there wasn't one. Brian's troubles still support this being a suicide, even though the gambling debt wasn't his. The guilt about not being able to keep paying might have been significant, if he had been willing to pay so much money in the first place."

Jazz sighed. Broken body, broken heart, broken relationships with his team. Brian had clearly been in pain, both physical and emotional.

"We have tomorrow," Clare said, pushing away from the table and reaching for Libby's hand. "Maybe we should let this simmer for now, return to it fresh in the morning."

They all nodded, and Jazz breathed a sigh of relief. They had circled back to where they had originally started with this case, and she had been worried that they would spiral through the details until they began to seem nonsensical. Too much of Brian's story was hearsay, filtered through the biases of the people who had known him.

"Wait," she said, causing everyone to drop back into their chairs. "I know it's inappropriate right now to contact his family and ask painful questions about his past, but Cappy, didn't you say that his coaches were like surrogate parents? Wouldn't the Canterwood coach know more about Brian's and Greg's pasts than almost anyone else?"

"You're brilliant," Cappy said, pulling Jazz into a sideways hug and kissing her on the cheek. She pulled out her phone and scrolled for a moment. "Thought so," she said. "Guess who has a game in Tacoma tonight?" No one answered, so she waggled her phone at them. "Canterwood Heights. You guys go get some rest. I'm going to drive down there and talk to him."

Jazz frowned. She had thought her idea might be a good one, but it was quickly getting out of hand. "You're going to drive to Tacoma alone?"

"I don't want to sound like I'm boasting," Cappy said, looking smug, "but I have even driven as far as Portland. All by myself."

Jazz waved off her sarcasm. "Yes, but this is an investigation. It could be dangerous, and I can't go with you."

"Of all the people involved in this case, I'm going to make the assumption that Brian's high school coach is the least likely suspect of the bunch. I just want to ask him a few questions. Try to get more of a fleshed-out story than we're getting from Greg, and see if I can understand Brian's past a little more."

Clare glanced at Libby, then back to Jazz. "Don't worry, I'll go with her. If I don't, she'll insult some parent's son or tell the coach what he's doing wrong and end up in Tacoma's jail."

Jazz sighed with relief. She doubted the coach would try to hurt Cappy for case-related reasons, though she might aggravate him to the point of murder with her commentary on his coaching skills. Still, she would feel much better if Cappy had Clare with her.

"Thank you, Clare," she said.

"No worries," she said, standing up and pulling Libby to her feet. "I'm going to go change."

They left the room, and Jazz turned to Cappy. "Just be careful, okay? I'm sorry I can't go with you."

"No, you're not," said Cappy with a laugh.

"Well, not really," Jazz admitted. Which would normally have been true. A high school football game? Really? She was assuming Cappy would want to stay and watch, too, not just talk to the coach and get out of there, like she would have done. Pop some Wagner on the stereo and drive back home. She had no doubt, though, that Cappy would have made the evening fun. "If I didn't have to work, I'd be there with you."

"I know. You be careful, too," said Cappy. "How late will you be at the library?"

Jazz shrugged. "I have a group of law students who are preparing for a mock trial, and I let them stay after hours sometimes. Should be a wild night."

"I'll stop by after we're done and let you know how it went. Maybe we'll be able to come up with some useful interviews to do after this. We have to make tomorrow count."

They stood up, and Cappy pulled Jazz into a tight embrace. Jazz leaned into her, feeling the rough scratchiness of her uniform and the firm pressure of her arms. Cappy moved her head back slightly to look her in the eye. "Thank you for this morning. I'm still afraid of hurting someone if they get involved with me, but I might be willing to try. But only if I'm trying with you."

Jazz smiled. "I'll be strong and help you through it," she said. "Unless I'm not feeling strong, and then you will be. We'll take care of each other."

"Sounds like a safe place to be," Cappy said, leaning forward and kissing her. It wasn't as all-out passionate as the one in Jazz's office last night, but it felt open to Jazz. Honest, as if Cappy wasn't holding anything back from her. That's what Jazz wanted. She could handle fear and baggage, uncertainty and exploration. As long as they were together.

A burst of loud laughter in the hall outside their room made them both jump, and Cappy smiled as she raised her hand and sifted it through Jazz's hair. Jazz sighed and closed her eyes, lingering in her touch until she finally pulled away. She gave Cappy another kiss.

"I'll see you tonight," she said. "Have fun at your game."

"Have fun chaperoning a bunch of law students," she said, then winced. "Sounds like I'm winning tonight."

"Debatable," Jazz said with a laugh as they walked out the door. Cappy headed to the locker room to change while Jazz and Libby walked outside into the misty afternoon.

"Maybe we'll all come by later," Libby said. "Bring you some food since you can't join us for dinner."

"That sounds nice," said Jazz, giving her a kiss on the cheek and walking back toward the library.

CHAPTER TWENTY-THREE

So. Road trip to Tacoma for a high school football game. Yay!" Clare said as she buckled her seat belt.

"That was an unconvincing yay," Cappy said. "But I'll take it."

"What are we hoping to accomplish, anyway? We don't even know if this coach stayed in touch with Brian over the past few years, aside from probably following his games, so I doubt he'll know anything about Coach Walker or Brian's money issues. Is this just to learn more about his past?"

Cappy frowned, unable to explain even to herself why she wanted to talk to this man, but the moment Jazz had mentioned him, she had been anxious to go. "I guess I'm trying to understand Brian better, so I can figure out what really happened to him. When I first started on this case, his situation seemed simple in my mind. Talented jock loses career opportunity." She shrugged. "Jazz's conviction about him having these new career dreams seemed far-fetched, but now even that's not enough. His relationship with Greg seemed to be a key one in his life, for good or bad, and it all started at Canterwood Heights."

"Makes sense. He was a complicated guy. They all are, I suppose, all the students. We just rarely get to dig this deep into their lives, so it's easy to make assumptions and snap judgments when we meet them. Sometimes that's helpful, since we need to make quick decisions on calls, but it's good to be reminded on occasion that they're normal, complex individuals."

"I wish I had done more, sooner," Cappy admitted, wondering how the case would have unfolded if she had taken Jazz's allegations more seriously. She hadn't known her then, but now she knew she would trust Jazz's instincts without question. She felt confident that she had put her heart into this case from the start, for Brian's sake if nothing else, no matter what assumptions she had originally made about his death, but still..."Now we're up against a deadline, and I'm panicking because we still might not find the answers we need. And once other people get hold of the evidence against Pryce, the focus will shift to him and away from Brian. We might never find out what happened to him."

"And so we rush to Tacoma on the off chance his old coach will be able to explain him a little more." Clare reached over and patted her shoulder. "Not the worst idea you and Jazz could have, partner."

"If nothing else, I'll buy you a hot dog and some nachos."

Clare laughed. "You should have mentioned food earlier. Then Libby would have joined us." She paused. "She told me what Jazz did for your gran, with the information about apartments. I mean, you mentioned it before when you got the Kibbles, but I hadn't realized the effort she made."

"Yeah, it was fantastic," Cappy said, shifting out of her pensive, worried mood at the thought. "We're going to look at a couple of them on my next day off. I wouldn't have even known where to start if she hadn't done that."

"I've learned that if Jazz does research for you voluntarily, without expecting you to fill out a formal request in the library, it's her way of showing she cares. All Libby's friends were very welcoming to me from the start, but when Jazz gave me a folder full of practice questions for the sergeant's test and study tips for people with dyslexia, I felt like I'd been given my permanent membership card to the group."

Cappy grinned. "Trust me, I recognized the importance of those color-coded packets. I could have done without the reminder to Gran about how much she loved cats, though."

"Please. I know I'm going to lose that bet to Jazz, and you're not going to let them go."

"You'll win, don't worry." Cappy merged to the left and passed a slower car. Her gran would definitely be taking those little furballs out of her apartment when she moved. Admittedly, she had been trying to convince her gran that she had allergies every time her gran sneezed, and that she should probably leave them with Cappy and just visit now and again, but Gran wasn't falling for it.

"You and Jazz," Clare said, with a shake of her head. "It makes sense, and I should have seen it coming, but I guess I didn't know that Valkyries were allowed to date mere mortals."

"She is amazing, isn't she?" Cappy said, focusing on maneuvering through the heavy traffic as they hit Tacoma's city limits. "Brilliant, funny, kind. And she smells like ferns."

"Ferns," Clare repeated. "Is that a compliment?"

Cappy glanced at her, hoping her heated cheeks weren't visible in the dim evening light. Apparently she was incapable of driving and self-censoring at the same time. "Of course it is. You know, like when you're walking on one of the woodsy university paths after it's rained, and the ferns have drops of water on them, and everything smells clean and fresh and almost a little minty. Like that."

She ignored Clare's laughter as she took the ramp to Highway 16, and then the Sprague Street exit. She might never live that one down, she realized, and she vowed that on the drive back she would pay at least as much attention to the conversation as to the traffic. If there were too many cars, she'd just need to shut up and not speak until they were back in Seattle.

She found a parking spot just a few blocks from the school, and they walked into the carnival-like atmosphere of a high school football game, bringing a wave of nostalgia. The exuberant but slightly out of tune sound of the local marching band competed with the shouts of the cheerleaders and the general roar of hundreds of people talking at once. The air smelled like popcorn, and the millions of colors usually seen in the world had been reduced down to bright green, yellow, purple, and black. On clothes, on faces, and on some scrawny bare chests.

Cappy paid for their admission, then they wove their way through the excited crowds and down to the edge of the field. The teams were warming up, and Cappy spotted Coach Rennick on the sidelines, giving one of the players either a pep talk or a loud scolding. It was hard to tell the difference. He was a big guy, with some muscle turning to paunch, and he had a gray crew cut. He didn't look like he was in the mood for an interview.

Clare must have been thinking the same thing. She held Cappy's elbow, possibly to protect her from running onto the field and getting yelled at.

"Maybe we should have gone to his school sometime when he wasn't in the middle of coaching a game. He's not going to want to talk to us."

Cappy waved her off, her eyes on the field as she watched the team running through its pregame warm-up. "He'll want to get us out of his way as quickly as he can, which means he won't bother taking the time to make up a lie. We'll get better answers. Fewer of them," she admitted, "but more honest ones."

"And then security will descend upon us. This night is just getting better and better."

Cappy made shushing sounds at her and ducked under the metal bar separating the people in the stands from the players. She approached the coach who was waving his hands around and giving instructions to players and his assistants. Cappy ducked, nearly getting sideswiped by the clipboard he was holding.

He glanced at her, and she quickly held out her badge like a shield. "Officers Flannery and Sawyer from the University of Washington Police Department."

He looked at her badge, then handed it back, remaining silent.

Cappy gestured toward the field. "Your cornerback, Lindholm, number twenty-five. He sure is fast, isn't he? Any chance he's applying to UW? We could use a strong corner."

"Do they send their police on scouting trips?" he asked, seeming confused more than irate, at least for the moment. Clare jabbed her in the back with her finger, probably reminding her to get back on track.

"No, just got a little distracted. We're here about Brian Keyes. Standard investigation anytime there's a death on campus."

He frowned. Well, glowered might have been a better term for it, but Cappy wasn't going to be intimidated. "Damn shame about what happened, but this isn't the best time," he said. "I'd be glad to talk to you later, if you care to make an appointment with the school receptionist."

"I'll be quick. Just five questions."

"Two."

"Three."

"Deal. Go."

Cappy cut right to the chase. "Did Brian have a drug problem in high school?"

"No way."

Cappy heard a strangled sound from Clare, and she knew she had asked for that simple response. No more yes or no questions.

"Greg told us that Brian owed him a favor because he helped get him off drugs. What do you know about that?"

"It's a lie," he said, possibly softening somewhat, but it was hard to tell. Can granite soften? "It was the other way around. Greg didn't handle it well when Brian transferred to us. He'd been big dog, and suddenly he wasn't, but what was I gonna do? You put your best players in the game. Well, Greg did a little experimenting with some amphetamines, but it obviously didn't do any good."

He stopped talking, as if realizing he had given her too much for one question.

"So Brian helped Greg get clean?" Oof, another yes or no.

"More than that, Officer," he said, giving her question more of a response than it deserved. Probably not because she had fooled him, but because he wanted her to know about Brian. "I was going to kick Greg off the team when I found out, but Brian threatened to quit if I didn't give Greg a second chance, so I did." He sighed. "Not my most ethical moment, but a player like Brian comes along once in a coach's lifetime."

"Were they close friends?" She was over her limit, but she had to at least try for one more. He paused before answering with a wry look on his face, as if letting her know he was on to her but would play along.

"On and off. Brian was the new kid, and as confident as he was on the field, he was kind of shy off it. He wanted to be Greg's friend, and Greg played along when he needed something. Eventually, Brian seemed to realize it, but he had gotten too deep into the role of caretaker for Greg. I always wished they had gone to separate colleges. Would have been good for both of them."

He shooed at her with his clipboard. "That was four. Now, scram. Oh, and tell that coach of yours to watch out for Lindholm's application. He's scholarship material."

She and Clare ducked under the bar again and climbed the stairs until they found a couple of empty seats. The players started clearing the field to get ready for the start of the game.

"That was exciting," Clare said. "There were a couple of times when I thought he was going to pummel you."

Cappy made a derisive sound. "I wasn't scared. I knew I had my partner right there, ready to protect me."

Clare waved over a vendor with a tray full of popcorn bags and bought two. "Hate to burst that bubble, but I was planning my exit strategy." She pointed off to the side. "I was going to run that way and shimmy up that little wall. Straight shot to the parking area after that, where I'd call for a lift back to campus. But, hey, I bought you popcorn."

"What more could I ask from my partner," Cappy said wryly. "So, what did you think?"

Clare sobered, her jokes disappearing. "Messy, codependent relationship. I think we were right that guilt might have been a factor in this, and not just Brian's need to have a friend. I actually thought the coach was very perceptive, wishing they had gone to separate schools."

"I agree. I had a feeling Greg was lying, so I can't say I'm surprised by this." She paused, thinking of the lengths Brian had gone trying to protect his…friend…from drugs. "I wonder. All the sneaking about and collecting evidence against Pryce. Maybe Brian was doing this for Greg again since he knew he was susceptible? Threatening the coach into not giving him drugs, or he'd turn him in?"

"Or threatening Greg to stay clean or he'd cut off his source." Clare said with a nod. "That would explain why he hadn't done anything with the evidence. He might have been using it as a shield to protect Greg."

"Makes you appreciate your friends, doesn't it," Cappy said. "At least Greg didn't hold him back as a player, but he sure did in a lot of other ways."

Clare bumped her shoulder. "Brian sounds like he was a good kid, just bad at setting boundaries. And Greg, well, he might have been a different person if Brian hadn't come into the picture and brought out his jealousy and insecurity."

Cappy sighed and settled back to watch the game. Had she learned anything vital for the case? No. But her image of Brian was growing clearer and more dimensional. Jazz would be grateful for this information, too. This glimpse into the young man she had tried to help. She sent her a quick text that they had talked to the coach and she would see her after the game. Jazz sent back a picture of Libby, Tig, and Ari gathered around her desk with takeout containers of food.

She showed it to Clare who smiled. "Now I'm hungry," she said, wadding up her empty popcorn bag. "Let's go find some of those disgusting stadium nachos you promised me."

Cappy drove them home after dark, feeling good about the evening. She and Clare had laughed and cheered throughout the game, and the coach had given her some insight into Brian's past. She felt ready to attack the next day, which was the last one she'd likely spend on this case, no matter the outcome. It would become something bigger than Brian's death and the question of whether he had died by suicide or was murdered. She didn't have any answers yet, and might not have any more after tomorrow, but she was going to do her best to try to find some resolution for Jazz.

She had been a constant presence this evening, too, whether just in Cappy's thoughts or through her occasional text. Tomorrow might bring the ending of the case, but it would also mean the chance for a beginning of a real relationship with Jazz, unencumbered by this investigation.

They sat in companionable silence on the drive, relaxed and sleepy, until Cappy's phone rang. Clare reached around to get it out of Cappy's jacket in the back seat and answered it for her, probably expecting it to be Jazz like Cappy was.

"Hey, I…Oh, hello…No, this is her partner, Officer Sawyer. Can I help you?"

Cappy pulled off at an exit near Boeing and parked at the top of the ramp, where she often saw state patrol cars parked and running radar on the traffic below. She turned her full attention to Clare, and dug out a pen and paper for her to write notes. Then she sat through the frustrating experience of listening to a one-sided call.

"Yes, it's good that you called. What exactly did he say?… Okay, and what did you tell him when he asked that?…Right. No, I'm not sure what he was looking for, but you made a good choice to call. Are you safe? With some friends?…Your roommate, good… No, I don't think so, but it wouldn't hurt to stick close to other people tonight. Officer Flannery will contact you tomorrow."

Clare finally hung up and handed the paper and pen back to Cappy. "You take notes, I'll talk," she said. "That was Justine. She tried calling Jazz, but it's after hours, so the library is closed, and that's the only number she had for her. She had your card, though. Sounds like Pryce contacted her just a few minutes ago and basically asked the same question Greg had, if Brian had given her something. He also asked about the tutor, if Justine had a way to get in touch with her."

Clare sighed, stopping for breath. "That's about it. It struck her as odd since Greg had been asking the same thing, minus the tutor. I wonder how Pryce heard about her? Maybe from Brian?"

Cappy frowned, chewing on the end of her pen. "Or maybe he heard about her the same place I did, from Brian's planner. It was just her first name, but I didn't have to search hard before I found a biology tutor named Mia."

"Pryce was one of our suspects for breaking into his apartment. If he knew about the evidence against him, he might have been searching for it."

Cappy nodded. "And Mia stood out on that planner since there was little else in there. It was part of a new life, starting after his accident."

She scrolled through her phone and found Mia's number. She answered and gave Cappy the same information Justine had told Clare. "Did you tell him about Brian wanting to show you something in the library?" Cappy asked.

"I did, but I don't know why it would matter. That was going to be something personal, and I told the coach that. It wasn't anything to do with football."

Cappy ended the call and frowned as Clare got out of the car. "Where are you going?"

Clare came around to Cappy's side and opened the door. "I'm driving. You can call Jazz, but I'm going to warn you that she isn't great about answering her phone, especially if she's taking care of late-night patrons, and I don't want you driving panicked. We'll go directly to the library to give you peace of mind and to make sure Pryce isn't prowling around searching for his envelope."

Cappy jogged around the car and got in, buckling her seat belt as Clare set off toward campus. She called and was sent to voicemail, then called again. She'd do it all damned night until either she was within touching distance of Jazz or she answered her phone.

CHAPTER TWENTY-FOUR

Jazz held the door while the group of law students, bleary-eyed and quiet, finally left the library. She shooed another three kids who had managed to sneak in after closing time and were scattered through the reading room. She hadn't had the heart to make them leave sooner, since she was there anyway, but now she was ready to shut down for the night. She'd do a full sweep before she set the alarm and locked the door. For now, she just locked it behind her before going upstairs to grab her bag and phone.

She smiled as she climbed the stairs. She usually didn't use her phone much, since she saw her friends every day, anyway, and knew their habits well enough not to need to call them beforehand. But tonight had been fun, sharing texts with Cappy and trading pictures of the ballgame and Jazz's shelving cart. She had enjoyed the near constant sense of connection with her, until it had been time to send the students on their way.

She was tired and ready for bed, but these late-night study sessions were worth the effort, when the library was closed to everyone but a small group of determined studiers, and she was able to catch up on her work, or just get into the stacks and shelve books. Now she had the possibility of some more texts from Cappy to look forward to. They didn't replace having her in the same room, but they were still good.

She was heading toward the darkened hallway leading to her office when the sound of books thudding off the shelves made her freeze. Her first thought was an earthquake, but the sound was isolated, and she didn't feel any movement. She edged forward from the staff hallway, peering around a large shelving unit, and saw a person in dark pants and a black hoodie pulling random books off the shelf and sifting through them before dropping them on the floor. She had already turned out the lights near her office, so they must have thought she had already left.

Given the proximity to Brian's carrel, she had a short list of suspects who might be searching for something in the vicinity, starting with Greg. He had been asking Justine about the envelope—maybe he had located Mia and heard that Brian might have had something secret near his workspace?

The person pushed the hood off his head, looking frustrated. Some long strands of thinning hair wafted in the air, loosened from their combover by the friction with the hood. He looked around, and Jazz narrowly managed to duck back again before he turned her way. Pryce Walker. Well, if anyone would want to find that evidence, it would be him.

Jazz hesitated. She wanted to storm over there and stop him from damaging her neat shelves and delicate books, but she knew what Cappy would say about that. What she needed to do was get downstairs and call the police from the phone behind the circ desk. Cappy's voice annoyingly told her to get the hell out of the building, but she decided to compromise and lock herself in the little circ desk office. She hated walking away from an intruder, especially since she was fairly sure she'd win, but she didn't know if he had a weapon. It would have been easy for him to come during the day and casually flip through books, but he had chosen to come here after hours. There was a distinct possibility that he had brought a weapon, since he was already committing a crime.

She had nearly made it back to the staircase when she heard footsteps coming up. She turned into the stacks and ran softly along the row of shelves, hoping she had come far enough from Pryce that he couldn't see her movement between books. She turned the corner and flattened herself against the endcap, nearly knocking off a display book but managing to catch it before it fell. She set it gently on the ground and moved back in the direction of the windows and study carrels, coming to a stop at the end of the row, on the opposite side of Pryce from where she had started. Yes, she had managed to box herself in the corner. Good job. She sighed and glanced at the carrels in front of her. If she could manage to get under the desks, she could work her way closer and find out who the second person was. If it was Cappy—and oh, how she hoped it was Cappy—she could simply stand up and watch her arrest Pryce for book vandalism.

She had less than a yard between her and the first carrel, but then she'd have to crawl under three more desks to get to the shadowy corner. From there she could move toward Brian's place. She took a deep breath and, feeling grateful for her usual black outfits but cursing her white-blond hair, dropped to her knees and moved quickly into the relative safety of the darkened right angle where the two rows of desks met. She nearly cracked her head on the underside of the desk when she heard Greg's voice. Was the entire fucking football team coming?

"Looking for something, Coach?" Greg asked in an arrogant sounding voice. She couldn't see him from her angle, but she pictured him dramatically sweeping his bangs out of his eyes.

She edged closer, unsure how far she could risk going before they would be able to spot her shadow but needing to hear what they were saying.

"Just looking for a book to read," said Pryce, dropping another one on the floor. Jazz ground her teeth together. "What about you, son?" He gave a bitter-sounding bark of laughter. "I knew you didn't really have that evidence Brian kept talking about. I could hear it in your voice when you tried to threaten me with it."

"Maybe I've been getting evidence of my own," said Greg. He might have been trying to sound belligerent, but he just sounded sulky. "I don't need to find whatever it was he had."

Pryce just laughed, a harsh and condescending sound. "I was worried about Brian. The kid would've done a thorough job of it. But you? You're just trying to keep up with him, like always, and failing. Like always."

"You have to listen to me," Greg said, his voice rising. "I don't need his evidence. I have the drugs. I can turn you in, and the police will do the same work Brian did, but better."

Jazz couldn't see Pryce shrug, but she heard it in his dismissive voice. "And you'll just bring yourself down with me, without Brian to bail you out this time. Oh, look at you, about to cry, poor kid. He was moving on, wasn't he? Even when he lost his leg, he was better than you. He had his own dreams to follow, and he wasn't going to take care of you anymore. You don't frighten me, son. All I need to do is wait, and your bookie friend will take you out of the picture."

"Oh yeah?"

Pryce mimicked his *Oh yeah?* in a babyish voice, which didn't seem smart to Jazz. Maybe he was hoping to intimidate Greg until he burst into tears and left, but Jazz worried he was just pushing him closer to snapping.

"What do you know? You're going to regret taking me off the team. And you'll be sorry for all the crap you gave me every day, comparing me to Saint Brian, the greatest player in the world. I'll show all of you that I'm even better than he ever was."

"Kind of hard to do when you're sitting on the bench, son. You had your chance, and you couldn't cut it." Jazz could picture the smirk on his face, judging by his tone.

"Kind of like you, Coach? You had your chance in the NFL, and all everyone talks about is how much you stunk up the place. Maybe I would have done better with a coach who could actually play the game."

Jazz rubbed her temples. That was it. Now they were going to get into a fistfight in the middle of her library, doing even more damage than Pryce had already done. She sighed. There'd be blood on the carpet, and Cappy and her police friends would shut the library down while they investigated—

Pryce's growl of anger turned into a shout of alarm, and Jazz pulled herself back to the situation at hand. Maybe she should focus on getting herself out of here safely before she worried about a few books and the old carpet. She heard Cappy in her mind, yelling *No shit!*

"What are you doing with that, you fool? Are you really going to shoot me?"

Jazz crouched down, trying to see what was going on. She saw Greg standing in front of Pryce, holding a gun in shaking hands. They weren't trembling enough to make it look like he wouldn't be able to do some damage if he pulled the trigger.

"It's amazing what you can buy from a bookie when you're already in debt and don't mind adding to the total. So now you're going to listen to me for once," Greg said, his voice suddenly cold. "First, you're going to put me back on the team. Second, you're going to help me pay this debt, just like you helped Brian. I'm going to find that evidence, but even without it, you have to do as I say, or I will find you and kill you."

Jazz sank deeper into the shadows, fully admitting that she was cowering. Greg sounded more than capable of pulling the trigger right now, and Pryce seemed to think so, too, because he had gone silent, probably trying to find a way out of this without losing his job or his life. Her mind was spinning. Greg, who had earlier admitted to taking drugs from Pryce. Who was now threatening to kill him, without a hint of doubt in his voice, and who had been told by Brian that he was now in charge of his own debt. She was out of the crawl space and standing next to Pryce before she had even decided to move.

"You," said Pryce. He turned and peered under the carrels. "What the hell were you doing down there?"

"Shelving books. What the fuck do you think I was doing?" She turned to Greg, too furious to care that the gun was now pointing at her. "You killed him," she said. "Brian. You brought your drugs and alcohol over to his apartment and got him started drinking until he didn't have the reasoning left to stop. Then you cleaned off your fucking glass, put it away, and then just walked out on the guy who had been your friend, who had paid your debt. Were you really that jealous that you had to kill him?"

The speech felt good, like a release of all the stress and confliction she had been feeling since Brian died. It was powerful, cathartic, and—she knew deep within herself—true. But when she finished talking, she went back to being just a nosy librarian standing in a dark library facing a murderer who had a gun. Yeah. Should have thought that through.

Pryce was staring at Greg. "Is it true?" he asked, with no *son* and no emotion in his voice.

Greg's gaze was shifting between the two of them, probably weighing his options, which were currently very limited. He might have been able to let Pryce go, as long as he promised to uphold his side of the deal, but now Jazz had shown herself, complete with accusations of murder, and his choices dwindled down to...Well, Jazz didn't want to think about them because none of them seemed like positive outcomes for her.

"I wasn't jealous. He sat me down, gave me this holier-than-thou speech about how he was turning over a new leaf, starting over. He said it was time for me to handle my own debt, and that I'd have the chance to do it now that I was taking over as starter. But that first game"—he made a choking sound and waved the gun at Pryce—"you set me up to fail. Didn't call the right plays, didn't give me the support I needed. Just because I wasn't Brian."

"You did the failing on your own. Don't blame me for that."

"Drop the gun, Greg," said Cappy, emerging from the stacks and facing him with her own weapon drawn. "There's nowhere to run, and you don't want to make this worse for yourself by shooting anyone. Just drop the gun, and we'll talk."

"No," he shouted, swinging the gun toward Jazz. "I'll kill her unless you let me go."

Jazz was amazed at the number of thoughts that sped through her mind in those brief seconds, but the primary one was concern for Cappy, who was living out the nightmare she had experienced with Clare and Libby in the woods, months ago. But this time it was Jazz in danger. She wanted to run to her, to comfort her, but she held still. Staying calm and not getting shot was the only way she could help Cappy now.

Cappy started talking to Greg again, her voice low and soothing, but Pryce seemed to have broken out of his stupor.

"You will not kill her," he yelled, launching himself at Greg and wrestling him for the gun. Suddenly, Clare was running around the other side of the shelves, and she, Cappy, and the two men were in a melee that Jazz couldn't untangle, until she heard a shot ring out and the sound of broken glass. They all stopped moving, and Jazz reached down to where she felt a stinging pain in her thigh.

"Ouch," she said, sitting on the ground and trying to keep her bloody leg off the carpet.

Cappy was there before she made it all the way to the floor, checking Jazz's leg with gentle hands, the roughness of her breathing the only outward sign of her panic.

Clare had Greg disarmed and in zip ties, while Pryce had dropped to the ground near Jazz. "I saved your life," he said, with wonder in his voice. "You never know how you're going to react in an emergency until it happens, but I was a hero."

"It's broken," Jazz said to him, leaning against Cappy.

"No, sweetheart, it's just a graze," Cappy said. "We'll get you checked, but I don't think anything is broken."

Jazz pointed over her shoulder at the window. "My library. He broke my library."

Cappy held her close, with her face buried in Jazz's hair, and laughed. "Don't worry. It's an arrestable offense," she said, then she sighed. "God, Jazz, if anything had happened to you…"

Jazz nodded, huddling closer to her. She heard the sounds of footsteps on the stairs, and the voices of other cops arriving. Pryce was repeating to Clare the story of how he had jumped to Jazz's rescue, but Clare wasn't looking impressed.

"He killed Brian," she said quietly.

"I heard. You figured it out. I wish you had waited until I was here and Greg was unarmed before you accused him of it, but you did it. You figured out the proof, for Brian."

Jazz rested in Cappy's arms and finally let herself cry.

CHAPTER TWENTY-FIVE

Cappy checked her reflection yet again in the mirror, running a comb through her hair and straightening the hem of her shirt. It was probably the most use her mirror had gotten in all the time she had been living in the apartment. She wasn't sure why she was so nervous. She had been on thousands of dates before—well, dozens, at least—and she had never gone through this sweaty-palms, quaking-knees experience. She sighed and shook her head at her reflection. Likely she hadn't been nervous in the past because she had gone into every relationship convinced it wouldn't, and couldn't possibly, last. She was going into this one with the unshakable knowledge that it not only could, but would. This was very likely the last first date she would ever have, so she was going to enjoy every stomach-churning moment of anticipation.

Still, tonight's dinner with Jazz barely qualified as a first date. They had spent hours together during the investigation, they had talked at the pizza party and in Red Square, and they had kissed in Jazz's office. But now the case was closed, and Cappy's entire world felt changed because of it. Tonight, it would just be her and Jazz. No one to interview, no questions about murder and motive to discuss.

Cappy tucked her phone in the back pocket of her jeans. It had been a stressful week, full of paperwork as they wrapped up the case and the melancholy experience of Brian's memorial service. His parents had cried as they hugged her and Jazz, thanking them for what they had done. Their investigation hadn't brought Brian back to his family and hadn't lessened the grief they were experiencing, but maybe knowing the truth about what had happened to him would be some small consolation during a dark time.

She was jolted out of her sad thoughts by a knock on the door, and she hurried over to let Jazz in, greeting her with a kiss and feeling all her nervous tension fade away.

Jazz smiled, looking as happy as Cappy felt. "You look amazing," she said, running her finger along the open front of Cappy's shirt. She stopped before she got to the good part, though, distracted by something over Cappy's shoulder.

"Oh, you kept the Kibbles," she exclaimed, walking over and picking up a tiny tuxedo kitten. "I won the bet!"

Cappy rubbed the back of her neck sheepishly. "Not exactly. Gran took those ones, and I sort of got these ones for myself. But, hey, I didn't cry when the original ones left, so Clare didn't win, either."

"Damn," said Jazz, adding the ginger kitten to her armful. "When Libby heard about the bet, she had to be part of it. She said this exact thing would happen. What are their names? And if you say Kibble Three and Kibble Four, I'm breaking up with you."

"Don't be ridiculous," Cappy said, trying to look insulted while she mentally searched for different names. "They're called Odie and Gaard, after my favorite library on campus."

Jazz snorted. "Odegaard isn't anyone's favorite library on campus. Sue and Zalo it is, then." She set the kittens down with a final pat and came over to Cappy, wrapping her arms around Cappy's shoulders and kissing her neck. "I've been looking forward to tonight," she said, her lips moving against Cappy's skin and putting all her nerve endings on high alert.

"Me, too," Cappy agreed as she slid her hands along Jazz's waist, feeling the softness of her sweater and the strength of the woman wearing it. "I made us dinner reservations at a Greek restaurant in Ballard, but we can order in and stay here instead, if you'd rather," she added hopefully.

Jazz laughed. "Let's go out," she said. She gently bit Cappy's earlobe before stepping out of her arms. "But we can maybe come back here after?"

"Definitely," said Cappy, wanting to reach for Jazz again and never let her go. She grabbed her jacket instead. "I eat really fast, by the way."

"Good. Me, too."

Cappy grinned, opening the door. "Clare recommended this place," she said as they left the apartment. "It sounds great."

Jazz groaned and leaned back against the closed door. "Did you tell her where we were going?"

"Well, yes, I texted her today. Why, does she have bad taste in food?"

Jazz sighed and looked toward the heavens. "Cappy texted Clare who told Libby who called Ari, et cetera, et cetera. The story of my life."

Cappy shook her head. "You really think they'll all be there? On our first date?"

"Did you say we considered it our first date, or did you just say we were going out to eat?"

"Yeah," Cappy said, running back through her conversation with Clare. "They'll all be there. Do you want to go someplace else?"

Jazz shrugged casually. "Do you?"

Cappy took a moment to picture the evening. Instead of an intimate dinner for two, there would be noise and laughter surrounding them. Holding hands under the table, their knees pressed close to each other. Friends and good food.

"Not at all," she said honestly.

Jazz smiled. "Neither do I."

Cappy nodded and they started walking. She stopped after only a few steps and faced Jazz. "But maybe they don't all have to come back here with us after dinner."

"Absolutely not," Jazz agreed with a smile, lacing her fingers through Cappy's as they walked down the hall.

About the Author

Karis Walsh is a horseback riding instructor who lives in the Pacific Northwest. When she isn't teaching or writing, she enjoys spending time outside with her animals, reading, playing the viola, and riding with friends.

Books Available from Bold Strokes Books

A Conflict of Interest by Morgan Adams. Tensions rise when a one-night stand becomes a major conflict of interest between an up-and-coming senior associate and a dedicated cardiac surgeon. (978-1-63679-870-7)

A Magnificent Disturbance by Lee Lynch. These everyday dykes and their friends will stop at nothing to see the women's clinic thrive and, in the process, their ideals, their wounds, and a steadfast allegiance to one another make them heroes. (978-1-63679-031-2)

A Marvelous Murder by David S. Pederson. When a hated director is found dead in his locked study, movie star Victor Marvel, his boyfriend Griff, and friend Eve seek to uncover what really happened to Orland Orcott. (978-1-63679-798-4)

Big Corpse on Campus by Karis Walsh. When University Police Officer Cappy Flannery investigates what looks like a clear-cut suicide, she discovers that the case—and her feelings for librarian Jazz—are more complicated than she expected. (978-1-63679-852-3)

Charity Case by Jean Copeland. Bad girl Lindsay Chase came home to Connecticut for a fresh start, but an old, risky habit provides the chance to save the day for her new love, Ellie. (978-1-63679-593-5)

Moments to Treasure by Ali Vali. Levi Montbard and Yasmine Hassani have found a vast Templar treasure, but there is much more to the story—and what is left to be found. (978-1-63679-473-0)

The Stolen Girl by Cari Hunter. Detective Inspector Jo Shaw is determined to prove she's fit for work after an injury that almost killed her, but a new case brings her up against people who will do anything to preserve their own interests, putting Jo—and those closest to her—directly in the line of fire. (978-1-63679-822-6)

Discovering Gold by Sam Ledel. In 1920s Colorado, a single mother and a rowdy cowgirl must set aside their fears and initial reservations about one another if they want to find love in the mining town each of them calls home. (978-1-63679-786-1)

Dream a Little Dream by Melissa Brayden. Savanna can't believe it when Dr. Kyle Remington, the woman who left her feeling like a fool, shows up in Dreamer's Bay. Life is too complicated for second chances. Or is it? (978-1-63679-839-4)

Emma by the Sea by Sarah G. Levine. A delightful modern-day romance inspired by Emma, one of Jane Austen's most beloved novels. (978-1-63679-879-0)

Goodbye, Hello by Heather K O'Malley. With so much time apart and the challenges of a long-distance relationship, Kelly and Teresa's second chance at love may end just as awkwardly as the first. (978-1-63679-790-8)

One Measure of Love by Annie McDonald. Vancouver's hit competitive cooking show Recipe for Success has begun filming its second season and two talented young chefs are desperate for more than a winning dish. (978-1-63679-827-1)

The Smallest Day by J.M. Redmann. The first bullet missed—can Micky Knight stop the second bullet from finding its target? (978-1-63679-854-7)

To Please Her by Elena Abbott. A spilled coffee leads Sabrina into a world of erotic BDSM that may just land her the love of her life. (978-1-63679-849-3)

Two Weddings and a Funeral by Claudia Parr. Stella and Theo have spent the last thirteen years pretending they can be just friends, but surely "just friends" don't make out every chance they get. (978-1-63679-820-2)

Coming Up Clutch by Anna Gram. College softball star Kelly "Razor" Mitchell hung up her cleats early, but when former crush, now coach Ashton Sharpe shows up on her doorstep seven years later, beautiful as ever, Razor hopes the longing in her gaze has nothing to do with softball. (978-1-63679-817-2)

Firecamp by Jaycie Morrison. Going their separate ways seemed inevitable for two people as different as Fallon and Nora, while meeting up again is strictly coincidental. (978-1-63679-753-3)

Fixed Up by Aurora Rey. When electrician Jack Barrow and artist Ellie Lancaster get stuck on a job site during a blizzard, close quarters send all sorts of sparks flying. (978-1-63679-788-5)

Stranded by Ronica Black. Can Abigail and Whitley overcome their personal hang-ups and stubbornness to survive not only Alaska, but a dangerous stalker as well? (978-1-63679-761-8)

Whisk Me Away by Georgia Beers. Regan's a gorgeous flake. Ava, a beautiful untouchable ice queen. When they meet again at a retreat for up-and-coming pastry chefs, the competition, and the ovens, heat up. (978-1-63679-796-0)

Across the Enchanted Border by Crin Claxton. Magic, telepathy, swordsmanship, tyranny, and tenderness abound in a tale of two lands separated by the enchanted border. (978-1-63679-804-2)

Deep Cover by Kara A. McLeod. Running from your problems by pretending to be someone else only works if the person you're pretending to be doesn't have even bigger problems. (978-1-63679-808-0)

Good Game by Suzanne Lenoir. Even though Lauren has sworn off dating gamers, it's becoming hard to resist the multifaceted Sam. An opposites attract lesbian romance. (978-1-63679-764-9)

Innocence of the Maiden by Ileandra Young. Three powerful women. Two covens at war. One horrifying murder. When mighty and powerful witches begin to butt heads, who out there is strong enough to mediate? (978-1-63679-765-6)

Protection in Paradise by Julia Underwood. When arson forces them together, the flames between chief of police Eve Maguire and librarian Shaye Hayden aren't that easy to extinguish. (978-1-63679-847-9)

Too Forward by Krystina Rivers. Just as professional basketball player Jane May's career finally starts heating up, a new relationship with her team's brand consultant could derail the success and happiness she's struggled so long to find. (978-1-63679-717-5)

Worth Waiting For by Kristin Keppler. For Peyton and Hanna, reliving the past is painful, but looking back might be the only way to move forward. (978-1-63679-773-1)